THE REBOUND

COURTING LOVE - A COLLEGE SPORTS
ROMANCE

SIERRA HILL

❀ Created with Vellum

REVIEWS FOR COURTING LOVE

I loved this story so much, that I read it in one sitting. A fast paced, sweet, and well written storyline flows smoothly. Sierra Hill's easy writing style hooked me from the beginning, while holding me hostage until the end. She added a twist that had me jacked up, as it didn't resolve itself yet. I'm super excited to read more of her work in the future, so I'm HIGHLY RECOMMENDING. – **The Power of Three Readers**

I recommend this read to all romance lovers, and I am looking forward to the next book. Well done Sierra, on a beautifully written love story. – **Wendy's Book Blog**

The build-up between these two will leave you laughing, swooning, fanning yourself and oohing the next. **LLEP Book Blog**

I was hooked in from the very beginning. And just when you think that this story is predictable, you quickly find out that there are still surprises. Don't miss out on the truly sweet story." – **Sweet Sexy Escape Book Blog**

OTHER BOOKS BY SIERRA HILL

Fast Break
Jump Shot

Reckless – The Smoky Mountain Trio serial
Reckless Youth
Reckless Abandon
Reckless Hearts
Reckless – The Smoky Mountain trio boxset

1

K ylah

IF SOMEONE CALLS ME '*A SWEET GIRL*' one more time, I'm liable to throat punch them. Not even kidding.

This boring description has been pinned to me since childhood – albeit fairly accurate. But now that I'm nearly nineteen and a freshman in college, it's not who I am, nor who I want to be. Unfortunately, it's still how I get viewed. I'm the sweet little sister of Cade Griffin – college basketball player extraordinaire.

I've tried to change my image over the first few months of college, and now that I'm back home on fall break, I'm hoping others will see I'm not the same girl I was before I left. All I want to do over the next week is let loose a bit and have fun. Enjoy my time back home – away from the stress of schoolwork, classes, and deadlines - spend time with my dad, my brother and his new girlfriend, Ainsley, and hang out at Cade's apartment with his roommates and friends.

Which is where I am right now. Sitting on the couch in

Cade's living room, watching an episode of *Game of Thrones* with my brother's roommate, Lance, and their teammate Van. The guys, along with my brother, all play basketball for ASU. I've been sitting here the last hour, waiting for Cade and Ainsley to return from a shopping trip they had to run. They'd invited me along, but I told them I wanted to get caught up with GoT.

Truthfully, I really just want to hang out with Van. I've kind of developed a little crush, even though I know he's completely off limits and out of my league. And the fact that he has a girlfriend. Which really sucks for me.

"Holy fuck!" Lance shouts, his body jumping off the couch in a herky-jerky motion, arms flailing over his head like the house is on fire. My head spins toward him, my cheeks flush in embarrassment that I may have been caught staring at the beauty of Van.

Lance's expression displays his state of horror, not over my obvious infatuation, but over something that happened on the show. I'm not exactly sure what I missed, but it must be a big deal. Since I've been lost in my own world and not really paying any attention to the TV, I have no idea what's got him so excited.

"I can't believe they killed him off! Un-fucking-believable!"

I look away from Lance and down at Van, who is sitting on the floor with his back up against the couch, shaking his head in disbelief. "Wow...I definitely didn't see that coming. They're always killing off the characters you'd least expect."

My attention swerves back to the TV, trying to clue into what's happening so I don't look like an idiot. Who could fault me, though? I'm sitting inches from one of the hottest guys I've ever met. I covertly glance over at Van underneath the protection of my bangs and the large-framed glasses I'm wearing today. I have contacts, but don't always put them in.

Van is sitting on the floor by my feet. His dark, shiny hair is pulled back in a low-man-bun, a black headband secured at his temple to hold back stray pieces. I'm not super into guys with long hair, or man-buns, for that matter, but it's a really good look on Van. My current location gives me the perfect vantage point to check him out without him knowing it. Unless he has eyes on the back of his head.

As the younger sister of a college basketball stud, I've been around my fair share of Cade's good-looking friends for as long as I can remember. Always watching from the proverbial court-side seats – invisible to them all. Sure, his friends and team-mates tease me unmercifully over my "sweet" and "cute" looks or gawky tendencies – I'm used to that. I've been known to trip over my own feet from time to time. But Van's attention these last few days has made me feel special.

Getting to know Van has been an entirely different experi-ence. He's treated me like an equal, not the younger, bratty sister of his friend. He's asked me about my interests, my favorite classes at school, my intended major and listened to me talk about some of the issues I've been dealing with during my first semester away. Like the high level of anxiety over expectations, as well as my constant cloud of homesickness. He's so easy to open up to that I forget to be my usual Nervous-Nelly around him. He's even cajoled me into regaling some of the embar-rassing moments I've had and related to me on the same level, which I find adorable.

And his sexy, gray-blue eyes – so dark they look like I've fallen into the deep ocean - seem to have taken notice of me as a woman, not some little girl. Unless it's my overactive imagina-tion at work, I think there may be a mutual attraction.

That attraction I have toward him has turned me into an idiot who can't keep a single thought in my brain when I'm around him. Or apparently, pay attention to really interesting storylines on my favorite show.

The only problem?

Van is taken.

He has a girlfriend.

The only guy I've ever connected with and feel like I can be myself around is in a long-term relationship with his high school sweetheart. The only reason I know this is because Cade and the guys constantly give Van shit about his "ball and chain" and say that he's crazy to be "locked down" when he could be getting tons of action from all the hoops hunnies that throw themselves at basketball players.

And believe me, I can see why they would. I'm not a girl who flaunts it or even knows how to flirt, but with Van, I'm inclined to try.

"Earth to Kylah." Van's smooth voice once again reminds me to get out of my own head. My body jolts at the mention of my name and my eyes flick up to his. He's now standing facing me and I have to crane my neck because he's so frigging tall. He's even taller than my six-foot-five brother.

"Uh, what?" I ask hesitantly, because I have no idea what he just said or asked me. Space cadet, much?

Van's low chuckle sends crazy vibrations through my nerve endings.

"I asked if you wanted something to drink. I'm going to run to the store and grab some beers and stuff. The fridge is nearly empty." He eyes me curiously when I don't say anything. "Or, would you like to get out of the house and come with me?"

My gaze darts around the room, trying to figure out what's going on. Apparently I'd been zoning out longer than I thought because the show is over and Lance is no longer sitting next to me. He's off in his bedroom, leaving Van and me together. Alone.

I swallow the lump in my throat, the massive ball of indecision bubbling up inside my chest. Yes, of course I want to go with him. I'd be crazy not to. I look down at the flip-flops I'm wearing, like they have the answer. I'm nervous – nothing new there. Being alone with Van has me questioning my sensibilities. He's giving me a look now that says he's probably questioning his own decision to ask me along. I probably should say no. But I don't.

"Um...yeah...sure." I stammer, sounding like a complete loser.

Pull yourself together, woman.

"Great. I could use the company."

He reaches inside his pocket and pulls out a pair of keys as we walk out of the apartment together. As we near his beat-up late model Nissan, I'm aware of his close proximity right behind me. He reaches down to the door handle, sidling up beside me, which startles me so that my head turns and my nose smooshes up directly into his chest.

Oh my God. The very first thing I notice is his scent. It's the best thing I've ever smelled. It's a combination of fabric softener, a crisp, clean deodorant and something else altogether very masculine. Maybe it's a cologne, but if I'd have to guess, it's just Van. Eau de Van. I sniff and then inhale a deep breath, taking him all in as he hovers over me. Realizing too late that he's staring at me, I jerk back against the car door and close my eyes in utter embarrassment.

When I gather enough courage to open them up again and dare a look, Van is smiling. At me. Not in an arrogant smirk, nor with mocking disdain. But with amusement. His dark eyes gleam with a sweet reverence and it has me tingling in awe over this giant of a man.

I quickly pull myself together, shoving myself into the passenger seat, immediately taking notice of the state of disarray that is his car. It's filthy! Littered with empty sports drink bottles, soda cans, chip bags, fast food containers, gum wrappers. You name it, it's on the floor, the dash, the middle console. I just pray I don't see an opened and used condom wrapper.

My body is contorted as I'm perusing the backseat when Van slides into his spot, his eyes flashing to mine and he shrugs apologetically, his neck and cheeks blooming in red.

"Sorry about the mess. I would've cleaned it up had I known I'd have company. It's not generally this bad."

"Psssh," I wave him off. "It's all good."

Van continues. "I just haven't had time to clean it out since I returned from Albuquerque. I returned late Sunday night and haven't had time yet."

My curiosity takes over. "What were you doing in New Mexico?"

Van is looking over his left shoulder out his car window as we merge onto the main road heading toward the grocery store.

"Um, my girlfriend Lyndsay goes to school there." His voice is barely a whisper. Like he's reluctant to say it.

I think my heart stops beating. Of course I know he has a girlfriend, but this is the first time he's brought her up, or mentioned her name. It just puts my crush into perspective. The reality is, I'll never have a chance with him. My heart wilts.

I try to school my facial expression, which I'm sure reads heartbreak, and place a mechanical smile on my face. I'm sure my voice sounds as fake as it feels to say this out loud, the tone overly cheerful.

"Oh, that's great! So do you see her...I mean, *Lyndsay* often?"

There's a pause and his eyes remain on the road – either for safety reasons or he wants to avoid the topic. As if he's uncertain what to divulge to me.

Van shifts his gaze over to me for a brief second, and unless it's my imagination, I see a flash of sadness.

"We try. Lynds doesn't have a car, so she can't come visit me often, unless she can find a ride. Our schedules don't always mesh too well."

He turns his face back to the road, his jaw flexing. He has a really angular jawline, that squares off at his chin, that is covered with a thin, dark stubble. My first instinct is to reach out and pat his arm – a gesture of empathy. I know that feeling of homesickness and loneliness all too well. And if I'm reading things right, he's got it bad, making me wish I could do something for him. But I can't, because he's not mine.

Instead, I grip my two hands tightly in a ball on my lap, fighting the urge to reach out and provide a consoling touch.

"I'm sorry to hear that. How long have you two been together?"

He heaves a heavy sigh. Almost in resignation.

"Since I was a senior in high school and she was a junior. We grew up together in Tucson. She got a scholarship for UNW and I came to ASU."

"Wow," I flatly acknowledge. "Four years of long-distance is a really long time. I'm impressed. How do you guys manage it?"

What I really want to ask is "how have you remained faithful?" Because, come on...he's a college basketball player, for heaven's sake. He's absolutely gorgeous. He must have girls tripping over themselves to get a piece of him. There's bound to have been some serious temptations over the years, that even the most steadfast and loyal of guys would fall victim to.

Case in point, the Midnight Madness after-party last Friday night. It was the team's first official practice of the season, and it was glaringly obvious that Van garnered the attention of more than one girl. Myself included. I, however, was more or less the self-appointed hostess of the evening, since the party took place at Cade's apartment and I knew his roommates, Carver and Lance, weren't going to be responsible for keeping things in check. As usual, Lance got so trashed he passed out around two-thirty a.m. As for Carver, I noticed him going into his bedroom with one girl, and then coming out later with another. Holy cow, two girls in one night. I've never...I mean, wow.

Yet I didn't notice any untoward behavior from Van that would make a long-distance girlfriend question his fidelity. He drank, he joked, he laughed, he casually chatted with girls – and guys - but there was no obvious flirting, and definitely not any hooking up.

Van is definitely a good guy.

"I honestly don't know," he says in response to my question. I watch his lips form a tight grimace, his side profile a view that could be a chiseled work of art. "I guess when you love someone enough, you have to believe that neither party will do anything to sabotage that trust."

He shrugs as he pulls into the parking lot and turns off the engine.

Turning toward me, he smiles brightly, all the tension vanishing with the light of his perfect white teeth.

"So, what'll it be? Beer or tequila tonight?"

Hmm. I'd opt for something else. Something tall, dark and handsome. Because Van gets me tipsy just by his presence alone.

Dammit. Why does he have to be taken?

an

LYNDSAY IS CHEATING ON ME.

I think.

No proof or evidence has surfaced to justify this claim, but something was off with her last weekend. I felt it during my visit. It was our first visit in over a month and only the second since the start of the school year.

Call it gut instinct or whatever, but something's definitely going on with her.

It could be just the strain and readjustment of getting back into the academic school year. We're both on the basketball teams at our respective schools, and team practices have just begun in preparation for the upcoming season. Lyndsay is also still grieving the loss of her dad, who died suddenly last May, right in the middle of finals.

We grieved together over the summer, in between basketball training camps and our summer jobs. She originally wasn't planning on coming home to Tucson, but after her dad's death, she came home to be with her mom and younger siblings. I was selfishly glad she did. I needed to be with her; spend time with her; remind her how good we are together.

But that didn't last long. Now that she's back in Albuquerque, she doesn't have time for me anymore. Or more like make the time for me. The vibe I got when I visited her is that I was a nuisance. She acts like it's a chore to hang out with me around her friends, her dorm – her life.

When I pressed her on the subject, asking what was going on with her, she brushed it off, scoffing at me like I was stupid to think there's something wrong between us. Or with her. Nothing has changed with me. I'm still the same. I'm still in love with her. But it hurts to know she may not feel the same way about me anymore.

My friends call me pussy whipped; I suppose I am. But Lyndsay is my best friend. We've been together for a long time. She knows everything there is to know about me. She's practically part of my family, and understands what things are like living with my older brother, Dougie.

My thoughts are interrupted when a basketball flies into my chest. Hard.

I rub at the spot, blinking through the pain as I watch the ball bounce off the court.

"Ow...what du fuck, man?"

My teammate, Christian Lancaster, a center power forward, gives me a mocking laugh.

"Dude, if you were paying attention to what's going on here, you wouldn't be whining like a pansy-ass." He struts over and stands facing me. "What is your deal today? What bug crawled up your ass?"

My eyebrows raise in question. "I don't know what you're talking about, bruh."

Another scoffing grunt and he jogs to the sideline to pick up the discarded ball, quickly handing it off to me as he returns to my side.

"Van, your head is so fucking far in the clouds, even Jesus and his angels can't reach ya."

What a dope. Maybe I am a little out of it today, though. I haven't slept well the last few nights. Got lots on my mind.

Specifically, I've been thinking about two girls. One that's possibly fucking around on me. And the other, quite honestly, that's fucking up my head.

Kylah Griffin.

My guilt over how I feel about her right now is so high that they should cuff me and charge me with indecent thoughts.

Nothing has happened between us – at all. And it wouldn't. I've been completely faithful to Lyndsay during my entire college career. I've never once touched or kissed another girl – even though I've had ample opportunity.

I met Kylah, Cade's younger sister, at the end of last week. She's home on fall break from her California college and has been spending time at Cade's apartment day-and-night. The same place I've been hanging around to keep my mind off what's going on with Lyndsay.

For whatever reason, Kylah and I have just clicked as friends. She's a sweet girl. Smart. Shy. Beautiful in the girl-next-door vibe. We've bonded over our interest in Game of Thrones and Marvel super-hero movies. Kylah is a bit of a geek-girl, which I find fascinating. And she's a great listener. Not that I've told her much about my personal life, because that would be a lot to digest, but she's been a great distraction for me. If I didn't have her around, I think I'd have lost my mind. The guys' have no clue what's going on in my life and there's no way I can tell them. They'd only make more fun of me for being such a love-sick pussy. Obviously I am, since I can't concentrate on a damn thing in practice.

"Sorry, man."

I dribble the ball down the court, weaving in and out of the red shirts we're working with on drills today. "I do have a lot on my mind."

At six-foot-ten, Christian pivots in front and blocks me as I take a shot from the three-point line. The ball leaves my hand, arcing up and then down, hitting the rim of the basket before ricocheting off, getting picked off by the red shirt team. Fuck. I've been working on my three-pointers over the summer, but apparently my technique is also off today along with everything else.

Lancaster and I run down the length of the court, posting up in our man-to-man defense. We do this for another twenty minutes – up and down the court – dribbling, passing, blocking, screening, shooting. Finally, the assistant coach blows the whistle and we head into the locker room to shower and change.

Cade, Lance and Carver all walk in front of me down the corridor, joking about something that happened recently at a party. I'm a few paces behind them when Cade holds back a little to allow me to catch up.

"Yo, Van. Heard you've been hanging with my sister this past week."

The expression on his face is unreadable. Is he pissed that I've been chilling with Kylah? Does he think something's going on between us? Shit. I've got to put a stop to any conjecture or misinterpretation of our friendship. Because that's all there is with Kylah. She's a friend.

Cade clamps his hand down on my shoulder. Actually, he has to lift his arm a bit, because at six-foot-seven, I'm taller than him by two inches. He outweighs me, though, by a good ten pounds. His grip tightens for a second and then he laughs.

"Whoa. You okay there, bud? You look like you're gonna pass out."

I wave him off. "Nah, I'm good. Didn't eat much this morning."

"Ah, man. I ate a shit ton. Ainsley made us all a huge breakfast. That's when Ky brought you up. She mentioned you'd been watching Game of Thrones with her."

I try to keep my breathing even and the timber of my voice to sound normal. Instead of jittery and nervous. I don't even know why the hell I am. There's nothing wrong with what me and Kylah have going on. Like he said, we've just been watching TV.

"Oh, yeah. That. It wasn't only us. Lance was there too." I sound kind of defensive now, like I am guilty of something.

Cade quirks his mouth up into a sideways smile and nods his head.

"That's cool. But Ky couldn't stop talking about you. Said you guys might go to the Twenty One Pilots show next month when she's back during the holidays."

Wow. The way he puts it sounds like a date, but that's not at all how it is. We did talk about going together, along with others, though nothing was lined up. We don't even have tickets yet and not sure we can even get some. I just happened to mention in passing that I was thinking about getting tickets because they're my favorite band. There's no way that Lyndsay would want to go with me. She doesn't like crowds or going to see live music. She's more of a country music fan – Luke Bryan or Eric Church. Where I'm not into the same scene.

"Maybe...we'll see. Not sure yet if tickets are even available."

We wind our way into the locker room and I open up my locker. My first instinct is to check my phone for any call or text from Lyndsay. Our schedules are so vastly different that it can be hit or miss on getting to talk to her any more. It's actually starting to piss me off. Our skipping daily chats has been happening more and more frequently and I don't like it. In fact, I'm becoming resentful and disenfranchised.

I press the button and the phone lights up with several text messages. Two from my mom about Dougie and his new therapist. The other from an unknown number. Much to my dismay, but not surprise, none are there from Lyndsay.

I frown.

Curious as to what the unknown number is all about, I open it up.

Unknown: Hi Van. It's Kylah. Hope you don't mind, but I got your number from Lance today.

Unknown: I know you're probably busy, but the new Avengers movie is out this week. I really want to go, but don't have anyone to go with. Thought I'd ask you. Want to go?

Unknown: With me?

Unknown: Or not. Whatevs.

Unknown: If not, that's tots cool. No biggie. Either way, let me know. TTYL.

I read the texts again, all coming in about an hour earlier in quick succession. A smile grows unbidden across my lips where the grimace caused by my girlfriend had just been hovering. I can envision Kylah, in all her shy awkwardness, getting up the nerve to text me. She's adorably sweet. She reminds me of a Ladybug. Or butterfly. One of those harmless, yet beautiful creatures, that always make you smile when they're present.

I glance over my shoulder to make sure no one is watching as I type out a text back to her.

Me: Hey Kylah. Just finished practice. Not sure if it'll fit in with my schedule, but we'll see.

I press send and then worry my response may be too brisk. Although I don't know her all that well, my guess is she has tender feelings and can get hurt pretty easily.

Me: Thanks for asking, btw. I'll let you know.

A response comes flashing across my screen a second later.

Unknown: Cool. Sounds good. And I totally understand if you can't go. No pressure. I can go alone, too. It would mean more popcorn for me, anyway.

I laugh out loud, garnering a sideways glance from Carver whose shirtless by his locker and about to strip out of his jock strap.

Hoping to avoid any further attention, I lock my phone and place it back in my cubby, and head toward the bank of showers. I pass my teammates, all in various stages of undress, and consider the exchange I just had with Kylah.

If we go to the movie together, would that be weird? I mean, if Lyndsay asked me, would it feel like a betrayal to her? Is it cheating if I go to a movie with a girl who's not your girlfriend? Kylah and I are just friends, like she said. I barely know her. And with the exception of a few rather impure thoughts that I've had about her, I'd never act on them. What guy doesn't have fantasies about women? I'm not a monk, but I'm definitely not a cheater. So regardless of whether my eyes or thoughts roam, my hands remain true.

Plus, there's also an issue with her brother, Cade. He's made it very clear that everyone is to stay away from his sisters. Yeah, Kylah has a twin sister named Kady. I haven't met her, but some of the guys who've knew Cade from high school, have been introduced. From what I hear, Kady is the wilder of the two twins and goes to school in Colorado.

I consider the whole movie thing again. Am I over simplifying it? Or trying to justify my actions? One thing's for sure. If I do end up going to the movie with Kylah, I will definitely tell Lyndsay about it. She deserves to know and understand that it's strictly platonic. There is nothing to be afraid of.

Convincing myself of that fact, though, seems a lot harder to do.

I'T'S STILL early in the afternoon and I've been back in my dorm for a few hours now. After the class I had this morning, and the energy-consuming early morning practice, my eyes can barely remain open to study. I've always been a pretty studious guy. Maybe it's because it keeps me out of trouble. Otherwise, I might fall into the trap that most college guys my age fall into – partying too hard and finding ways to hook up with every girl they meet. By keeping my head in the books and solely focused on basketball, I've stayed clear from the temptations that surround me. I don't ever want Lyndsay to doubt me.

Yet it feels like that's backfired on me, because I'm the one who suddenly doubts her faithfulness.

My phone sits on top of one of my books…like a proverbial 'little red devil' tempting me to respond to Kylah with a "I'm in" reply to her question about the movie. It's all I've been thinking about since I read the text earlier.

Dropping my highlighter into the crease of my stats book, I run my hands through my hair, which I left loose after my shower, and exhale a deep and frustrated sigh. I fight the urge to text her back, by instead dialing Lyndsay.

It rings three times and then she finally answers. She sounds out of breath.

"Hey," she answers, the noise in the background nearly drowning out her voice. "I was gonna call you later."

I've never doubted her intentions, but for some reason, I do right now. I called her last night and again this morning and never heard anything back from her. Just the thought that she may be ignoring my calls makes my blood boil hot. And it's obvious in the tone of my reply.

"Yeah, when exactly? Next week, perhaps?" I shut my eyes tight, angry more at myself for letting my frustration get to me.

There's a pause on the line. A rustling in the background. A muffled voice.

What the fuck?

"Where are you right now?" I snipe, barely holding on to my contained rage and jealousy.

Her response doesn't douse my anger, but instead ignites it even further.

"Just at a friend's. We're watching a movie."

"Which friend?"

"Julia and Izzy's."

Plausible. They are her two best friends and teammates. But it's three o'clock in the afternoon. Why would they be watching a movie together during a school day?

"What movie?" I sound like an interrogator and she's the perp I'm questioning. But something's not sitting right with me. My bullshit meter is off-the-charts. I've never had reason to doubt what she says and honestly, I don't know why I do right now. Everything about this makes me twitchy inside. Uncomfortable. The fact that I don't trust her and what she's saying makes my gut hurt. Sick to my stomach, in fact.

"Uh…I can't remember the name. It's with Steve Carrell."

Now I'm even more suspicious. Lyndsay has never been a fan of comedies. She likes the sappy, chick-flicks like *The Notebook* and *The Vow*. Whenever I tried to get her to watch a comedy of any sort, she turned it down. Or if she did watch it with me, she'd be on her phone the entire time, browsing Facebook or Twitter. Which was fine, because I watched those types of movies with my brother or friends. The fact that she's watching one now…with her two girlfriends, has the hairs on the back of my neck tingling.

I hear another muffled sound in the background. Then she lets out a noise that sounds an awful lot like a moan. Then silence. Then she speaks again.

"Hey babe...can I call you later? Julia just told me to pipe down so she can hear the movie. I'll call you tonight after dinner. K?"

I'm fucking pissed. I haven't had a real conversation with Lynds for several days and now she's fucking blowing me off so one of her friends can watch a movie?

Instead of calling her out on her bullshit, I decide to use a different tactic. See if she bites. Find out if she's interested in me at all right now. I know it's a passive-aggressive thing to do – like stooping to the lowest of lows - but it's what I feel.

"You can try, but I'm going to a movie tonight. With Cade's sister Kylah."

Without even a shred of question, she responds without hesitation. "That's nice...sounds fun. I'll call you tomorrow then. Bye, babe."

And before I can even say goodbye, the call ends and I'm left with a rock in the pit of my stomach. I just told my girlfriend of nearly five years that I'm going to a movie – with another chick – and she didn't even blink. Not so much as an ounce of interest, worry or concern.

I stare at the phone clutched in my hand, looking at it as if it has some hidden answer as to what just transpired. I'm not even sure I can put a name on what I'm feeling right now. The most descriptive term would be hurt.

Lyndsay's reaction to me during that brief one minute and thirty second conversation is something that has never occurred before. I've always been a priority for her, and vice versa. She'd drop everything to talk to me if she could. That's how our relationship has worked. We don't have the luxury of seeing each other every day, so we made good use of our phone time, Face-time and Skype sessions to talk and stay connected. And let me tell you, a lot of phone sex occurred.

This? This utter disregard for me and the quick brush off she gave me? It's only heightened my awareness that something is horribly wrong. And I will find out as soon as I am able.

But in the meantime, I shoot a quick text to Kylah to let her know I'm interested in seeing the movie with her.

At least one thing is for certain.

My friend Kylah wants to spend time with me, even if my girlfriend doesn't have the time of day for me.

And whether she knows it or not, I need Kylah's friendship to sooth the hurt that's growing like a weed in my heart.

3

Kylah

I JUST ABOUT shit a brick when I read Van's response to me late yesterday afternoon.

Van: I'm in for the movie. How about 7:30 tomorrow night. Meet at Cade's?

He'd accepted my invite to go see the movie with me. I've been bouncing off the walls ever since, barely able to contain myself. I'm sure in the lives of most girls, this isn't such a big deal. A movie date with a guy they like. But for those of us who have only been on a few dates in our lives, this is huge.

It's not a date.

I have to keep reminding myself of that fairly significant detail. Even though I am crushing on Van like nobody's business, I'm not stupid enough to think this is anything more than a friend outing. We are clearly in the friend zone, for more than one reason.

In fact, he's probably right this very minute asking himself how he can get out of it. He's my older brother's friend and likely views me just like all of Cade's other friends - like the sweet little sister they love to pick on. Just as Carver is doing right now as I sit at the kitchen table in their apartment, waiting not-so-patiently for Van to show up.

"Aw...isn't that cute? Ky-Ky got all dressed up for her big, hot date tonight!"

I glare at Carver with all the meanness I can muster. Which isn't much. He sees right through me.

"It's not a date, Carver...so stop saying that. And don't you dare say anything remotely similar to Van, either. We're just friends, you jerk."

Carver's right, though. I did put a lot of effort into my wardrobe tonight, including hair and make-up. My light auburn locks are hanging at my shoulders in loose waves, created by the styling wand my mother got me last Christmas. I'd slathered on some mango-spice body lotion my dad brought me back from his trip to a tropical island last year, and slicked on a peach tinted lip gloss.

Instead of wearing the usual T-shirt, shorts and Converse, I chose a flirty floral print jumper with wedge sandals. It barely hits my knees and exposes a lot of leg. My legs are definitely my best assets, in my humble opinion. I actually pulled the ensemble out of Kady's closet, because I own nothing as sexy-cute as this outfit. She wore it once this past summer and left it behind when she went to school.

I looked nice. Date-worthy, even though it's definitely not a date.

Wishful thinking. I need to get that idea out of my head. It will only come back to hurt my heart.

It's then that I feel something bounce off the back of my head. I look across the table and see that Carver threw a wadded up napkin at me.

"Rude much?"

Carver just laughs as he stands up from the couch where he's been parked the last half hour and walks over to sit at the table next to me, turning the chair around and straddling it. He's wearing a blue-tank that on the front says, "*It's not gonna suck itself*" with an arrow pointing down to his nether regions. Carver is never subtle and always up for a good time. He probably doesn't even need to advertise with a shirt like that. Most girls would do it on their own accord.

He wears a serious expression as he leans his arms over the back of the chair, adjusting his baseball cap backwards too.

"As the older and wiser of the two of us, I feel it my duty to instruct you on the important rules of dating..."

I tilt my head to the side, my curiosity peaked.

"It's not a date..." I refute once again, even though I know it holds no weight. "But what is this sage advice you have, o'wise one."

Carver reaches out his hand, gently taking mine in his very large palm. He stares down at our joined hands for a moment, as if he's in deep thought, ruminating over whatever he's about to say to me.

And then he smiles. The smile that only Carver can give women. It's his '*I know I'm pretty and you'd love to get down on your knees for me*' smile. Many girls have, of that I have no doubt. He's the captain of the team and is never at a loss for women admirers and hoops hunnies. In fact, it surprises me that he's home tonight without company of the female persuasion. Present company excluded.

"It's very important, Ky, that when the time comes..." He pauses for emphasis, lowering his voice so that I have to lean in to hear him. "That you always swallow. No spitting."

"Oh my God, Carver!" I shriek, jerking my hand from his grasp and shoving him on his shoulder. Carver throws his head back in laughter, howling at his clever tactics and perverted advice.

"That is so disgusting! Ugh! I can't believe you just said that to me!"

His laughter dies down and a genuine smile returns to his face as he looks me over with a sympathetic concern. Because I know he knows...although I don't know how, exactly...but he somehow has accurately concluded that I am still a virgin.

Yes, I know...it's most certainly not what I had hoped for myself as a college freshman and a few months' shy of my nineteenth birthday. But it is what it is. I can't go back through any time travel mechanisms to change my past. I've been extremely unlucky in fulfilling the right of passage that most girls my age have already checked off their bucket lists. It's just never happened for me because I've never had the opportunity. And I'm also incredibly awkward and shy. A homebody that isn't out there flirting and messing around with boys.

I had my first kiss when I was seventeen with my prom date, Billy Bloomquist. It was wholly unsatisfying, very wet and extremely awkward. He was in my biology class in high school, a member of the debate team, and a friend of the boy I really wanted to go to prom with. But I didn't have the nerve to ask him – and Charlie didn't ask me – so Billy was runner up.

I went on my one and only other date in high school, but that was a set-up, double-date with my friend Brittany and her boyfriend. Nick went to another school and there was no connection between us at all. Toward the end of the night, as Brittany and Alec got it on in the backseat, Nick groped and fondled me in the front seat in the most dispassionate way possible, until I finally just told him to stop. It was embarrassing. For both of us.

My hope was that college would fix all my problems. That by some miracle, the boys would have matured and I would turn into a less-bumbling, gawky girl who practically swallows her own tongue any time a guy talks to her.

Swallowed. No pun intended.

So with my very limited experience with an actual boy, my hands, mouth or eyes have never even actually seen a real live penis up close and personal. So I guess it isn't so surprising that Carver would catch on to my inexperience. He probably has some virginity radar, where he can easily detect the good girls from the bad. I assume he always goes for the naughty ones. What is a surprise to me, though, is that I'm about to ask him to elaborate on the whole swallowing thing. Lord help me.

"Carver," I say, my face heating from the blush coloring my neck and cheeks. "When you're with a girl...um...does she...well, how does it get from point A to point B?"

His eyes go round and wide as they flick to me, apparently trying to assess whether my question is for reals. I can't look him straight in the eye, so I glance away, staring instead at the table. Finding whatever he was looking for, Carver nods his head and scoots his chair in closer, as I inch my way back. While I don't like him like *that*, his closeness is a bit overwhelming. He is pretty damn hot.

"Didn't mommy and daddy ever tell you about the birds and the bees, Ky-Ky?"

I roll my eyes. "Shut up, dummy. That's not what I mean. I just...like, who makes the first move? Do you like girls who take control and just go for it? Or do guys like to be the instigator?"

"It depends," he says with surprising sincerity. "Some guys like the coy girls who flirt and flaunt, but act all innocent until it's time to get down to business. And some like the dirty girls who just take what they want. I happen to like them all. I'm an equal opportunity lover."

I snicker. My face is heated from the topic of discussion, but if anyone can tell it to me straight, it's Carver. And he might make fun of me, but I know he has my best interests at heart. He's a good friend to Cade, which by proxy, means he's a good friend to me.

Leaning my elbows on the table, I reach for the wadded up ball her threw at me earlier and begin to play with it. Nervous tick.

"What if...well, if the girl is inexperienced. Do you...or guys...will they just automatically take the lead?"

His answer is thoughtful and not what I expect to hear from him.

"Believe me, Ky-Ky, even guys worry about getting rejected. So if I'm with a chick who I think may be hesitant to go any further, or seems genuinely nervous, then I ask her for permission. A good guy should always that. If he doesn't, and he just races to the finish line without taking into account your needs, then he's an asshole who deserves to get blue balls. In my book, the girl is always in control, even if I'm leading the way. And I know it's hard to believe, but I've even been rejected before."

Wow. For being a certified man-whore, Carver is actually human just like the rest of us. And it appears that he even has a morality clause and can be a gentleman. Now that's a surprise.

My head nods in understanding, even if it still doesn't answer my question. Maybe it's a case by case scenario, but I'm dumbfounded by the mechanics of sex. It's obvious that everything starts with a kiss...and it requires some level of attraction to move forward. Hands and mouths are involved. And then there's naked body parts to account for. But the entire process is just foreign to me. I wish there was some kind of manual, or instruction sheet, that I could read to help me learn how things go down. My analytical-brain needs that type of direction.

Kady and I have talked about these things in the past, but hearing it from her can be akin to a Mexican telenovela. She's light years ahead of me in the boy and sex department, and is over-dramatic in the descriptive nature of things. She lost her V-card when she was sixteen in the back of a Tahoe and hasn't looked back since. The problem is that I don't own the same confidence level that she possesses. Kady is a born flirt. Rebel. Risk-taker. Renegade.

And I am not.

With Kady away at school in Boulder, it's not easy to pull her away from the various activities she has going on to have a serious heart-to-heart. And there's no way in hell that I'd ever discuss this with Cade. Good grief, he'd flip shit if he knew I was even considering something like this – with Van or anyone else for that matter. Carver seems an obvious choice to open up to. He's experienced, non-judgmental, and won't treat me any differently. I also know without a doubt that he will keep this in confidence.

"Okay, thanks C. Good talk." I pat his hand and start to get up from the table when he latches on to my wrist to stop me.

"Ky-Ky, this thing with Van...you know he has a girlfriend, right?"

Of course I know, you idiot! I want to scream at him, but it wouldn't do any good. In my dreams, Van's stupid girlfriend doesn't exist. It's just me and Van. But reality is a cruel bitch, where Van is head-over-heels for his high school sweetheart. And I'm just the lonely, pathetic, virginal school girl who pines after someone she can't have.

"Yes, I'm fully aware of his relationship. Thank you for enlightening me, though. As I've already said, Van and I are just platonic friends. I'm going to a movie, he's going to a movie, that' it. For the last time, this isn't a date...in fact, if it would make you feel better, you're more than welcome to come with us tonight, since it's obvious that you think I need a chaperone."

Carver scoffs like that's the stupidest thing he's ever heard.

"Sorry – no can do. I've got plans with Teresa and Sadie

tonight." He waggles his eyebrows suggestively. His transition from Dr. Drew to porn star Carver is astoundingly fast. "I just don't want you to get hurt if you have expectations of being boyfriend/girlfriend with him. Okay, Ky-Ky?"

Carver leans across the table and kisses me on top of my bent head. Cade and Carver have been friends for a long time, so I've come to expect his annoying habits and crazy theatrics. But this Carver is sweet and loveable. Too bad he hides that from everyone else most of the time.

Our heads turn in unison when we hear a throat being cleared behind us. I glance over my shoulder to find the oh-so-dreamy Van standing in the doorway, hands buried in his front pockets, eyes clearly taking note of what's going between us. I see a brief flash of something across his face, before his lips turn up into a warm smile. I shift back into my seat and straighten my back, feeling the warmth move across my spine.

"Hey guys."

Carver leans back, his eyes bouncing between the both of us until they land on Van again.

"Yo, what's up, bruh? Heard you're taking our lil' sis here out to a movie. Better keep your dick in your pants, though, or Cade'll kick your ass. And I'll have to join him."

I roll my eyes and groan. At this rate, no one will ever touch me, for fear of suffering the wrath of the entire ASU men's basketball team.

I stand up and grab my purse so I can hurry Van out the door, just as Carver bolts up and leans down to speak in a low voice at my ear.

His breath tickles my cheek and my face turns hot when I hear what he says.

"Remember to swallow."

I gasp loudly, slapping at his back as he quickly retreats

down the hallway chuckling, leaving me and Van alone in the kitchen.

Van slowly ventures forward into the room, a look of uneasiness washing over his features, as his gaze flits between me and the spot Carver just departed.

"What was all that about?"

Shrugging my shoulders, I bend my head back to look him in the eyes.

"You know Carver. Crude, rude and disgusting at every turn."

He grunts loudly, seeming to accept my answer as I scoop up my Gap denim jacket off the back of the couch.

"You know it's like ninety-five degrees out, right?" His voice holds a hint of amusement in it.

"Thanks, Mr. Weatherman," I retort, bumping his hip with mine. Technically, my hip hits his mid-thigh because of his height. "Movie theaters are always so dang cold, so I need to bring something to keep me warm."

There's no response, so I chance a peak up to his face. His gray eyes are now filtered with a dark shadow, eyes narrowed into slits. They blaze with intensity and for a second I feel trapped in his gaze. A spark ignites low in my belly and it ribbons its way up my spine.

Immediately the spell is broken when the door swings open and in steps Cade and Ainsley. Instinctively, we shift apart, as if somehow our bodies had been magnetized together in the moment before, closer than we realized, and now we are forced to recreate a suitable amount of personal space.

Maybe that's just me romanticizing the moment. I'm hopeless.

It's then that I notice Cade staring between us – first at me, then Van, then back to me. He wears a deep frown, squinting at us both.

"What's going on? Where are you two going?" He looks at his watch, his grimace growing wider. His tone is accusatory.

Van breaks the tension by greeting Cade with a strange handshake slash bro-hug, leaning down and giving a quick hug to Ainsley. Her usual bright smile is greeting us without a hint of any suspicion – either she's oblivious to the unusually high level of weirdness or finds it all rather amusing.

Whatever it is that she sees, she wraps her hands around Cade's bicep, which seems to be a natural elixir to his obvious stress. I have to admit, since they started dating, she has changed him in such positive ways. He's not as angry, or high-strung, as he once was. Ever since mom and dad divorced, Cade's found ways to avoid family obligations and has become self-absorbed. Ainsley has been a positive influence on him, and for that, I adore her.

We haven't had much of an opportunity to hang out much, but when we have had conversations, I find that she's just super chill and easy to talk to.

"Hi Cade. Hi Ainsley," I say, giving them both a small wave. "I invited Van to go to a movie with me tonight. None of my friends in town are available and he'd mentioned wanting to see it." It pains me to have to say what I say next, because I really don't want to make the offer. But if I don't, it will look weird.

"Do you two want to come with us?"

Cade immediately asks, "What movie?"

Ainsley says, "No, thank you."

And then they look at each other and burst out laughing. Cade concedes without argument.

"Nah, guess not. Me and Ainsley haven't seen each other in a while, so we have some catching up to do."

There's a naughty twinkle in Cade's eye and I blush at his inference. They'd recently gotten back together after a short break-up, and their alone time is few and far between these days with everything they have going on. I can't say as I blame them. If I were them, and that much in love, I wouldn't ever want to be apart for too long from my lover, either. Although, what would I know about lovers anyway?

Ainsley gives me a shy, apologetic smile. "Thanks for offering, though. Under normal circumstances, I'd say yes. But Cade and I aren't going to see each other much in the next few weeks."

Thank God for alone time.

All I want is to spend my own alone time with Van, without everyone else getting in the way and reminding me that he has a girlfriend. It's not like I can forget. Is it so bad to want to hang out with him because I like him as a friend? Friends go to movies together. Big deal. Plus, he doesn't like me that way, anyway. He's probably just being nice because he didn't want to turn me down.

Just because I have the constant urge to jump his bones shouldn't factor in to our movie-going plans.

"Okay, maybe another time then."

I give my brother a reassuring smile, trying to convey to him that everything is A-Okay. Nothing to worry about here. "We'll catch you later, Cade. Will you be over at Mom's on Sunday for brunch? You, too, Ainsley. Before I leave back to school?"

Just mentioning my return to school has my heart deflating, like a discarded birthday balloon that's been hanging in the corner of the room and is now slowly losing its air. My soul has felt lighter, freer, from the anxiety I feel about school. Since I've been back home. Since I've met Van. Geez, I'm such a loser. Why do I have to be crushing on the one guy I can't have?

"Of course we'll be there, Ky. We wouldn't miss it. And we'll bring gramps, too. Right, Ains?" My brother turns to look at his girlfriend, who happens to be a nursing student and my grandfather's nursing assistant at the adult-care facility where he lives.

"Absolutely. If Simon is feeling up to it, we'll bring him with us. I'm sure he'd absolutely love it."

My thoughts shift then to my parents, specifically my dad. He and I have gone out to dinner a few times this past week during my fall break. I know he and my mom are still on speaking terms, but definitely not friendly. And he and my grandpa - my mom's father – have never gotten along. To say I have a fairly dysfunctional family is an understatement. I guess all families have some form of drama.

As I consider this, I wonder what kind of drama Van has in his family? He hasn't discussed it much. We've talked a lot about school, movies, music, our favorite foods. Stuff like that. Nothing serious, though. He's also been pretty tight-lipped about his girl-friend, Lyndsay – only bringing up the things I already knew about her. She's apparently a junior at University of New Mexico. Is from the same hometown as him; is also a basketball player. And that he doesn't get to see her as much as he'd like to during the school year.

We leave shortly after confirming plans for Sunday. Although I have a car, which is shared between me and Kady when we're at home, Van says he'll drive. He's parked at the far end of the parking lot in one of the few visitor spots in front of Cade's building. As we near his car, he walks in front of me to the passenger side and opens the door.

My heart beats in the rhythm of an African drum cadence. *Ba dum. Ba dum. Ba dum...bum bum bum.*

Hiding my eyes from his watchful stare, I slide into the seat. "Oh, thanks."

He moves quickly around the hood of the car and into his own driver's side seat, starting the engine as the music blares through the speakers.

We both jerk in our seats over the loud intrusion and my hand automatically reaches toward the volume button to turn it down. Our hands collide, as he reaches in at the same time. My head is usually filled with a million things at any given time, day or night, but in this instant, I couldn't even have told you my name. Everything shuts down as our fingers touch, the spark of electricity that explodes between us is enough to render me speechless.

I pull my hand back with a mumbled apology, squirming in my seat. It's then that I notice my shorts-jumper has crept up my legs, exposing more than what might be considered an acceptable amount of flesh. I brave a glance over at Van, who I find is staring at my hand that's gripping the edge of the material. I have to lift my butt slightly to readjust my outfit and I see his eyes track my movement, the dark gray irises roving over me. He licks his lips as they part slightly. As if he wants to say something.

Then they snap closed and his eyes fly back to the front, where his hands grip the steering wheel tightly.

He barely says a word to me on the drive over to the theater, just a few Yes and No answers to questions I've asked him. All of a sudden, tension fills the car and I feel I've done something wrong. His mood changed from conservative to downright cold. I might need that jacket on sooner rather than later.

Maybe this was a mistake asking him to come along with me. I could've just as easily gone by myself. I've done that before.

He seems angry with me for some reason and I'm not sure why. I think back to our exchange prior to leaving and nothing comes to mind. Or maybe it has something to do with Cade and the awkwardness between us.

Hopefully the movie will give Van some time to decompress or something. He seems really tense and stressed suddenly, which is very unlike him. His natural demeanor, at least from what I've seen, is normally calm and chill. As we get out of the car and head into the movie theater, I say a quiet prayer that whatever is eating at him won't last long and we can go back to the way things were, when we were laughing and talking freely.

This Van - the stoic, grim and closed off guy - seems a far cry from the one I've gotten to know over the last week. Based on his expression at the moment, he seems almost tormented by something. Part of me wants to let him off the hook and tell him to take me home. But the other part wants to make him feel the same way he's made me feel.

Like I matter.

4

---

an

THIS IS TORTURE.

Pure fucking torture.

We're an hour into the movie, barely halfway through it, and I'm finally realizing what a bad idea this was to come with Kylah.

My nerves are shot and I'm hanging by a thread, trying to control myself around her. If someone asked me at this very moment what movie we are watching or who's starring in it, there's no way I could tell them. I have no clue because I haven't paid an ounce of attention to it over the last hour. All my focus has been on watching Kylah out of the corner of my eye.

Every little thing she does – the way she moves, her gasps of breath when something big happens on screen, and her laughter over witty lines – has me aching to touch her. And not in a friendly way. I want so badly to reach for her hand, the one that's been toying with the flimsy material covering her thighs. She's probably completely unaware that her fingers move constantly, fluttering along the soft, smooth skin of her legs.

Ugh. It's killing me.

And so is my guilt.

She was staring at me earlier with wary eyes. I know she noticed my demeanor had changed. That happened the minute I walked into the apartment and found Carver practically sitting on her lap. My jealousy spiked to a raging-green level over seeing him lean in to whisper in her ear. I wanted to be the one who got that gasped reaction from her sweet mouth, not him.

God, what is wrong with me? I have absolutely no claims over Kylah. I've barely known her a week and we're just friends, goddammit. I have a fucking girlfriend.

None of that seems to matter to my body, whose chemical reaction is like an exploding atom bomb. The minute I noticed what she was wearing when I picked her up, my body lit up with desire. Kylah is usually dressed casual in shorts and a vintage T-shirt. One day she wore a red print tee that said, *Have a Coke and a Smile.* Another was a Return of the Jedi shirt. And yet another, it was an old, worn Wrigley's gum T-shirt that said, *Double the Fun.* Which was actually pretty ironic, since she's a twin and all. And for the fact that she'd told me her sister was the wilder of the two.

That's what I find so refreshing about Kylah. She doesn't take herself so seriously. She knows who she is and has a self-deprecating humor about it. Although, over the short time I've spent with her, I've put together bits and pieces about her anxieties over school and the pressure she's under to do well. I know the feeling.

What I wasn't expecting when I picked her up tonight was to see her dressed in this short little number she's wearing. It's one hundred percent sweet – and way too sexy. And unless I'm mistaken, she isn't wearing a bra. The spaghetti-thin straps of her outfit show no signs of a bra underneath, and I can see her nipples poking out against the material. *Fuck*. That, along with how incredible her smooth, tan legs look decked out in the tiny jumper, had me adjusting my semi-hard chub after I shut the apartment door and walked to the car. Thankfully I walked behind her and covertly handled business.

The tension only grew worse on the drive to the theater. I was mesmerized by the sight of her legs and the creamy flesh that left little to the imagination when her jumper rode up her thighs. I had to stop myself from reaching over and running my finger along the curve of her knee, up the inside seam of her leg, skimming the exposed flesh at the edge of the material.

The torment is a thousand times worse now that I'm sitting right next to her in a dark theater, with only a puny arm rest separating us. My dick has turned into a steel rod from every casual brush of her satiny skin against my legs. I'm surprised I haven't broken the armrests with my crushing grip.

My brain is warring with my body. I honestly don't know what's going on with me. I've never had these types of thoughts for anyone else outside of Lyndsay. There's something about Kylah, maybe it's her pheromone make-up or whatever, that drives me absolutely crazy with desire. My thoughts have been all over the place when I'm both near and apart from her. And those thoughts are anything but friendly.

My current fantasy, not withstanding, has me slipping my hand off this armrest and placing it gently on her leg, as my fingers casually maneuver along the sweet expanse of her thigh, inching their way underneath the edge of the material. I'd follow the linear path up her leg and slide my thumb between the V intersection of her body, finding her panty less and very, very wet.

My X-rated thoughts are interrupted as a flash of movement to my right catches my attention. I turn to find Kylah struggling to pull on the jacket she brought with over her shoulders. Sure enough, she was right. It's like an icebox in this theater, which is great for me because I've been sweating bullets the last hour due to my hot train of thought.

Without blinking, I grab the jacket from her small hands and unfold it so she can slip it over her arms. In the process of sliding it up her shoulders, my knuckles skirt over that silky skin of hers and I feel the goosebumps breakout across her back. It does something to me that I can't begin to describe. Lust, sparking through my veins, electrifying me from the inside.

She shivers again, her hands reaching up to lift her hair away from her neck, as I quickly drop the material across her shoulders and let go. Terrific. Now I know exactly what her skin feels like. Like the petals of a rose bush.

Her fruity, mango scent lingers around me. Maybe it's from her shampoo, or her perfume, but it is a concoction that lights me up. Has me hearing the sounds of birds singing, or some shit like that. Jesus, I'm a sap. All I know is that she smells edible and it takes every ounce of strength I have to return my focus on the screen ahead of me. Otherwise, I might just act upon my desires.

But before I do, she lightly touches my arm with her hand, bringing my attention to her face. Her smile glows against the light shining from the movie screen, as she mouths the words, "Thank you." I nod and sit back against my seat.

Here's my problem. Not only is Kylah a temptation – with her sweet, innocence – like an auburn-haired angel – but she's also off limits. Off limits because I'm not available to pursue anything with another girl. I'm also forbidden to do anything with Kylah because of my relationship with Cade. Even if Lyndsay and I weren't together, there's no way Cade would ever be okay with me dating his sister. It's completely out of the question. So I might as well shut down these inappropriate thoughts of mine right this minute.

Kylah is off the table.

Even if I can easily picture her spread out on that table – naked and writhing underneath me as I kiss a wet path up those sexy thighs of hers.

Oh fuck. This is so not good.

I pray for the ending credits to roll. Either that, or just shoot me now. Because this pain I'm enduring is requiring Marvel Avenger-like strength.

"So what did you think?"

My head snaps toward her, the guilt probably written all over my face, wondering if she can read the dirty thoughts that have been running through my head the past two hours.

When I notice her curious stare, I realize she's asking me about how I enjoyed the movie. That makes more sense than her potential mind-reading capabilities. We're walking out of the theater and over to the food court in the mall, since we both decided the large popcorn she'd purchased didn't cut it for dinner. Nothing wrong with grabbing a bite to eat with your friend, right? Absolutely not.

"Oh," I stammer, trying to recall what the movie was even about. "It was good. Action-packed. I liked it."

Kylah laughs, her giggle doing something to my insides. Twisting my stomach up in knots that feel like the display in the Auntie Annie's shop we just passed.

"I really like the character Tony Stark," she admits with a shy grin. "He's so full of himself, but he has a right to be. The guy's a genius and engineered this super cool weapon to help protect human kind."

I give her a thoughtful nod, a smile cropping up at the corners of my mouth. "Sounds awfully familiar, Miss Scientist." I playfully bump her shoulder with my arm and I'm once again startled by the current that jolts through me from the touch of her skin. I clear my throat. "Isn't that what you and brother want to do? Find meaningful ways to save lives, either through medical science or mechanically engineered efforts?"

Kylah turns her head away from me, but not before I see the blush that's creeped up along her neck and cheeks. When she turns her head back to me, she's chewing on her bottom lip. To my knowledge, it's not meant to be seductive or coy, but it's turning me the fuck on. Her lips are nearly as plump and perfect as Scarlett Johansson's from the *Avengers*.

In fact, now that I compare the two, she could easily be compared to Scarlett. Kylah has this sweet seductive quality – kind of sex kittenish. Yet she doesn't know it or flaunt it. It's just part of who she is. It's a natural beauty that is sexy as fuck.

She shrugs one shoulder, lifting her bluish-green eyes to me. Her medium-length bob is styled tonight in a wavy-do, and it covers her cheeks. Without thinking it through, my hand brushes the wisps of hair away on one side, pinning it behind her ear. Those innocent eyes grow wide as the ocean and she smiles.

My heart stops. If I was walking, instead of standing at the moment, I would have tripped and fallen on my ass from the detonating power her smile has on me.

It's then that I realize something different about her tonight.

"Hey, you're not wearing your glasses." Yeah, just call me Mr. Observant. Maybe if my eyes hadn't been glued to her legs or her boobs earlier, I would have noticed sooner.

Kylah's hands touch the sides of her temples, like she just realized the same thing. Her smile turns shy as she squints up at me, her long lashes fluttering.

"Oh, yeah. I decided to wear my contacts. I usually don't take the time to put them in, but I didn't want the glare that can happen when I watch a movie on the big screen."

I consider this for a second before I respond.

"That makes sense. Well, it's the first time I've actually noticed your eye color. You have really pretty eyes."

And she does. They look like that beautiful sea green glass of the Caribbean waters. Or a mountain lake reflecting the forest green of the Evergreens around it. Tranquil. Calm.

She blushes. "Thank you."

"Do you and your sister look identical? Can people tell you apart?"

"Most people can't tell us apart until they get to know us. Our eye color is different. Hers are deep blue. But as we've gotten older, she's changed her looks and style a lot more than I have." She shakes her head in amusement.

"What do you mean, her style?"

She lets out a deep breath, as if she's always trying to explain this to someone. "Kady's a very colorful person, to say the least. Ever since we were old enough to dress ourselves – maybe three years old? She just liked to make a statement. I can't say that I blame her. Being a part of a pair is hard and it's difficult to separate ourselves from people always associating us together. And now that she's on her own and away in college," she laughs, reaching for a strand of her hair and looping it around her finger.

"When she left for school, she had long hair dyed pink on the ends. But when we Skyped last week, she'd shaved the sides of her head and the hair is now blue. I wouldn't be surprised to find her with a Mohawk when I see her over Thanksgiving break."

I'm a little shocked. I get that crazy-colored hair is all the rage now with both guys and girls, but I don't get why people mess with it. I kind of like the classic looks. Like on Kylah. She could easily be described as a classic beauty. Her style is simple, yet classy.

"Wow. That is really...unique."

"What about your family? Didn't you say you have a brother? Do you look like him?"

I open the door to the Paradise Bakery Café, allowing her to step in front of me, and give myself a second to consider my response, while also doing a quick perusal to admire her ass.

Had Dougie, my older brother, not been born with a debilitating condition, we probably would look a lot more alike. We share the same hair color – deep chocolate – and dark gray eyes. But's that where our similarities end.

"Um," I clear my throat. This is the part I always hate when I have to tell someone new about my brother. Not that I mind, but it's the reaction I get when I do. Pity. My family, and especially Dougie, is not to be pitied. He's an amazing guy, with the biggest heart of anyone I know.

"In some ways we do. Except in one pretty obvious way."

I take a quick glance around the room, as we move forward in line toward the counter. "My brother was born with CP."

"CP?"

"Cerebral palsy. Well, actually, he wasn't born with it. It became obvious around the time he turned three, just about the time I was born. He was struggling to walk and gain balance. He couldn't grasp or hold on to toys. His speech became slurred and mumbled, until he could no longer talk at all with the exception of really loud, high-pitched squeals."

Kylah's hand touches my shoulder and my eyes track to where we're connected. Her touch is soft and warm. Reassuring. Comforting.

"Wow. That must've been so hard on you growing up. And your parents. I'm sure it was difficult dealing with all the complexities of adjusting to that type of disorder in their child and then bringing a new baby into the world at the same time."

I'm floored by the capacity of empathy and understanding that Kylah has about my family situation. Most people are sympathetic to our plight. They feel sorry for me having to live in the shadow of a brother who takes all my parents' attention and focus. Kylah, though, seems to get the truth behind the situation.

Her next words are spoken softly, but with confidence. "That's one of the reasons I want to go into molecular biology. I'm fascinated by the human body and the diseases within them. How DNA is mutated to create human afflictions that we have no cure for and no way to stop."

I must be looking at her with a weird expression because she suddenly stops and slaps her hand across her mouth, eyes filled with worry.

"Oh my God. I'm so sorry. Sometimes I don't filter what I say and just blurt things out that other people don't care about. I'm such a dork. I'm sorry." Kylah turns her ahead, anxiously glancing around the room trying to avoid any further eye contact.

That just won't do. I place my index finger under her chin and press lightly, returning her attention back to me. She bites down on her lip and chews nervously.

"Ky," my voice is low as I speak directly to her. "You're not a dork. I think that's the coolest thing in the world that you know what you want to do with your life. I admire that about you. So don't ever downplay your ambitions, with anyone."

Before I can think twice, I lean down and place a chaste kiss on her forehead. I may linger a bit, taking in her tropical scent. Just then, the cashier calls us to the front to take our order. I place my hand on the small of her back and gently press her forward.

After we've both ordered, we move to the end of the counter to await our orders. Kylah stands next to me, but turns her head, moving the hair out of her face as she smiles up at me, her eyes bright and beaming.

"Thanks, Van."

"For what?" I ask.

"For understanding me. For being my friend."

5

K ylah

FOUR WEEKS Later

Returning to school after my week long break was a difficult transition – maybe even more so than my first week of school. I felt a longing – and a loss – that I'd never felt before. Homesickness, sure. But this emotion was different. And it was all due to Van.

I'd made a decision on my travel back to California. Even though it would likely kill me, I've decided that it is better to have Van as my friend than not to have him in my life at all. So friend-zoned it is. At least if I had to suffer with this achy longing I felt every moment of every day, I'd still have him in my corner.

Just not my arms. Or my bed.

Over the last four weeks since I've been back at school, he's proven to be an awesome friend. It's amazing how close we've grown through our texts, emails, phone calls and various other exchanges we've had. We've talked about everything. I've shared more personal details with him than any of my other friends – even my roommate Sienna. Well, with the exception of that tiny fact that I'm still a virgin. Whether intentional or not, we've steered clear of the sex topic altogether and avoided anything of a sexual nature. Probably a wise thing because I think I'd die of embarrassment if we got to talking about him and his girlfriend.

For example, when he returned last weekend from his visit to New Mexico to see Lyndsay, Van was specifically vague about details related to the time they spent together. Apparently I'm a masochist though, because I wanted to know everything they did together. Is that creepy? Yeah, probably.

Unfortunately – or maybe fortunately for me – Van was tight lipped about his weekend of love, offering very few details and only yes or no answers when I tried to pry deeper. Maybe that's a typical guy thing, I don't know. With my sister, she's always been loose lipped about spilling the beans about her torrid affairs. I guess it makes me respect Van even more that he's not willing to share all the intimate details of his love life with his girlfriend. That says a lot about his character.

Yet, the jealousy dwelling inside me, not knowing what they did together, is eating me up. There's absolutely no reason I should be envious or feel betrayed over his relationship with Lyndsay. It's illogical and stupid of me, really. He's been dating her for years and has only known me a little over a month. But that doesn't stop the hurt whenever he says her name – which is fairly often in conversation. It just proves that he's consumed with thoughts of her, and I'm simply consumed by him. Every single waking hour and in my dreams at night, Van is with me. I'm so pathetic.

In fact, it may be nearing the point of obsessive. I think I've become a bit of a stalker, following him on Instagram, where really rarely posts anything other than basketball-related updates. And Lyndsay's account is private, so I can't see what she posts on her page. We've also added each other on Facebook, but again, Van isn't great with social media. Just a few quotes here and there and lots of shared videos – some of which I find rather humorous that we talk about when we chat on the phone.

The first time he called me was one night three weeks ago. We'd been texting throughout the day and the conversation had veered into some deep territory about feeling anxiety over life and school and family. That is something we share in common. Although, he seems to have a better grip on it than I do. My shortcomings are very visible, where his are tightly guarded and well-hidden from the general public.

Anyway, I'd asked him via text what weighed on him the most. And his response was:

Not measuring up.

Whoa. I had just started to type out a response back when the phone rang in my hands. It surprised the heck out of me and I just stared at it incredulously for several seconds in disbelief. Like it was some prank. Because honestly, it wasn't often that I received phone calls. My two best friends from high school were now in different schools and leading their own new lives in college. And my sister had already called me earlier in the day, so I knew it wasn't her. My mom was off doing something with her new boyfriend, John. And Cade...well, suffice it to say, he never called me.

So I answered the phone with a circumspect tone in my voice.

"*Hello?*"

I was already aware it was Van because his name popped up on the display.

"Hey. It's me." He stated for the record.

"Hi," I responded, a big cheesy grin plastered across my face. I'm such a sucker for this guy. My insides turn all gooey at the sound of his voice, like the way a marshmallow melts over the heat of a campfire. "What's going on?"

I can hear his keys jingling in the background, and then the electronic dinging noise generated from his keys in the ignition. He's obviously going somewhere or coming from.

"I just got done with practice," he explains, as if he could read my thoughts. "And I didn't want to leave you hanging. I feel the need to clarify my last text."

The sound of his deep breaths had me vividly imagining what he looks like at practice. How he pushes his tall, muscular body up and down the court; running, sprinting, jumping. The sweat pouring down his chest. Crap. I needed to stop this train of thought otherwise I was liable to self-combust.

"Okay...so tell me. Who do you think you're not measuring up to?"

Someone meeting Van for the first time would never believe that he suffered from any insecurities. He just exuded coolness. Like nothing ever fazed him or ruffled his feathers. Never once had I heard any of Cade's friends or teammates say a bad word about Donavan Gerard. He was a class act in every way, both on and off the court. Van was always thoughtful, hard-working and considerate of his teammates.

Van heaved a deep sigh, seeped in frustration. "I don't know...everyone, I guess. My parents are at the top of the list. I feel this incredible pressure to do well for them, to make them proud, you know? They've been dealt a shitty hand with my brother – the financial problems, the physical demands – all of it. I don't ever want them to worry about me or be a burden to them. They have enough to deal with."

I slouch down on my bed, the pillows bunched behind my head as I burrow in and get comfortable. Hearing him open up to me sends a thrill down my body, even though we're talking about some pretty heavy stuff. It feels good to know he considers me a trustful ally to share these personal thoughts with.

I'm genuinely outraged by his confession. "How could you not make them proud, Van? I mean, you're an All-Star basketball player on a Pac-12 team. You're intelligent and have a brilliant future ahead of you. And to top that off, you're a genuinely kind person. What parents could ask for more than that?"

I'm not sure if I pushed him too far or said something wrong, because there was a really long pause. In fact, it went on so long I had to jump in to make sure he was still on the line.

"Are you still there?"

"Yeah, I'm here. Thanks for that, Ky. But that's not all... it's...well..."

"What is it?" I prompt.

"*Shit*," he cussed, causing me to jerk my shoulders back into the pillows behind me. It's rare that he swears out loud. At least, I haven't heard him curse much. "The thing is...God, this is hard to admit. But I'm not sure Lyndsay is...I don't think she's interested in being with me anymore."

This drew a loud gasp from my throat. Holy crap. Van had no idea what those words did to me. I felt an overwhelming sorrow for his obvious heart ache over this. That was my first reaction. The second is difficult for me to admit even to myself. The jealousy lessened its tight rein over me, opening up like the wings of a butterfly that's been swaddled in the confines of its cocoon.

"We got into a huge argument last weekend. I left without even staying the night. I confronted her about something I'd been holding back on for a while and she just blew up. Told me to leave. So I left her apartment, drove around for a little while and then went back because I couldn't drive all the way back to Tempe without finding out what was going on with her. When I got back to her apartment, she wouldn't even let me back inside. She just said she couldn't deal with it then and told me to go home. I mean, what the fuck was I supposed to do? Make a scene? Tear down the door?"

"Oh, Van. Oh my gosh. I'm so sorry. That had to have been awful for her to treat you that way, especially after all this time together." Even as I choked out the words, I knew they sounded lame. Who was I to make commentary on long-term relationships? Or lover's quarrels? I've never even had a boyfriend. I literally had no clue what it felt like for him. But it didn't stop me from adding, out of morbid curiosity.

"Have you spoken with her since?"

Although I can't see him, I instinctively know his head is bent forward and his eyes are closed. The sound of his breathing comes through the connection, slow and easy. I want so badly to be there for him, to wrap my arms around him and just hug him tight. It kills me that he's feeling so down. I wish I could find the right words to say that will make it better. But I can't. I have none to offer.

Plus, I'm not the one who has what he wants or needs right now. Lyndsay holds all the cards.

"She called me yesterday," he said and I mentally calculate that it's now Wednesday. She obviously took her own sweet time. "She apologized, if you can call it that. She said she's confused and she doesn't know what she wants. Said that things are just too crazy with school and ball. And the distance makes it even worse."

I erupt with more indignation than I should probably feel. "But you've been doing the distance for years...this isn't anything new for her."

He huffs. "Yeah, I know. I said the exact same thing."

A few seconds lapsed until we spoke again.

"Van." I say his name like a prayer. Soft. With reverence. A gentle plea. A whispered touch. "Where do things stand between you two right now?"

As horrible as it sounds, the hope in my heart is building with every pass of our conversation baton. Of course I don't want Van to suffer this type of hurt and heartbreak. As his friend, I should want him to be happy...and at one time, Lyndsay did make him happy. But right now, she's stabbing his heart out and filling him with despair. And for that reason alone, I hate her. I hate what she's doing to him. Van is an amazing guy and doesn't deserve the horrible way she's treating him.

If I were any other kind of girl – maybe one who was brave and true to herself – I might find a way to confront her and let her know just exactly how much of a bitch she is. Kady would do that. But me? Probably not. Plus, it's not my war to meddle in.

"God, Kylah. I don't know. I told her I'd give her time to figure things out. What else can I do? Thanksgiving is in a few weeks and we'll both be back home in Tucson. So I'll give her 'til then and we'll see what happens."

"So you're just going to let her have all the control? All the power in this one-sided situation?" I nearly slapped my hand over my mouth, in disbelief that I actually said that with such malice.

An apology is on the tip of my tongue when he says, "I know it seems like I'm a fucking wuss. I suppose I should just tell her to go fuck herself, but I can't. So if that makes me weak, I guess that's what I am."

Kill me now. If I wasn't already laying down, I would've fallen to my knees from the sounds of his desperation. My heart longs to be there for him. To show him she's not worth it and he deserves so much better. Whether that's me, or not, it doesn't matter. He just is too perfect to be shit on like this.

"Van," I say, the phone to my ear as my hand crosses my chest to rub the spot at my breast bone that aches for him. "I know it's not much of a consolation, but I'm always here if you need to talk. I may not be able to give any good advice, but I'll listen. I'll commiserate with you, if that's what you need." I would also be more than willing to learn how to make a voodoo doll and extol some harsh pain in Lyndsay's keester.

I hear the smile he gives me across the phone connection.

"Thanks, Ky. I really appreciate it. I can't talk to the guys about this stuff. They'd either make a joke of it and rub in that I'm just pussy whipped, or tell me to just go fuck her out of my system."

I swallow the lump in my throat, wanting to throw up my hand to offer my services if that's what he decided to do. I don't know what to say to that, though. Since I'm not a guy, neither of those things would ever cross my mind as the solution.

"Wow." Is all I say in response.

"Sorry. I know that sounds crude."

"No. No, I understand. I think you have the bad end of the stick right now. But you're handling it the best that you can. And I'm sure that she'll come to her senses and realize what a great guy she has in you..." He scoffs on the other end of the line but I don't let him get away with it.

"I'm serious, Van. I know it sounds totally cliché to say it, but if she doesn't appreciate what she has with you, then she's off her stupid, mother-trucking rocker. And it's her loss."

The loud laugh that fills the line surprised me with a deep resounding vibration that I can feel all the way down to my toes. This is the first real laugh that I received from him the entire phone call.

"Mother *trucking*? Did you really just use a kiddie version of profanity, Kylah? You are just too damn sweet for your own good."

Oh great. Here we go with the sweet girl comments again.

"Would you prefer I cuss? And say mofo?"

More laughter and I can picture him doubling over, slapping his knee in a fit of hysteria.

Finally, he seems to catch his breath. "Holy shit, Ky. You crack me up. Do I need to give you lessons on how to curse properly? Here, repeat after me...Fucker, fucker, fucker, *fuck, fuck, fuck...*"

My snicker turns into full-fledged giggles until I snort out in laughter, tears running down my face. I thrash around my bed, grabbing the pillow and shoving it over my face trying to muffle my sounds. My suitemates are right next door on the other side of the wall and are very studious. They don't like noise after ten o'clock. Party poopers.

Once our laughter died down, I stretched out on the bed, sighing a contented sigh. Although Van is dealing with a tough situation, it felt so good to laugh with him again and joke around. He makes me feel so...carefree.

"Woo-hoo! Earth to Kylah...come in, Kylah Grace Griffin."

My eyes snap open to find my roommate, Sienna, staring at me from the foot of my bed wearing a robe, a turban-towel wrapped around head, and a toothbrush dangling from her mouth. She has one hand on the toothbrush handle and the other on her hip, which juts out in her always-sassy stance.

I liked Sienna the moment I met her – the day we became roommates. She's a small-town girl from Northern Cali who lives a big-city life. In fact, sometimes, she is larger than life. Honestly, she reminds me of Kady, maybe that's why we get along so well. We've definitely found our own groups to hang out with in school, but she's become an important fixture in my life and a great friend. She's definitely helped ease my homesickness on more than one occasion.

Sienna knows almost everything about my newfound friendship with Van and hasn't hassled me about the situation. She's not stupid – she knows I have the hots for him, even though I haven't come right out and admitted it to her. Sometimes it scares me even admit it to myself. It gives me a guilt trip to like him so much. Like his issues with Lyndsay are somehow my fault because of my attraction to him. Stupid, I know. But that's how I think.

"Are you coming out with us tonight?"

I give her a blank stare and she huffs out her reply.

"Matt Keene's party. How could you forget already? We just talked about this yesterday."

Uh, maybe because I put it out of my mind as soon as we did. Parties hold no interest for me. Where my sister, along with Sienna, love to socialize and go to every party they can, I don't find the appeal. I'm a wallflower by nature. I don't drink to get drunk and I find it incredibly boring to be around a bunch of intoxicated nut jobs.

Sienna sits down next to me on my bed, slurping at the remnants of her toothpaste. *Gross.*

I give her an eye roll to demonstrate my displeasure over her manners before grabbing my pillow and cradling it within my arms in front of my chest. She caught me mid-daydream over Van. A place I would love to return to right about now.

She flashes a stern glare. "I hate to state the obvious, here. But how the hell are you ever going to lose your virginity if you don't get out and embrace the college lifestyle? Let your hair down and party like a rock star?"

One of the characteristics that I find enduring about Sienna is that she is very supportive and non-judgmental. Maybe that's because she recently came out as bisexual, I don't know. But when I told her about my lack of sexual experience, she didn't make fun of me or exclude me in conversations about her newfound sexual proclivities. Instead, she gently prodded and coaxed me into opening up and sharing about my past and what I wanted in the future related to dating and sex.

What I've shared with her is that while I don't need a boyfriend or commitment, or anything serious, I definitely don't want to just hand over my V-card to just any one-night stand. Perhaps I'm sentimental, or old-fashioned, but I feel it should be given up to some guy who a) knows what he's doing, and b) has some stake in the game related to my heart. And now that I know Van, and the way he makes me feel, he's the expectation the guy has to live up to.

I shove Sienna's shoulder, knocking her over on the bed. "I'm pretty darn sure I won't find the man of my dreams tonight at Matt's party."

She scoffs. "Who says anything about the man of your dreams? I'm not suggesting you find your Prince Charming, but you have to at least go where the guys are to get the dirty deed down and over with. Unless..." she waggles her perfectly plucked eyebrows suggestively. "You're looking for a chick to help you out."

My eyes flash wide and my mouth gapes open. Okay, maybe I'm a little naïve, because I have no idea how two girls could... well...do that? Sienna seems to understand what I'm thinking because a sly smile creeps up into the corners of her mouth.

She pats one of my knees, which are in a crossed-legged position.

"Oh, my sweet little Chery Pie," she chides sarcastically. "Do I have to spell it out for you? You of all people, studying the sciences and biology, should know that virginity isn't necessarily a medical condition. You can still lose it with someone of the same gender."

I feel my cheeks color in a bright blush and glance away from her. It's almost as embarrassing as the day my mom sat me and Kady down and had the "talk." It was too late for Kady, however, who'd already done it and informed me of all the ins-and-outs (pun intended) of sex.

Waving my hand in the air to stop any more talk, I jump off the bed to find my shoes.

"Okay, okay...please don't go into detail. I get it. But I'm not going to go to a party to lose my virginity. I've got some major reading to get done this weekend, anyhow. My paper is due before I leave on Wednesday."

Sienna pops off the bed and turns toward our dorm room door.

"Fine, I won't pressure you. But you know you're always invited with me, and whether you get laid or not is irrelevant. We'd have fun regardless." She blows a kiss in my direction before closing the door, heading into the small bathroom we share with our suitemates.

I got so lucky with my roommate assignment. There is no doubt that she has become a good friend and we will be friends for a long time to come.

But the friend I really need tonight is four hours away, at a completely different school, in a completely different state.

And likely thinking about a completely different girl.

6

Van

ALL I CAN THINK about lately is seeing Kylah again during Thanksgiving break, even though I should want to spend time with Lyndsay.

My basketball pre-season began in early November with several non-conference games – both were away games and on the road. We lost both, mainly due to being down two of our good players. One was Cade Griffin, who'd been suspended due to his recent legal issues. The accounts of his arrest, sentencing and probation all came out in a press conference back in September, at which time, Coach Welby announced that Cade would be benched for the first three games of the season.

While some of the team was disappointed in him, as well as many of his supposed fans, I stuck behind him. I respected the hell out of him for taking accountability for his actions and turning things around. He's a role model any young kid could easily look up to.

The other player we lost was Jeremy Munson, one of our junior forwards, who tested positive for anabolic steroids and is now suspended for the entire calendar year. Not only did he screw his scholarship, but he severely hamstrung us this season. Now our team's balance is completely messed up.

Unfortunately, I can't blame either Cade's absence or Jeremy's suspension for our loss last weekend. That one is entirely on me and was all my fault. I am the one who let everyone down – the coaches, the staff, the team, the fans. I got ejected from the game for a flagrant foul. I got in a fight with Jalen Hawkins.

I wasn't in a good headspace going into the game that night to begin with. Right between the team warm-up and game time, I'd been talking on the phone with Lyndsay, who normally called to give me a pep talk and wish me luck.

Instead, she mentioned the one thing everyone dreads hearing when they're in a relationship. The *"we need to talk"* announcement. Truthfully, I would have rather had darts thrown at my naked body or suffer an excruciating loss to UNC than to sit through the agonizing conversation about what I'm doing wrong in her eyes or how I don't stack up anymore.

I know something's going on with her. I just don't know what's changed or even when, but it has. As far as I'm concerned, we're still the same people we were at the beginning of the semester. I know I haven't changed.

Looking back now over the summer we spent together back home, I thought we had a great time together, like we always did. Or so I thought. The sex was still good, in my opinion, although it wasn't as frantic as it was when we first began. I guess the old adage is true, everything can become routine if you let it. Maybe we were just too comfortable with one another and I didn't give her the same level of attention as I did in the earlier years. In those days, we'd spend every waking hour together, as much time as we could. In the evenings, after our work days were done, we'd take a drive, go swimming in the lake near our house, and layout on blankets with our faces to the stars and talk.

That was then. This is now.

Since September, I'm lucky if I even talk to her once a week. At one point a few weeks back, I became so worried that something bad had happened to her because I hadn't heard from her in over five days. I actually called her sister, Lara, to see if everything was okay. Lara seemed hesitant at first to discuss it, but made some lame excuse about Lyndsay's school schedule and all the work she had to do.

Even at the time it didn't sit right with me. I fumed for several days. It was on my list of things to talk about when I saw her over break. That was until my confrontation with Jalen on the basketball court.

Jalen and I, we go way back – since we were in traveling select basketball leagues back in our formative years. He now attends Rice University in Houston and is a rising All-Star who we all think will be drafted at the end of the season. We aren't the best of friends, but we hang out whenever we're in the same city.

Although we aren't tight, it still makes our confrontation on the court disheartening. We'd just returned from halftime and started the second half, eighteen minutes to go. My team was down six points, but we were fired up after our halftime locker room pump up session.

A Rice player had just taken a shot and I'd rebounded, passing the ball swiftly to our point guard and captain, Carver. Sprinting down the court, I positioned myself outside the three-point line, allowing the remainder of the team to set up for one of our offensive plays, which Carver signaled with the verbal cue of "Eileen". That meant that I was to head to the top of the key, receive the pass, and dribble it in to shoot and get the points under the basket.

As with any sport, there's a fair share of taunts, jeers and trash talking. This game, in particular, was fueled with a lot of lip. Due to my easy-going nature, I normally let those comments slide. They're only meant to get me ruffled so I lose focus.

I'd just received the pass from Scott, one of our forwards, and was dribbling it in, watching the shot clock, as Jalen stood guard in front of me.

"Yo, Van...saw your girl last weekend. You two not together anymore?"

Normally, I'm in the zone, and zingers about my mama or team don't bother me. This one, though, had my attention snapping from the ball and basket to Jalen, my eyes narrowing at the audacity of what he was implying.

"What the fuck, bro?" I shout, noticing the clock is quickly dropping to under five seconds and I hear Coach yell from the sidelines to take the fucking shot. Keep in mind, I've been playing basketball since I was old enough to run. I know every diversion tactic there is on the court. And in that moment, I know Jalen is just trying to get in my head. But what he said next had me fucking losing it.

A smirk the size of the Rio Grande appears on Jalen's face.

"Just calling it like I see it...since she was sucking Cody Leach's dick and all, I figured you guys were over."

It was then that I lost control of the ball and before I could recover from his comment, Jalen had swiped it from my hands and started dribbling it down to the opposite end of the court. The entire place erupted in an audible gasp, the sound a sleeping dragon might make upon waking to find his lair infiltrated.

My brain caught up with my body as I launched myself at Jalen, encircling him with my arms and tackling him to the floor. Yeah, not my finest hour. For a minute there I forgot I was a basketball player and not on a football team. That tackle would've been sick out on the grid iron.

The problem with this little attempt to stop him mid-court? In the game of basketball, a player cannot touch, grip or make physical contact with another player who has the ball. In this case, it's considered an intentional foul.

However, it quickly turned into an all-out brawl, as the ball got jarred from his hands and I started wailing on him. All my frustration over what had been going on between me and Lyndsay over the last few months came out in a blur of punches, kicks and curses.

"What the fuck you say, motherfucker?" *Jab. Kick. Punch.*

Jalen squirmed underneath me, rocking left and right to try and protect his face from my fists, which was unleashing like a plane propeller.

"Get the hell off me!" He blocked my next punch and his knee got a good jab at my balls. "No wonder your girl is fucking someone else. You're fucking crazy, man!"

All I saw was red. My vision blurred, my ears filled with a white noise so loud it could drown out a New York city street during rush hour. I can't remember what happened next, all I know is someone pulled me off and I was being held against my will as I struggled to get loose.

The next thing I know, I'd been given a technical foul by the ref and ejected from the game. I was quickly escorted back to the locker rooms by one of the assistant coaches where I stewed over my anger the remainder of the game. It was a colossal fuck up.

I fucked up colossally.

After I'd cooled down enough to realize what had just happened, my first thoughts were of my parents and my brother. If they saw my melt down on Sports Center or on the news, they'd be embarrassed by my behavior. I wasn't the type of player that got into pissing matches. I never lose my cool. That's just not who I am.

I apparently have a breaking point and a hot button. My second coherent thought was what if what Jalen said was true? Or was it just a trumped up lie just to get me riled up and into my head?

I thought back to all the games we've played together in the past, and although he was always talking trash, he never personalized like this. He'd never attacked anyone down to the quick like he did with me tonight. So that meant there must be some validity in his statement. And to get to the bottom of it, I'd have to confront the only person I knew who had the real story.

After the game, I tried calling her –*five times* – each one went directly to her voicemail. On the fifth and final attempt, I left her what was probably an accusatory, incoherent message.

"I want to know why you don't answer my calls anymore, Lynds. Why the hell can I never get ahold of you? Where are you all the time? Why are you always too busy to talk to me? And oh yeah…please tell me you're not fucking *Goddamn Cody Leach.* You better believe we're gonna have a talk when I see you next week. If the rumor is true…goddamn it, Lyndsay. I don't deserve that."

I'd hesitated a second, pushing back the tears that had gathered behind my eyelids. I blame it on the anger and the adrenaline of the fight. But I know it ran much deeper than that. "I thought you loved me."

I couldn't get out another syllable without choking on the words or crying like a pussy, so I simply pressed the end button and hung my head in my hands. I felt the crack in my world that instant – the chasm breaking my heart in two. My life as I had known it for years was about to change without my permission – collapsing down around my feet.

The pain was excruciating

~

I'M PARKED outside Lyndsay's house, waiting for her to come out so we can go to dinner.

She'd called me back the night of the game, after I'd drowned my sorrows in one too many beers. I was still sober enough to hear her guilt over the phone. She was too smart to openly admit that she was fucking someone else, but she did have the guts to tell me that yes, indeed, she was at a party with Cody Leach and that she would tell me about it when we got together at Thanksgiving.

So here I am, tapping on the horn to let her know I'm here. I should go up to her door and say hello to her mother, who is still grieving over the loss of her husband just six months ago, but I just can't seem to find the nerve to get out of the car. My fingers curl around the steering wheel with a death grip, my knuckles turning white.

The car door opens but I will my eyes to stay focused in front of me. I will not look over at her, for fear of losing it right here in my car. Lyndsay's familiar scent fills the interior, surrounding me with memories of my youth, and I have to close my eyes, trying to avoid all the moments that bombard my brain. Images of our first kiss; our first date; lying together naked after we both lost our virginity together, limbs entwined as if we were each other's lifeline. All of it was too much and I have to bite my lip to restrain myself from reaching over and pulling her into my arms.

But I don't. I won't fall for the nostalgia.

She shifts in her seat. "Hey, babe."

When I whip my head in her direction, she has the decency to look apologetic for using the pet name in greeting. I'm sorry, but she does not have the right to throw out a term of endearment right now.

Her voice softens, offering up a bargain in its wake. "Can we swing by The Blue Horse and pick something up to go? Head out to Coal Springs?"

"Yeah, sure. That's fine." My voice is tight and dispassionate.

We get to the restaurant and order a pizza to go, as we make small talk in the waiting area. As we stand together, I notice a few nuances in her physical features that I hadn't noticed the last few times I saw her.

She appears thinner than she's been in the past few years – her blouse hangs loose at her shoulders and her waist is drawn in where it's tucked in at the hem of her shorts. As an athlete, Lyndsay is tall and has carried a lot of muscle. That muscle is still there, but she looks gaunt.

It's in her face, too. Her eyes are shadowed underneath and her skin holds a gray pallor.

"Lynds," I say her nickname and her eyes flit to mine in surprise, as this is the first time I've actually said her name since I picked her up. "Are you okay? You're not looking so good."

She appears to think about my comment, which is far from a compliment, and just as she opens her mouth to respond, our order is called. I walk up to the window and grab the box, and we head back out to the car. All of this triggers memories for me. We've done this so many times I can't even count. Picking up food and heading out to our favorite spot at The Springs, which is really just a big pond by an old coal mine.

As soon as we're back on the road, Lyndsay returns to my question.

"I don't think I'm okay, Van..."

Her voice is laden with sorrow. Weariness. Truth. Consequences.

"What is it?" She has me worried now. Especially after her father's sudden death earlier in the year, it's made me extra mindful of how brief life can be and how quickly it can disappear.

On autopilot, I reach over and grab her hand that's gripping the edge of the car seat, but she pulls it from my grasp.

"Van, I'm pregnant."

Oh shit.

That was not what I expected to hear.

I'm literally speechless. And I'm counting back to the last time we had sex. Did we use protection? Yes. We were always super careful. She has an IUD and I typically use a condom, unless we're drunk and sloppy.

It was a joint decision we made when we first started sleeping together. We didn't want to be young parents trying to raise a child without college degrees or careers. But we'd talked about it; what our lives would look like in the future. Our family that we'd have.

Someday. But not now. Not yet.

All my hostility I'd been carrying around with me evaporates. I pull into the gravel lot at The Springs entrance where only a handful of cars are parked. I lean over to - do what, I'm not sure? Touch her? Hold her? Whatever I intend, she dismisses by crossing her arms over her chest and turning her face in the opposite direction, avoiding my scrutiny. In search of answers somewhere outside the window.

"Wow, okay. You're pregnant...not the end of the world. What do you want to do, Lynds? I'll do whatever you want. If you want to have it, we'll have it. We'll get married. We'll..."

And then that crack in my world splits wide open, the San Andreas fault opening up inside my soul, swallowing me whole and sending me careening down to the bottom pits of hell.

"Van, it's not yours. It's not your baby."

I can't quite fathom what she's just said. It's a jumble of

words, bouncing around in my head, and I'm unable to make sense of them.

"*Whatdoyoumean*?" I mumble.

She finally turns back to me, tears streaming down her face, agony written all over it like graffiti on a wall.

"I'm sorry," she stammers, body shaking from the violent sobs escaping. "I'm so sorry..."

Well, I guess that puts an end to my questions over Lyndsay's faithfulness.

You want to know what's worse than finding out your girl-friend of five years is sleeping with another guy?

Finding out she's carrying his child.

7

K ylah

I LOVE THE HOLIDAYS.

Let me rephrase that. I used to love the holidays when we were all one big happy family.

My mom would go all Martha Stewart on us, fixing all the most incredible festive dishes. And she'd go all out with the baking and decorations. When everyone else was out at the malls shopping on Black Friday, mom would have me, Kady and Cade taking down all the boxes of Christmas decorations from storage and filling every nook and cranny in our house with holiday cheer, all the while Christmas music played in the background.

This Thanksgiving, however, would be decidedly different, to say-the-least. Divorced parents, a mom who is dating our neighbor, and three college students reconvening in the house seem to up the weirdness quotient exponentially.

But I am more than thrilled to be back in the same house

with my siblings – especially Kady. I've missed her so much. I've missed her annoying habits, which include leaving make-up and gobs of toothpaste on the bathroom counters, but also her light and bubbly personality. She's always happy – carefree and effervescent. Kady has this light about her that illuminates everyone and everything around her. When I am down, she lifts me up. And I'm in much need of that right now.

It's Friday evening, the house smells like baked goods and cinnamon sticks, and the music in the background is full of holiday cheer. But I am not cheerful, because I haven't heard from Van yet. The last time we spoke was on Wednesday evening, right before I flew back to Phoenix. He said he would give me a call on Thursday. I was well aware he was going to have his "talk" with Lyndsay and he promised he would call and update me.

That may seem odd to others to know he was going to tell me about the intimate conversation he had with his girlfriend, but I was his new sounding board. He'd already told me all about the reason he was ejected from the game last week and the subsequent phone calls with her. I also know that he was seriously worried. I can't say that I blame him. From what he told me, there is a serious chance that she might break up with him.

What a horrible thing to happen over the holidays.

Sadly, I don't know how I should feel about that. My emotions are all over the board on the topic.

Obviously, as Van's friend – the only one he claims he can talk to about these matters – I want to hate Lyndsay with all my guts. How can she do this to such a nice guy? I realize there's always two sides to every coin – just look at my parent's break-up for example. While my brother likes to pin all the blame on my dad for leaving my mom and the family, my mom has confided to me a little that she was also at fault. She said over the years she'd lost herself a little more with every passing year, until she realized she was just a shell of a woman. And who can love someone who doesn't even love themselves? Her words, not mine.

Van shared with me that the distance had a major impact on them both. When at first it made their relationship stronger, over time he said it just weakened the areas that had started to decay and crumble. The weeks and months that went by without visits, along with their crazy schedules during the season, had put a strain on things. Their weekend visits became stilted and uncomfortable – like they were strangers trying to relearn the things they loved about each other.

I don't want Van to be unhappy. I care too deeply for him. So if finding a way to work out whatever their problems are and remaining together will make him happy, then I'll back him one hundred percent. I'll bury my crush in order to remain friends with him. Even if it means my lustful fantasies will never have a chance of coming true.

On the other hand, if they do break up, I want to be there for him in whatever capacity he wants. I doubt Van thinks of me as anything more than a friend, anyway, but if in the off chance that should ever change, and if he feels the same attraction as I do, then I'm ready. I'll gladly be his rebound girl. See what I did there? Rebound? With a basketball player? Sometimes I'm a funny girl.

Needless to say, if I'm to do any of those things, however, it would require hearing back from him. It's like he's dropped off the face of the earth. He hasn't returned any of my calls, and my texts have remained unanswered. It worried me at first. But now I'm hurt. Frustrated. Even a little angry that I'm so easily forgotten in the presence of Lyndsay.

We're all finally settled down on the big L-shaped couch in the family room, tired out from the long day of activity, about to watch a movie. Kady's picked *The Sound of Music* – her favorite – and we all do a sing-a-long. Everyone except Cade, who just bitches, moans, grumbles and curses while his head is buried in his phone or laptop as me, my mom and sister belt out the all-too-familiar songs.

Cade and I are already sitting on the couch waiting, my mom fixing up some plates of cookies and hot chocolate in the kitchen, and Kady's upstairs in the bedroom changing into her pajamas. It gives me a chance to share with Cade my thoughts on his girlfriend.

"I'm glad Ainsley and her sister got to come over for dinner yesterday. I really like her, Cade."

He looks up from his phone, where I presume he's either looking at a sports website, or is texting with Ainsley or one of his friends.

He gives me a cheesy smile, one that demonstrates how smitten he really is. "Yeah. She's pretty great, isn't she?" He and Ainsley have been dating since earlier in the school year and it's something I never thought I'd see. Cade with a serious girlfriend.

"It's such a small world, too. The fact that she is grandpa's nurse is so weird. Cool, but weird." Cade isn't the only one in love with Ainsley. My Grandpa Simon is head over heels for that girl. I'm pretty sure he thinks she farts rainbows and unicorns.

He gives me a small grunt, returning to his phone, a frown forming on his face where is grin had just been.

"What's wrong?" I ask, wondering if something's going on with Ainsley.

He shrugs before typing again. "It's Lance. He says Van is over there drunk as shit and cursing up a storm, looking for trouble."

"What do you mean? That's not like him. Why is he upset?" I'm pretty sure I know why. That means it may not have gone too well with Lyndsay. My tummy flips and rolls with a wave of worry.

Cade's eyes zero in on me, curiosity flaring over the concern in my voice, which I couldn't hide even if I tried.

"Yeah. I guess he's ranting on about this ball player, Cody. Says he's going to go fuck the guy up."

I push to my feet, sliding into my flip-flops next to the lounger and grab at Cade's hand to help pull him up, too.

"Come on. We've got to get over there...this is not good. He needs my...I mean, our help."

I'm not sure Cade even knows what to make of my sudden call to action, but he doesn't protest. Instead, he reaches into his pocket for his keys and slips on his shoes.

I run down the hall and then take the stairs two at a time, grabbing my purse from my dresser before rushing into Kady's room.

"Gotta go...not sure when we'll be back home. I'll call you later."

I hear her shout my name, but I'm already down the stairs and grunting out a good-bye to my mom, who stands in the hall looking confused, and then I'm out the door and jumping into Cade's awaiting car.

My mind is racing a million miles an hour as we drive the twenty minutes to Tempe, although it feels more like two hours. I imagine a plethora of scenarios and it only heightens my fear. I'm uncertain what we'll find when we get there, but if Lance's description is accurate, it could be a pretty ugly mess.

Poor Van. This can't be a good sign that things went well yesterday. I guess I understand, even though I'm a little miffed, why he didn't call me. I just hope that it's not too late and I can talk him down off the ledge when we get there. He's gotta be hurting pretty good right now.

Pulling into Cade's parking spot in the front of his complex, we can already hear Van's loud and agitated voice carrying from inside the apartment.

"Shit," Cade laments, slamming his car door. "The neighbors are going to throw a shit fit. If we get the cops called again this semester, we might be thrown out on our asses."

We make it up to the front door when we hear a loud crash from inside and then Lance's voice shouting at the top of his lungs.

"Dude, calm the fuck down! Do I need to shoot you with my tranquilizer gun?"

Huh? Why in the world does Lance have a tranq gun? I'll leave that question for another time.

Cade pushes open the door just as Van comes barreling into us full force. I'm knocked to the ground as Cade tackles Van right beside me. We all three groan in unison. Rolling to my side, I rub my hip that seems to have suffered the brunt of the fall, as I watch in horror as Cade flops on top of a flailing Van's stomach.

"Get off me, man." Van slurs, unable to move an inch.

"Not happening until I know you can be trusted to be calm." Cade twists his butt deeper into Van's abdominals. "Are you going to calm down?"

Van wiggles and grunts, and then finally lets out a whoosh of air, followed by a very slurred "*fine*". Cade jumps to his feet, extending a hand, first to me and then to Van.

I don't say a word as I stare up at Van. Mainly because I'm in utter disbelief of what I'm seeing. He looks awful. His T-shirt is stained with sweat, or maybe vomit, and he smells disgusting.

Cade seems to agree with me. "Dude, you reek. What the fuck is wrong with you? Go take a shower, it'll do you some good. I'll grab you some shorts and come back out when you're ready. I'll have coffee waiting."

Van laughs. Out of all the laughter we've shared together, I've never heard such a desperate sound. If I could, I would throw my arms around him right this minute. Hold him. Tell him how much he means to me. That I'm sorry he's so hurt. But I can't because my brother and Lance are here. Watching our every move.

And if my brother ever found out I had a crush on Van Gerard, he'd throw a hissy fit of ginormous proportions.

Instead of doing any of those things, I reach out my hand to lightly touch his, barely skimming the top of his knuckles.

"Come on, Van. I'll help you. Just follow me, okay?"

My brother touches my shoulder. "He'll be fine. I'm sure he can handle it on his own. It's not your mess to clean up, Ky."

I wave him off, already reaching around Van's solid waist to help move him toward Cade's master bathroom where there's a walk-in shower.

"I got it. It's not a problem. I'll yell if I need anything."

Cade chuckles, but lets me go with no argument. "Suit yourself." And then he gives Van a death glare. "Touch my sister and you're dead." I groan in embarrassment but keep on walking.

It's not until we get into the bathroom, Van's head bobbing back and forth like a dashboard ornament, that I realize this could end badly. I don't know what I'm thinking trying to take this on myself. Really, how am I supposed to manage to get a six-foot-seven drunk basketball player into a shower? What if he passes out on me? Falls down on me so I can't get up? And then there's the teeny-tiny problem of clothes removal. And a potentially naked Van in front of me.

This sounded better in my head when I was just trying to calm him down. Although the Naked-Van sounds pretty darn good.

Taking a deep breath, I get to work. Van's propped up against the edge of the counter, eyes closes, body swaying gently. I grab the bottom edge of his shirt and start to pull it up and over his head. Unfortunately, I hit a roadblock. Mainly, his size. I'm a fairly tall girl, but still a full foot shorter than him, and I can't reach, even on tip-toes, past his shoulders.

"Van, you need to help with this. I can't do it."

His eyes are dark, gray slits – only half open. But he follows my direction and yanks the material from his body, tossing it on the ground next to our feet. My eyes are now pinned on the dark smattering of curly hair on his chest. Another time, another place, I might have had the guts to reach out and run my hands across his pecs and down his tight, smooth abs. Down the dark happy trail leading underneath his pants...to maybe find some other form of happiness. But sadly, tonight is not the night and it's not happening now. No matter how much I want to do it.

Truth is, I probably wouldn't be brave enough to do it anyway. If anything ever happened between us, Van would have to be the one to make the first move. I've never been assertive in any way, especially with guys. Not like I've had much experience in that department, anyway. Plus, Van wouldn't dream of making any move on me. His friend. The shy girl who is his buddy's little sister.

Van teeters like a huge Redwood tree above me, swaying in the wind. The only thing that keeps him upright, evidently, are his hands which grip the edge of the counter behind him. I watch his face, the bright light of the bathroom casting shadows on some of the confliction etched in the lines on his forehead.

He leans forward, bending his head until our noses touch. I gasp, because this is the closest we've ever been, except for a few brushes of our hands and knees when we went to the movie together last month. But this touch is intentional. His eyes are severely unfocused but I watch them openly drink me in.

It feels like he's weighing on a decision to kiss me. *Please, kiss me.*

Please, please, please kiss me.

I don't think I breathe as I wait. His voice is raspy and gravely when he finally speaks. It comes out like a torpedo from a submerged submarine.

Fast. Furious. Pummeling its target full force.

Blasting me to smithereens.

"She's fucking pregnant."

Who's pregnant? What in the world is he talking about?

It takes me a second to figure out who he's referring to. We've talked about Lyndsay often, usually just trivial facts about her or that he'd talked to her. Van did give me clues that things weren't all sunshine and roses between them recently, but he never spoke ill about her or mentioned anything about their sexual relationship. So to hear him tell me that she's pregnant...well, I'm more than stunned.

He said it with such loathing, mixed with despair. Van is definitely not happy about it.

"Um...wow," I manage to squeak out, because really? What am I supposed to say to that? "That's...not a good thing, I take it?"

I have no idea what I'm supposed to say in a situation like this. Gee, the boy I have the hots for just knocked up his girl-friend of five years. I guess congrats are in order? Even though I still want to sleep with him. I'm despicable.

I'm not prepared for the snide, sarcasm that drips from his reply. Or the gorgeous smirk that beautifully contorts his face – in pain and hostility.

"Not when it's not mine."

Holy shit. I take an involuntary step back, hitting the wall with my butt. There's now about three feet between us, but all that space is filled with questions. My head is spinning from the prox-imity to his naked torso. From the admission of this horrific truth.

"*Wha-*"

He snorts, interrupting me before I can even get the word out in its entirety. "She's been fucking some other player for months. Since last May. Behind my fucking back. She's been together with him and didn't have the guts to tell me or to break up with me. She's lead me around by my ball hairs and I look like a chump. A fucking idiot. I. Am. A. Fucking. Loser."

"No!" I blurt emphatically. Hard and loud enough for him to rear back, his eyes flaring wide in surprise.

I get it. Sweet, docile Kylah doesn't raise her voice. Ever. But dammit, I will not have Van feeling he is to blame for this situation.

"Don't you dare feel embarrassed over her errors in judgment or her despicable behavior. Oh my God, Van...I can't believe her. How could she do this to you?"

His hand rubs at his temples before gliding down his face, as if trying to stave off a headache. His eyes remain closed, head bent toward his feet which are crossed at the ankles.

"I've been in love with a cold-hearted bitch. It makes me sick."

I can't imagine what's going through his head right now. My thoughts veer to Lyndsay, wondering why the hell she would string him along all this time if she was with someone else. How could she be so cruel? Why didn't she just cut him loose earlier on, before all of this happened? He's right about her being cold-hearted. It's a shitty thing for her to do.

As bad as it sounds, and as horrible as I feel for thinking it, I hope she gets what she deserves. Her cheating behavior is reprehensible.

My internal berating is interrupted by a groan from Van. My eyes fly back to his, and I see the sudden look of horror in his eyes, his face turning a vile green.

He growls, an animalistic noise, as he moves so fast I barely blink before I see him crouching down over the toilet. "I'm gonna be sick."

The contents of his stomach splash into the bowl. My own gag reflexes lurch for a second, but I quickly move into action. I pull a washcloth from the rack on the wall and wet it under the sink before I kneel down next to Van.

Laying a hand in the middle of his back, which is now covered in a sheen of sweat, I place the washcloth against his neck. I feel, before I see, his body shiver, the goosebumps climbing over the thick cords of muscles of his shoulders and arms. I pull the cloth away and make a swipe across his face, his hand coming up to take it from my hands.

"Thank you." He mumbles, pushing his sweat-drenched hair away from his face.

He'd been wearing a man-bun tonight, so most of it was pulled back into a messy roll, leaving only a few wisps escaping at his temples. Most of the time he left if down, either with an elastic sports band tying it back, allowing his gorgeously angular features to be prominently displayed, or he'd wear a beany over his locks. But it was his iconic man-bun that I'd grown to like. I'd only seen his hair down and loose one time before – the day of their pre-season press conference. I'd nearly dropped to my knees when I saw the picture of him wearing a suit, his white shirt collar opened at the top, and his shiny, dark locks brushing at his shoulders.

Unbidden, my hands go to each side of his head and I smooth back the loose hairs, tucking them behind his ears. He gives a soft moan and then shifts off his knees so he's sitting on his butt, sagging against the side of the tub, his head resting on my shoulder. I dare not move, but take a quick peak over at him. His breathing is still labored, but slowly returning to normal.

"I don't want to move you, but I think I should go get you some water. You need to stay hydrated."

My knees are pulled up to my chin, and his large hand lands on top of my kneecap, applying gentle pressure. The zing of pleasure rockets through my legs and my toes involuntarily curl with joy.

"No, not yet. Just...wait a bit."

I nod my head, because yes, regardless of the circumstances, my body doesn't want to move from this spot at the moment. I realize that we're sitting on my brother's bathroom floor – and ew, who knows when it was last cleaned – and that Van just puked his guts out and the booze he'd consumed is still leaking out his pores – but honestly? I wouldn't want to be anywhere else.

It's crazy, but my brain feels wonky just by his touch and his nearness – as if I was the one who was drunk. I have tingles at every point of contact between us and it feels unimaginably good. Better than anything I've ever experienced before.

We sit there for a good fifteen minutes. My butt has become numb from the cold tiles, but despite that fact, I'm warm from the furnace heat emanating from Van's body. If it feels this good just sitting next to Van, what would it be like to be wrapped up in his embrace? For his arms to be slung around me tight. If he were on top of me, pushing inside of me, slow and deep.

I jolt upright from the sound of my brother's voice. I must've fallen asleep and was dreaming about Van. And from the sound of the soft snores at my shoulder, I know Van is asleep, too.

"Jesus Christ...what happened here? I got worried that Van was taking advantage of you."

Ugh. Stupid big brother.

I press my index finger to my lips, telling him to shut the hell up so we don't wake my sleeping giant. My shoulder itches a little from the scruff on Van's jaw and chin, but I would go numb before I move him.

"Shhh. He needs to sleep this off. But first, can you go grab a bottle of water for him? He's going to need it tonight."

Cade shrugs and turns to head back out to the kitchen, leaving me and Van alone once again.

"Kylah?"

It makes me sad to lose the connection that we just had, as Van lifts his head off my shoulder, rubbing out a kink in his neck.

"Yeah?" I whisper, running my fingers over the spot where his scent still lingers.

"Thanks for being with me tonight. I may have drunk too much."

I give him a dismissive wave and then turn my head to face him, smiling softly. "Ya think? What was your first clue?" I wink, trying to add some levity to the already uncomfortable situation. I can't help but use the moment to ask the question that's been burning on my mind.

"What are you going to do, Van? About...*you know*...Lyndsay."

He sighs, the weight of the world being exhaled in that one breath.

"What can I do? She's made her choice. We're through. As far as I'm concerned, we had our last conversation last night. I don't ever want to see her again. She can live happily ever after with her baby daddy."

I suck in a gasp at the venom in his tone. Not that I blame him.

"Do you think it'll be that easy? Just letting go like that and never talking again? I mean, you two were together for such a long time."

Obviously, I don't know a thing about relationships, except my parents. And I know it's different when a couple has been married for over twenty years, but it took a long time for my dad to be completely out of the picture. So I'm not sure what happens in a break-up like Van and Lyndsay's.

Is it truly over just like that? Or, are there lingering and residual feelings and complex dialogue after-the-fact?

Well, if there is, Van doesn't seem to want any part of it.

"If I never see her again, it will be too soon."

His eyes lock on mine and I see the sincerity there. And the conviction when he says the next thing that hurts more than I could ever imagine.

"And I'll never be in another long-distance relationship again."

With that, my heart deflates and lies limp on the cold tile floor – right along with the remnants of his own battered heart and soul.

8

Van

I SPENT the last three weeks in a state of perpetual angst and sleepless nights. Our basketball pre-season is in full swing and we are playing every weekend in out-of-town tourneys. It's utterly exhausting and my head and spirit aren't fully in the game. Which is a source of frustration for my teammates.

So much so that Carver, our point guard and team captain, has been in my face the last two games because my rebounding and shooting ability has diminished significantly. Oh, and I've fouled out the last three games because I'm playing too aggressively under the basket.

In my power forward position, it's my job in both offensive and defensive play, to be the guy under the basket who 'posts up' to block and rebound in the man-to-man zone defense. And to put up the ball when I do end up rebounding. While being aggressive in play is rewarded by increasing team effectiveness and shot advantage, it doesn't help when I'm fueled by anger, versus competition, and don't temper my playing techniques.

Like tonight, for example. I was down in the paint, my back toward the basket. I was posted up to protect the ball as Scott Wagner, our small forward, was setting up for a three pointer. He missed, and both me and Eli Blanchard from Marquette, went up to rebound. He picked it off the rim, his elbows out as he guarded it against me. I had other plans, though, as I reached in to the pocket he'd created and grabbed hold of the ball, working to pull it free from his grip. The ball came loose and we both dove for it before it went out of bounds.

At that point, I'm not sure what happened. All I know was Eli was about to grab for the ball, and suddenly he's on his back and about to pass it to one of his team players. I jumped to my feet, and was about to run back down the court when I hear him mutter a comment...I couldn't even tell you what he said, but it was lewd and it was a snipe at me. So instead of running toward the ball in play, I stomped on his stomach with my foot, using him as a human launch pad.

It wasn't an accident and it was very apparent that it was on purpose. So when the ref's whistle blew and I was charged with a foul, effectively booting me out of the game, I tried to defend myself by getting in the ref's face. I lied to cover my butt, arguing that it was an accident. I tried to play it off like I just lost my balance and Eli just happened to be in my way. You know, it's basketball. Accidents happen.

Unfortunately, I'm a terrible liar and didn't convince anyone of my innocence.

So I got my last foul and had to sit the bench the remainder of the game. Luckily, the second half clock was already winding down. But it still didn't prevent Carver from getting in my face after the game.

Now I'm sitting on the bench in the locker room, waiting for everyone to come back in so we can hear from the coach. We did end up winning the game, barely squeaking out with a five-point lead. It was touch and go for most of the final half.

My head is lowered, my elbows on my knees, as I watch the sweat drip down onto the tiled floor. It's then that I see a pair of size twelve shoes planted in front of me. I raise my head to see a very pissed off Carver glaring down on me, his brow furrowed and his lips in a tight line.

It takes a lot to ruffle Carver. He has a pretty even-keeled personality. On the court, he's a force to be reckoned with and the boss in three-pointers. Off-the-court, he's just as amiable.

But right now, he looks like he wants to take a swing at me. Hard.

"You want to tell me what the fuck is going on with you, bro? Why is your head in your ass? I've never seen you play this shitty. And never have I seen you do something like you just did to Eli. You pulled a fucking Laettner, you twat."

He's referring to Christian Laettner, a former Duke University power forward/center who is one of the most hated basketball players of all time. Great player, but questionable ethics. Mainly because he stomped on the chest of a Kentucky player during a 1992 regional final. Personally, I always revered Laettner because he was one hell of a ball player. The clutch shots he took and the number of titles he had under his belt were impressive.

Sadly, he'll always be remembered for two career-defining moments. One was the clutch shot, turn-around jumper, buzzer-beater and the other is the bullying chest-stomp.

I shake my head that's still in my hands, disgusted with myself. "I know...I know."

Even though I keep my eyes averted, I can feel Carver's eyes boring into my head. When I do finally lift my head, he wears a scowl that would make most people run in fear. He's a mother-fucking badass, his tats covering the majority of his right arm, and biceps that could (and probably have) lifted tractors.

"Dude, just get over her. You got a future here and plenty of other chicks who you can fuck to get her out of your head. Women aren't worth it. They'll fucking ruin ya."

If that's supposed to be a pep talk, it's the worst one in the history of all pep talks. Seriously. Why the hell would I take rela-tionship advice from Carver, who to my knowledge, has never had a serious girlfriend and doesn't know shit about love.

I scoff and stand up, towering over his six-foot-three frame. By most standards, he's tall. But not in this locker room, where the average height is six-five or more.

Out of respect for Carver, I don't shove him like I want to. A fight would feel really good right now, but I'm not stupid enough to throw a punch at my team captain. That would be one sure way to get myself suspended indefinitely. So I move around him and grab a towel from the bench, heading toward the showers.

Before I turn the corner, I glance back over my shoulder to where he's still standing, hands on his hips, lips pursed like he still has something to say.

"I respect you, C...but you don't know shit about what's going on. So lay the fuck off."

Carver and I aren't extremely close, but we respect each other as team mates. I have never spoken so bluntly to him, and I'm a little worried by the look in his eye that he might clock me for speaking out of turn. And when he comes barreling toward me, I barely have time for my hand to instinctively cover my balls, as he slams me into the locker, his forearm pressed right up against my throat.

My eyes bug out wide, but I hold my ground. I'm not about to fight him, but I won't back down like a fucking pussy.

"Don't tell me what I do or don't know, because you're the

one who doesn't know shit. I get it, man. It sucks what she did to you. But it's motherfucking life. You're not human if you haven't lived through a broken heart. But my advice to you, bro, is that you need to man up and pull your shit together before you spiral out of control." He releases me and steps back, allowing me room to breathe, my fingers massaging at my neck where he had me pinned.

My eyes take in the room around me, where the guys are milling about, trying to look inconspicuous and uninterested in what's happening between us, even though I know they want to know. It's probably all over the interwebs by now.

"Just take it from me, man," he continues, running a hand over his sweaty mop of hair and down the back of his neck. "If you don't get control of things, the girl wins by default."

Carver's eyes are hazel, but when he looks me in the eye they are darker than I've ever seen them. They're filled with the same pain I feel right now. Interesting.

It's gone in a flash and he uses both palms to smack my chest, right above my pecs.

"Okay...good talk. Now, let's go out and celebrate our win tonight by getting drunk off our asses. And maybe get laid in the process." He turns and then flicks his gaze back to me, his eyebrow quirked up. "Well, at least one of us is getting laid. And it ain't you, buddy."

Carver laughs boisterously and turns the corner, leaving me standing there wondering what just passed between us. What he just said makes me wonder if he really does know the heartache of a break-up. I suppose there's a lot I don't know about Carver. We all have a past. Maybe he's just hiding his better than the rest.

I decide to go out with the guys after the game and it does feel good to let loose. We don't drink much during the season, but the holidays are nearing and the semester is almost over, so we need to get in some final hurrah's before we all leave for break.

I'm a little drunk – but not wasted - as I head back to my dorm when I realize I haven't checked my phone since earlier in the day. Pulling it out, I notice several texts and voicemail notifications, along with my Twitter and Instagram feeds. A lot of congratulations on the win – from my parents, friends and family. A couple of girls I'm in classes with have texted offering to come celebrate with me. I consider it for less than a second, when my eyes land on a text from Kylah.

I laugh out loud when I read it.

Kylah: What's next? Kicking an old lady when she's fallen and can't get up?

Kylah: Geez, Van. You big bully, you.

Kylah: Remind me never to get on your bad side. Or fall down in front of you.

Kylah: Cuz your foot's bigger than my head. You could do some damage.

Kylah: Anyway, glad you won. Now be nice from now on. BTW – when does your break start?

This was the last one she sent and it came in over an hour ago. I check the time and wonder if it's too late to call her. It's after midnight, but I know she's a night owl. She's very studious and serious about doing well in school, so I'm guessing she's up. Just in case, I text her first.

Me: Yeah, not my finest hour. It's been a pretty shitty couple of weeks. But no excuse. I did apologize to Blanchard afterwards. We good.

Me: And I'd never do that to you. You're too sweet.

I laugh again because I know she hates being called sweet. During one of our recent conversations she admitted wanting to shed herself of that reputation, although I don't see how she could. It's just her nature.

I see the three dots pop up and know she's up and responding.

Kylah: That's good to know. But hey - I am NOT SWEET!

Me: Oh yeah? Prove it. Tell me one thing you've done that was mean?

I wait for her response. I can just envision her, sitting cross-legged on her dorm bed, pondering her recent actions and behaviors, hoping to isolate one instance where she wasn't the nice girl that I know she is. A nice girl who's smoking hot, none-theless. It's not like I haven't been affected by Kylah.

Even though I'm not in a good place emotionally right now, that doesn't mean my body hasn't taken notice of her. In fact, the night I got wasted at Cade's apartment, after the bomb was dropped on me, there was a moment when we were in the bath-room where I was about to put the moves on her. I wanted to kiss her so bad – to get a taste of her pretty pink lips. To lean in and suck at the indent of her throat, where I knew she would take like mango or something just as fruity.

Looking back, I'm glad I did get sick that night, because chances are I would've done something stupid to ruin our friendship. I was strung so tightly, I felt the coils would've burst and she was right there to help me unwind the fury and rage that had me so wrapped up in anger.

Just then, a thought hits me, smack in the head. Although we've gotten to know one another over the last few months and spent a few hours in each other's company, nothing has happened between us. We've only been friends this whole time because...well, because of Lyndsay.

But now Lyndsay's out of the picture. For the first time in over five years, I'm free to date whomever I want. Kiss whomever I want. Fuck whomever I want. Ah, shit.

It's like my brain finally peeled back the covers on what I'd tried to keep hidden away in the dark corners of my mind. The fact that I *really like Kylah*. And I know she really likes me.

I'm not being cocky or full of myself. It's fairly obvious when she looks at me that she wants something more. I've denied the attraction up 'til now, but she makes me horny. She's funny. Smart. Adorably geeky. And she has a smoking hot body. Just the thought has my dick chubbing-out.

I'm screwed.

What the hell am I going to do with this attraction? Absolutely nothing. Because Number one, she goes to school in California and I vowed that I am never doing a long-distance relationship again. I'm not about to get trapped into having to trust from afar, only to find out I've been played by someone I love.

And Number two -- Cade.

Enough said.

He would go ape-shit if he knew I was fucking around with his little sister.

My resolve kicks in, knowing there is no way I can touch Kylah. She is off-limits. No matter how much I want her, we have to remain friends.

My attention returns to my phone as it pings with her response.

Kylah: I told someone to fuck off this week.

I chuckle, because Kylah doesn't swear. See? Sweet.

Me: Sure ya did.

Kylah: I did! It was this guy in my Comp class. He told me he'd go down on me if I helped him write his term paper. Gross!

I stare down at the screen and reread the words. I'm in utter shock that she just told me this. My brain is firing off strange signals to my body. My hand grips the phone in a tight fist. I can feel a jealous scowl grow across my face. I think I even growl.

And my next thought is...Did she let him?

Jesus, Mary and Joseph. Am I jealous of some guy who wants to eat her pussy?

Hell yes, I am.

Me: What a fucktard. He actually said that to you?

Kylah: IKR? He's really creepy, too. He always tries to walk with me after class.

I'm still digesting her response. She obviously told the kid to fuck off...but does she think that he's gross, or that the *act* is gross? Now my dog-on-a-bone curiosity needs to know the answer.

Me: Wait, go back...what did you find gross? Him or being eaten out?

Kylah and I, while friends, have not ventured much into the sexual territory. We've stayed on very neutral topics, veering from anything that could be considered flirting or sexual innuendo. There have been times when I really wanted to make a wise crack over something she's said because of her innocence, but I've held back. Now, I want to know.

I have no idea how much experience she has. I know she hasn't had a boyfriend – she told me that much. But she's been in college a whole semester now. That's plenty of time for drunken hook-ups at parties.

Truthfully, I can't see Kylah doing that, though. Part of me hopes she is still innocent because the jealousy is already a living and breathing demon inside of me. Maybe I don't really want to know these things...since we are just going to be friends.

The three ellipses pop up on my screen...then I can tell she's deleted the text and starts again. Then deletes.

Fuck that shit. I decide to call her.

Kylah answers with a breathy hello.

I lay back on my bed, feet hanging off the edge, and place my left arm under my head.

"So tell me, sweet girl...is it just the guy who grossed you out about it, or don't you like it when a guy goes down on you?"

Her response gets me so hard, my shorts are tented, and my mouth salivates with possibility.

9

K ylah

"OH MY GOD! I can't believe you just asked me that."

I'm so glad that this conversation is over the phone, because my cheeks are burning so hot, I know my face looks like a little red balloon.

This topic is too embarrassing for words. What the heck am I supposed to say to him? Do I tell him the truth, because that's what friends do? Or should I play it off, pretend I'm not an innocent school girl who's never even had a boy's hand in her pants?

Ugh. Admitting this will be so humiliating. I just can't do it.

On the other end of the line, I can hear Van rustling around, like he's in motion. I wonder where he's at right now. Is he sitting at his desk? Or on a chair in the corner? Or maybe on the bed. Just thinking about what he looks like sprawled out on his bed makes my girly bits tingle. I unlock my legs from my crisscross position and lay back against my headboard.

Van's voice is low and deep.

"It's a serious question. I've heard some girls don't like it. They think it's too intimate or makes them feel too vulnerable or something."

"Do *you* like it?" Redirect...there, that's good. Now I don't have to lie about it.

Holy crap. I cannot believe that question just came out of my mouth, though. What am I thinking? Oh, right...about him and his tongue. *Down there.*

He clears his throat and I can hear the tension in his voice.

"Um...yeah." There's a level of amusement in his tone. "I like eating pussy."

My mouth is gaping open. I'm so glad we aren't Skyping right now. I would die. Literally, keel over and die.

"So...um, what about you? Do you enjoy giving head?"

I cough and throw my pillow over my face to bury my squeal. If Sienna were in here right now, she would be laughing her ass off at my expense. How the hell did this conversation even start?

Oh right...I was trying to prove to him that I'm a naughty girl, and not at all the sweet one he thinks I am. Even though I totally am. Now I'm doomed.

His laughter on the other end of the line has my ears perking up.

"You find this funny?"

He makes a throaty sound. "Nah...it's kind of a turn on, actually."

Whoa. Van is turned on? By me? Holy cow.

I'm seriously at a loss for words. I never expected in a million years having this type of conversation with Van. All our previous discussions have been on safe topics. I, of course, was curious about his relationship with Lyndsay, but we never discussed their sex life. Nor did he bring up the subject of my sex life (or lack thereof).

Now I have to get creative. What am I supposed to do, come

out and admit that I've never even seen a dick up close and personal? I'm nearly nineteen years old. In fact, Kady's and my birthday is coming up on December twenty-ninth. We were almost New Year's Eve babies.

"Oh." I say lamely.

"So, do you?"

Oh no. What's the question? Do I what? Do I like giving head? Or do I find talking about this a turn on? Geez.

"Yes." I admit, but have no idea really what I'm agreeing with.

"Yes, you like giving blowjobs? Or yes, you're turned on too?"

My heart is breaking records right now at how fast it's beating. It feels like it's speeding down the Autobahn and has no breaks to stop it from beating out of my chest.

"Both." My response is a whisper. Maybe if I don't say it too loudly, the lie will be real. Because I'm sure if I had the opportunity, and really liked the guy, I'd definitely like sucking dick. A lot of girls do, so why wouldn't I?

Or maybe I'd only like it if it were Van's.

"Ky." Van says my name like it's a prayer. It's beautiful in the way that it floats through the airwaves, touching me like a feather across my heart.

I swallow the lump in my throat. I love it when he calls me by my nickname.

"Yeah?"

"I think about you a lot."

If my body wasn't amped up before this, it is roaring to life now. My hormones are like piranhas in a feeding frenzy. They are going insane.

"Me, too."

"When do you come home for Christmas?"

I mentally count down the days. I have two more finals to take and a paper due before Tuesday. Then I'm back home for three weeks. Now I can't wait. My tummy flip-flops with antic-ipation.

"I'm back on Tuesday."

He blows out a long breath. "I leave for Tucson on Thursday."

My heart boomerangs and then hits a wall, careering to the floor. I'll only have a few days with him. I can feel the tears of disappointment welling up in my eyes.

"But I'll only be home for a week. I have to come back for practice right after Christmas."

"Oh, good. I'm glad. You'll be back for my birthday." I don't know why I let that slip. Why should he care about my stupid birthday? All we ever do is celebrate with our family.

"Really? That's awesome. You gonna have a party?"

"Probably not. It's always lame because it's during the holi-days, so Kady and I usually just go to a New Year's Eve party and call it good. But I'm kind of hoping I get those tickets for the concert I want to see. I hinted to my parents that I wanted to go, but I don't know if it'll happen."

I don't know if Van remembers or not, but we talked about this back in October. We'd been discussing our musical influ-ences and the type of music we listened to. He said he was into mainstream country, and some hip-hop, but really liked Twenty One Pilots. They are literally my favorite band. I'd mentioned that they had a show planned for the week after Christmas. I'd told him that if I got tickets, he could go with me.

I'd actually been dreaming about the show for months now. I imagine us standing there in a pit full of people, his arm wrapped tightly around my waist, holding me against his tall, hard body as we sway and move to the beat of the music. In my head, it's romantic and not a love-sick fantasy at all.

In reality, it probably wouldn't happen.

"That's right," he says, the enthusiasm in his voice helping to alleviate my insecurities. "If you do get them, and if the offer is still good, I'd love to go with you."

I pump my fist in the air. Yes!

"I'd like that. It'd be fun."

I hear him yawn loudly and realize it's after one a.m. Crap, I have more studying to do tonight.

"I better let you go, Ky. It was good talking to you." He pauses for a second, leaving me to wonder if he fell asleep. But then he continues.

"I'm looking forward to seeing you next week."

I can't contain my smile. I feel like this is a turning point. Like he's finally seeing me as more than a friend. And now that he doesn't have a girlfriend, maybe there's room for me to grow into something more.

"Me, too."

"I'm really glad we're friends."

And just like that, my hope is dashed. Killed in a fiery wreckage aptly titled the friend zone.

10

Van

EVERY PART of our conversation runs through my head over the next three days. I think I may have made a mistake and crossed a line I shouldn't have crossed.

Because now, I can't stop thinking about Kylah. And not as a friend, but something more. Specifically, Kylah wrapping her lips around my dick and sucking me off so hard that I can't see straight. Or me pulling up her skirt, wrenching her legs open, and finding her sweet, tasty center. Kind of like a Tootsie Pop. I wonder how many licks it will take to get her off.

I shake my head and stare down at the exam in front of me. My head is definitely not on the Econ test I'm supposed to be finishing right now.

I'm in the School of Business, majoring in Finance with a minor in Economics. Boring, I know. But it's what my dad does – he's an analyst for a large financial firm in Tucson - and

numbers have always come easy for me. Not having any particularly strong gravitational pull toward one specific career, per se, I
figure this degree will work well for the future. I may get
licensed as a CPA and work for an accounting firm. Or maybe
not. Perhaps I'll end up working in the banking industry. Who
knows? I haven't thought much farther than the right here
and now.

That's a lie. All I've been thinking about is what will happen
when I see Kylah next.

As for the long-term future, I know I'm not bound for Wall
Street or anything like that. I'll stay in the southwest and find a
job that pays well. It'll be a far cry from the NBA, where a few of
my fellow teammates are looking to go – namely Carver and
Lance. It's all they ever talk about, aside from getting laid.

I stare blankly at the test sheet, trying desperately to
remember the factors that influence fluctuations in market and
economic stability. It's hard to do when my dick is aching and all
the blood rushed down to that head when I started imagining
what Kylah would look like naked in my bed.

This whole thing is just confusing. I've only ever been with
one girl my whole life - my now pregnant ex. She was my first
and only up to this point. I don't even know where to start with
someone new.

Regardless of all the ribbing I've received from the guys, I am
not just going to go out and fuck a random girl. That's not my
M.O. Maybe it was how I was raised. My parents are very religious, right wing conservatives who believe in the sanctity of
marriage, church and government.

Obviously, I don't share all their beliefs. But love factors in
the sex equation. Getting into a girl's pants one time doesn't
necessarily appeal to me like it does some of the other guys. I
don't begrudge them for wanting what they want – but I want

something solid. A connection. Someone I can rely on, not just for sex, but for companionship. Because no matter how many male friends I have, being with a woman whom I can talk to is a pretty amazing thing.

I shared my hopes and dreams with Lyndsay. I told her about my insecurities related to my brother's condition. My fears. Everything. Now that she's gone, I've found myself opening up a lot more to Kylah, too. She's been such a healing presence for me.

It makes me nervous how much I've come to rely on her so quickly. I don't want to subconsciously use her as a rebound. I'd never want to hurt her just because she was an innocent by-stander.

Maybe I'm one of those guys who always has to be in a monogamous relationship – never able to be alone without female companionship. There's nothing wrong with that, I suppose. Some dudes are lone wolves. Me, not so much. I like being together with a girl. Having that partnership.

Now I feel empty inside. Except when I'm with Kylah. Once again, the timing of this attraction is not great. I just can't see us making a go of it, so I should shut it down now, before anything starts. There's no way we can be together. I've put a lot of thought into how I should proceed with her. I don't want to lead her on or use her just because she's convenient. She deserves someone who has the time to give her. And has a less fractured heart.

I'm still mulling this over as the class TA tells us that time is up and to finish our remaining problem. My head flies up as I take in the scene around me. There's only three other students in the room, and they are packing up their bags to leave. I return to my attention to my test and realize I have three remaining questions left unanswered. Shit.

Thankfully, my grade in this class was fairly high going into finals, so it shouldn't ruin my chances of passing. I'm angry at myself, though, for being so distracted lately. The professors all understand that for athletes, we have a lot of other priorities that can interfere with coursework. It's just a fact of life for college basketball players during the season. Up until now, it's never been a problem for me to divide my time. Sure I've gotten sidetracked every once in a while, but never so far off course that I bombed a test or a class.

With defeat and self-loathing, I pick up my test and my backpack and head to the front of the classroom where I hand my paper in to the TA. Her name is Margarita and she's from Spain. Gorgeous by any standards, with a seductive accent that can turn a guy on just with one syllable from her mouth. I'd not given her much notice until this second. Now that I'm the only one in the room, she's leering at me with these big, brown eyes. If we were in a bar, I'd say they were 'fuck me' eyes.

"How'd it go, Señor Gerard?" She rolls her R's and it's really sexy. Very Salma Hayek-esque. I swallow the lump in my throat and push away any porny-thoughts that crop up. Sweat trickles down the crease in my back.

"Oh, you know. Okay, I guess." I shrug, letting go of my grip on the test between us. When I return my gaze to her face, I see her lick her lips.

Shit, have I been this oblivious this semester? My brain scrambles to recall any previous interactions we had that maybe I'd misconstrued or completely overlooked. She was always hovering near my desk when she lectured, and kept her attention on me a lot, but none that seemed out of the ordinary.

She leans in toward me, her button-down blouse hanging low enough so that I can easily see the cleavage displayed and a peek-a-boo of her pink-lace bra. She coyly peers up through long, inky lashes, pinning me with the sexiest stare I've ever encountered.

"I would have gladly helped you study, Donavan. Your time must be in limited supply with your extra-curricular activities. I wish you would've called me so I could've helped you...perhaps in the Foreign Currency and Exchange Rates principles."

Is this innuendo for something else? Good God.

Her hand juts out to land on my bicep, which she squeezes before sliding it down the curve of my arm down to my wrist. My eyes are glued on her hand as I watch this transpire. She lets out a soft moan as her hand makes its way back up my arm, and then to my chest.

What the hell is happening, here? I think I've gone into shock because I can't get my body to move or my mind to conjure something to say. Nothing. My tongue feels three times larger than normal, my mouth dry. Feet rooted into the floor.

"If you're worried about your test score, perhaps we can meet later to discuss? In my office, where it's quiet and I could conduct an oral exam." Again, the roll of the R sends the blood flowing south.

I stammer at the suggestion. "Um...wow...that's really nice of you to offer."

"Mm-hmm. It would be of benefit to you, si?"

We are interrupted by this surreal conversation when my phone chimes. Shaking my head to clear my thoughts, I pull it out of my shorts pocket and check the display. Margarita lets out a sigh of frustration. I blow out a sigh of relief.

I pull back, her proximity almost cloistering, and give her a little wave. "I gotta take this. I'll see you next semester."

Pivoting on my Nike-clad heels, I exit into the hallway as fast as I can before I stop and lean against the brick wall of the concourse. My heart is hammering and my cheeks are hot, red and blotchy, I'm sure. I have a tendency to flush easily when I'm embarrassed. Just a trait that I was born with and that brings a lot of attention to my face when I'm in front of reporters during press conferences.

I open my hand and look down at the display. It's Kylah. I feel guilty for even thinking this, but I consider not answering it. Getting involved with her, no matter how much I want to, will only prove difficult. Not that she's difficult. She's great. It's just the damn timing and circumstances that bum me out.

The picture I took of her the night we went to the movie is the contact photo. We'd been goofing around after we'd eaten dinner and before we went back to Cade's and she was laughing hysterically over something we were talking about. I just couldn't help myself. I opened up my camera app and snapped a picture. Her hair is disheveled, her eyes are squinty because her smile is wide-open and takes up most of her face. And her chin is pulled up, head back. She looks gorgeous. Happy. Irresistible.

So how can I not answer her call?

"Hey, Ky. What's up?"

I hear her form a soft 'O', like she's surprised I answered the phone.

"Oh my gosh," she stammers. "Hi, Van. I didn't expect you to answer. I thought you'd still be in class. I was just going to leave a message. But now I don't have to." She's rambling nervously and it's pretty cute.

"Where are you?"

"I just got home."

"Really?" I ask. This is different than what she originally mentioned. "I thought you weren't expected back until tomorrow? Isn't that when your flight was scheduled?"

After our hot and sexy conversation the other night, things felt a little awkward. Or maybe it was just me for feeling like I steered us into uncomfortable territory. So I'd made up an excuse the next day that I had been really drunk that night and I apologized for my participation in that discussion. I told her I was sorry for bringing the blowjob thing up and I'd hoped she could forgive me and we could still be friends.

Her reaction was a little weird. It was like she was angry with me. She didn't come right out and say it, but things seemed a little stilted after that.

We moved on to other topics, though. One being her expected return to Phoenix. She said her parents booked her flight for Wednesday afternoon and her last final was on Tuesday. Same as mine. And today is Tuesday.

"Yeah, I was supposed to fly in tomorrow. But I finished early and booked it to the airport and flew standby. So here I am!"

"That's so awesome."

Part of me is disappointed when she says she's at home and not at Cades, because then I can't go over to see her. On the other hand, it saves me from seeing her. I'm afraid of being around her too much. Afraid of what might happen. Of what I might do. I want her so bad. And I'm pretty sure she wants the same thing, but is too shy to admit it.

If this isn't the biggest conundrum ever, I don't know what is.

"Well, I'm at home for now. My mom is making us dinner tonight. She said she has an announcement and was waiting for all of us to be home together to tell us. I'm hoping it's about our Christmas gift. Last year we went on a four-day cruise and it was amazing! My mom loves cruises. We never went as a family before because my dad hated them."

"Huh. Cool. How are things going with your dad? Are you going to see him much while you're home?"

I walk out the building and head toward my dorm. I'm one of the only senior ball players that still lives in the dorms, but I wouldn't trade it for the world. I love my privacy. Because of my status, I get a private dorm suite. It's small, but I have a small couch in my room, along with a bed and desk, and my own bathroom. It's not a palace, but it definitely allows me the luxury of being by myself when I need the quiet. It was also a big plus when Lyndsay would...

Shit. My brain needs to eliminate her from my thought patterns. She's my ex. We're over. Done with. Kaput.

It's not like I'm missing her or anything like that. It's been over a month since we broke up and there's no chance we'd ever get back together because of the charming circumstances involved in our split.

That brings me back into our conversation about Kylah's dad. She'd told me that her mom and he divorced a few years back and she's still reeling from the split. Said it's really difficult trying to spend equal time with each of them – especially now that she's away at school. Apparently Kylah's the only one of the kids that actually like her dad. I know for a fact Cade's relationship with him was really rocky for a while.

"Well, depending on how things pan out, I'll spend this week with my mom and we'll be there for Christmas Eve and day, then the following week with my dad. I'll be at Cade's New Year's Eve, and I don't have to return to school until January 5th. So I'll wing it 'til then."

She says all this with a flare of excitement. She seems happy and animated now that she's home, and it only increases my desire to see her. To charge my batteries with the power of her positivity.

My parents already know to expect me at home only until Saturday, when I'll return to school. We have practice, but no games during the week between holidays. It'll be great to have some downtime for once. Although my parents know that Lyndsay and I broke up over Thanksgiving, it does create a little weirdness with our families. Her parents and mine attend the same church and spend a lot of time together in various social circles. Thankfully, we don't spend Christmas with them.

"So how about you? You mentioned you'd be home with your family for a few days in Tucson, right? And then what?"

Walking up to my third floor dorm room, I unlock the door and throw my bag down on my bed. Before I can think better of it, and because I can't think of anymore more than I want to do, I invite her over.

So much for keeping my distance.

"Hey, Ky? Since you're back in town, would you want to get together tonight? After you have dinner with your mom, of course."

I can just imagine her chewing on her bottom lip, analyzing how she should respond.

"Um...you mean...meet up over at Cades?"

I chuckle, because that's what we've done in the past. But now, we can do whatever we want. I can tell she's nervous and maybe unsure of where I'm going with this. I kind of like that. We haven't talked about anything of substance related to who we are to each other. Only that we're friends, first and foremost.

"I was thinking you could come over here, to my place. We can hang out. Play some video games. Watch a movie. Whatever." Netflix and chill was on the tip of my tongue, but that wouldn't be happening for sure.

I must be a glutton for punishment. I'm torn between wanting something to happen between us, and adamant that nothing should happen. In this case, I can't have my cake and eat it too.

"Yeah," she says quietly. "I'd like that."

"Cool. I'll be here whenever you want to come over. I'm in Cholla, suite 301. Just buzz in downstairs at the door since it requires a key card and I'll come down and get ya."

"Okay, I'll see you later. I'm not exactly sure when. Probably around nine."

"Perfect. I'll see you then."

I hang up and run my hand through my hair, my fingers picking through the long strands that hang loose. This is probably a really, really bad idea.

But on the other hand, having Kylah alone in my room with me sounds *really, really* good, too.

11

K ylah

THERE ARE certain aspects of being a twin that are automatically inherent with multiples. The biggest advantage is that you can read your twin like a book, without having to say a word. While Kady and I are vastly different in every aspect of our lives, she is still my best friend.

We share everything. So it's no surprise that she knows how I feel about Van. In fact, the first thing she did when she got home was to pounce on me for information.

The other thing that is always associated with multiples? One of the two will always be the older one. In our case, Kady was born seven minutes before me. A fact that, like horoscopes often do, the birth order seems to dictate personality type. Between the two of us, Kady is the natural leader. The bossy one. The lion. And I'm...well, meek and moldable. More like a little lamb.

I'm in my bedroom, unpacking and unwinding after a long

week of finals, when she comes bounding into my room, bare-foot and in yoga shorts and a tank. Flopping down on my bed on her stomach, chin in her hands, she just grins up at me.

Knowing exactly what she is thinking, I play dumb, raising my eyebrow at her. "What? Hello to you, too."

She rolls to her side and props herself up on her elbow, her blue hair piled high in knot on top of her head.

"You've got a goofy smile on your face. And you're humming. You must be thinking about your dreamy boy-toy and the action you're going to get tonight." She chuckles at her witty remark. She already knows that Van invited me over and that I am super nervous to be alone with him.

She's undoubtedly the more experienced of the two of us. Kady is self-assured and confident in a way that I could only hope to be. I wish I had her poise – or even an ounce of her level of self-esteem. She, on the other hand, has told me that she envies my singular focus and ambition, knowing exactly what I want to do and how to succeed. We hold a healthy dose of competition between us, but it's never hurt our relationship in any way.

Where Kady is the wild one, who socializes like she was born to be the center of attention, I'm a homebody. A fact that my roommate, Sienna, would love to change. She's tried valiantly the last semester to get me to go out and have 'fun' and has grown a little tired of my lack of interest in leaving the library or our dorm room.

But I'm okay with who I am. I'm not a girl who needs to surround myself with a lot of friends at all times. I have my sister – my confidante – and other close friends to share my life with. I'd also say I'm pretty close to Cade, too, as far as older brothers go.

But there's no freaking way I could ever share any of my personal feelings about Van with Cade. He would freak out and find a way to sabotage any change I have at seeing Van, I'm sure. I'll likely tell my mom about Van at some point, if anything progresses between us, but right now my mom is in her own little world of romance. She's been dating our neighbor, John Roberts, for a while now.

Now that's a little weird. I'm not opposed to my mother dating. She's a beautiful woman who deserves to be happy. But it's Mr. Roberts – *our neighbor*. He's totally fine and all, albeit ten years older than mom. But he seems to treat her like a queen and is a very nice man. Anyway, it just leaves me no opportunity to sit down with my mother and spill my guts about my friend-slash-crush.

Plus, where would I start? I honestly don't even know what's going on between me and Van. He's been unavailable since I've known him. As in, already taken. We haven't really touched. Or kissed. Or made out. And definitely not hooked-up. Yet there's a closeness with him and I feel more comfortable around him than any other guy I've ever known.

I whip a T-shirt that I pull from my bag at my sister, who grabs it with a giggle, falling back onto the bed.

"Shut up. I don't know what you're talking about."

Kady props herself back up on her elbow and she rolls her eyes at me.

"Come on...he's free now. And he likes you. He's going to want to fool around. Maybe even fuck you." She mocks me with smoochie kissing against her hand and loud, dramatic moans, emphasized with hip gyrations. Good grief she's disgusting. Next she'll be dry-humping my bed if I don't stop her now.

Yes, I think he likes me, but I'm not sure to what level. If it is more than a friend, and we end up having sex or whatever, I don't think I'd want to be a rebound fling for him. I don't want him to leave me high-and-dry when he realizes he moved too fast from one girl to another. Although, based on what I know of him, I don't believe he's a womanizer or a player. That title belongs to Carver Edwards.

"He's not over Lyndsay yet. Nothing's going to happen between us."

I turn around and place my folded clothes into my dresser drawer. That's another difference between me and Kady. I'm the neat one and she's a complete disaster in terms of organization. I don't know how her college dorm mate handles it. Thankfully, I never had to share a bedroom with my sister.

But I have been thinking about sharing my bed with Van. In the Biblical sense, that is. He lights me up from the inside like a Chinese lantern by simply the sound of his voice on the other end of the phone. My body responds in a way it's never done before. Like it's getting shocked from an exposed electrical wire, charging through my nerve-endings in high voltage watts.

"Bullshit," Kady argues, pushing up to a sitting position. I can see her reflection behind me in the mirror. "It's been over a month since they broke up. That's more than enough time for a guy to get over a broken heart. Believe me. Chad was over me within two days after we'd broken up."

I can't argue that. Chad Danon was Kady's high school boyfriend. They'd dated the last semester our senior year and broke up right before she left for college and he left for basic training. Sure enough, the week after they broke up, she spotted him at the mall with Deanna Burgman. They were making out like nobody's business.

I shut my dresser drawer. "That's different." I protest. "Van was with Lyndsay for five years. He has history with her. She was the love of his life." I'm not exactly sure about that. Van told me he loved her, but were they soulmates? He's never said.

Kady jumps off the bed and begins rummaging through my suitcase, picking up shirts, shorts and various unmentionables while shaking her head.

"One thing's for sure, Ky. You're never gonna get laid in these undies." She tosses a few pieces away on the floor like they are garbage. "What the hell? Why do you have granny-pants? Ew."

She says it in such a scandalized tone. Maybe I should have considered my wardrobe and underwear situation a little more. It's just never dawned on me to wear anything sexy. I dress for comfort. Not style or what I think a guy would like to see.

My face flushes as I bend down to pick up the discarded underwear, putting them in my top drawer. "These are my period pants, for the record."

She scoffs, blowing a piece of her blue-colored hair out of her face.

"For the record, they are disgusting. We need to get that little booty of yours into something smoking hot. And I have the perfect thing for you. I picked them up in this cute boutique in Boulder. God, they have the most awesome corsets. You should see the one I wore on Halloween! Brandon just about dropped his load the minute he undressed me. It was classic."

My brain manually flips through the lists of names she's mentioned over the last four months like a rolodex. She goes through guys faster than I read books – and I'm a speed reader if that gives you a clue. I think Brandon was some frat boy she met at a party in October. They lasted about three days.

I ignore her comment, moving to my closet and opening the doors. I give an assessing stare at the contents. Hmm. Maybe Kady has a point. I have nothing that I can wear to hang out with Van that isn't frumpy or geeky. I have a sundress that my mom bought me for our high school graduation party last May, but it's December and not appropriate attire to play video games in.

Turning my head, I glance over my shoulder in defeat. "Okay. Fine. Help me find something to wear...but," I qualify, ensuring she understands I'm not trying to be her. "It can't show cleavage. It has to be comfortable. And there are no high heels in the mix. Got it?"

Kady gives a little grunt, but claps her hands in glee as she runs up behind me and wraps her arms around my middle. "Can I do your hair, too?"

"Don't push it."

We both dissolve in a fit of giggles, knowing full well I'll give in to her request. That's what sisters are for.

AN HOUR LATER, we descend the curved staircase and head into the dining room where my brother and Mr. Roberts, I mean, John – both sit, chatting about basketball. My mom is in the kitchen putting the finishing touches on the meal she's prepared for tonight's dinner.

As we take our seats, Cade finally notices me, his eyes smiling first at Kady and then widening in shock when he locks with mine.

"Whoa," he exhales, setting his beer down on the table in front of him. "What happened to you?"

I bite my lip, glancing sidelong to Kady who's sitting next to me. My eyes plead with hers not to say anything that would out me and Van. I definitely do not want to get into this with Cade tonight. Or ever. It's complicated enough as it is. No need to throw a protective, older brother into the mix.

"She's going out tonight." Kady intercedes, glaring at Cade from across the table.

Cade's eyes narrow. "Where? With who?"

Kady lobs one over again – she always has my back. I feel like I'm watching a tennis match and my social life is the ball. "None of your business."

She gives him a feisty head tilt, begging him to push it. I

watch as Cade's lips press together, the blue of his eyes dimming to a dark denim. He's about ready to respond when my mom saves the day.

"Okay, let's eat!"

All our heads turn as we watch her walking into the dining room carrying a large tray of food, the succulent smell wafting through the room. My mouth instinctively waters and my stomach grumbles. It's been far too long since I've eaten good home-cooked meals. It's definitely true what they say about the Freshman Fifteen. I'm at a five-pound weight gain already and I still have a half of a year to go. All the weight has gone to my ass, much to my chagrin. I had hoped it would pad my bra a little more than it did, but no such luck.

I'd asked my mom earlier if she needed any help with dinner and she just shooed me away. John was in the kitchen with her, sipping on a glass of wine and chopping up veggies. It was kind of cute to watch them together. He is a nice guy and I'm happy they get along. I've finally come to the realization that my parents are over for good. I'm not gonna lie. It still hurts that our family, the way it was at one time, is no longer a unit. From the looks of things, though, it's better for my mom.

I saw my dad at Thanksgiving and before that during fall break, and he seems to have mellowed a bit. Dad is a Type-A personality, which is a good thing in his line of work. He's a criminal lawyer and has made a living defending some really high-profile cases. I've seen it wear him down over the years, though. Moving from childhood to adulthood, I've noticed the affects it's had on him. He drinks more. Spends more time away from home. It definitely drove a wedge between he and my mom, as well as between he and Cade.

I still love my dad and have the closest relationship with him out of the three of us kids. Cade is my mom's pride and joy.

Kady...well, let's just say Kady has given both my parents more trouble than all of us combined.

My mom never told us what we were celebrating tonight but my guess is the meal is some sort of pre-holiday celebration. She set wine glasses at all our seats, so that means it's a special occasion. She'd always give us a little taste when we were teenagers and now that we're in college, apparently it's okay to drink at the family dinner table. I'm not a big drinker to begin with, and Kady doesn't hide the fact that she enjoys the sauce.

John stands and pushes his chair back from the table, bringing his wine glass in front of him, suggesting a toast.

"Thank you, Kristine, for inviting me to your family dinner table tonight. And for being the most wonderful woman in the world. I love you. Cheers."

My head turns to look down the other end of the dining table, where my mom sits, her cheeks stained red and the smile on her face is bright and cheery. She's glowing. I don't think I've ever seen her looking so beautiful. And she is a beautiful woman.

A chorus of 'cheers' goes up from everyone, including myself, as we clink our glasses together. It's strange to think that we've all grown up around this table and yet we've never been witness to this kind of genuine appreciation or affection from the man sitting at the head of the table. I'll admit, my father wasn't the kind of guy who let compliments slip out that readily. I don't ever recall seeing him embrace my mom in a hug, kiss her on the cheek, or even offer her any praise.

My mom brushes the hair from her face, the smile receding a bit, as she takes a large gulp of her Pinot. As she places it delicately in front of her plate, she looks across the table at John and returns the sentiment.

"I love you, too, John." I notice a twitch in her cheek as she swallows what appears to be a lump in her throat. "I'm so happy you're here with my family tonight. And I hope that we will continue having these opportunities for many years to come. Kids..." She takes turns gazing at each of us lovingly – with hope.

"John and I have an announcement to make."

It hits me then. The reason for this dinner. The celebration. Johns' presence. Holy smokes. My stomach plummets as it fills with an emotion I can't quite place. Hostility? Anger? Uneasiness?

"John has proposed and we are going to be married right after Christmas. I wanted to do this when you're all home and we're together as a family."

There's a collective gasp around the room and then it feels like the oxygen is sucked out from around us. It feels like an out-of-body experience as I look around the table at my siblings. Kady, who sits to my left, looks astounded, her eyes wide as saucers, mouth agape. I'm surprised, too. I thought John and my mom had only been casually dating. I had no idea it was this serious. Married?

Cade has a smile on his face and he's toasting John and my mother in congratulations. The bastard doesn't seem fazed by this announcement at all...which means he already knew. What the hell? I realize he's closer to home than Kady and me, but that shouldn't preclude us from being in the loop.

All of a sudden, I'm struck with the hard realization. My mom wouldn't just jump into another relationship that easily or quickly. It dawns on me, then, that maybe this has been going on for longer than she initially let on.

For some reason, anger spikes in my blood. I feel duped.

"Are you serious? Have you been lying to us, mother? How long have you been seeing each other?" At that moment, another thought pops into my head. What if...holy shit. What if they were having an affair before my parents got divorced?

"Did you cheat on dad while you were married?" I practically scream this as all heads turn to me in utter shock.

I don't even realize that I'm now standing, gripping my wine glass so tight that it feels like it could shatter between my fingers. The heat rises in my neck and to my cheeks, which is customary when I get embarrassed or angry. I'm horrible at hiding my feelings.

Kady reaches a hand for mine, reassuring me with her presence. It's always been like that between us. We're connected in ways other people don't understand. She calms me without saying a word.

But I'm too angry to be mollified. I notice John stiffens in his chair, the glass that had been halfway to his lips now placed down on the table. My gaze shifts to my mother, who slowly stands from her seat and walks toward me. Hesitantly. With a level of uncertainty that I've never witnessed before.

My mother is the epitome of cool and collected. Never ruffled. Always poised. Magnificently proper.

My body shirks out of Kady's grip and I pull back when my mom tries to offer me a hug.

"Don't touch me." I snarl.

The biting tone of my response has my mother appearing stunned, unable to comprehend this is me, her mellow child. She takes a shaky step back, allowing me space I desperately need to keep from lashing out further.

"Honey," my mom says quietly, her eyes filled with unshed tears. "It's okay to be upset. I understand. This is something you weren't expecting. But please don't think that I would ever do that to our family. To your father. John and I were only friends until a year ago. We've been together for the last year."

My brain tries to formulate a picture of the last twelve months. I must have been oblivious when I was living at home, before we graduated high school. How was I not aware they were dating? Why did she keep this from us? She apparently didn't trust us to know the truth. I hate her for keeping it from me.

I turn my head to glare accusingly at Cade. "You knew, didn't you?"

He shrugs, quickly glancing at the table to avoid my icy stare. "She's happy, Ky." He says, returning his eyes to mine. "Doesn't she deserve that?"

No! I want to scream. She doesn't if it means she lied to me. To us. That she hid a part of her life from her own daughters. Why does she get to spring this huge, life-altering decision on us like it's nothing? It's huge!

I've got to get out of here before I do or say something I'll regret. I know my family is wondering what the hell has come over me because this isn't how I normally react. Kady is normally the fueled-by-emotion member of our family. Then Cade. But me? I'm the less reactive of the three of us. I don't get upset or angry, or ever talk back.

Maybe I'm finally cracking under the pressure of my life's instability right now. The stress of college, of being away in unfamiliar territory. Having to grow up and be comfortable on my own for once. Of having my first taste of a crush that I don't know how to handle.

Whatever it is, I've lost all sense of who I am.

And all I want to do is find myself in the arms of Van.

12

Van

THE KNOCK on my door startles me as I step out of the shower.

I'm dripping wet, my hair damp and hanging at my shoulders, drops of water running down my back. I grab the towel that I threw across the curtain rod and make my way toward the door. The clock on my nightstand tells me it's still too early to expect Kylah, so it must be one of the guys on my floor. Although, most everyone has taken off already for Christmas break and the dorms are an empty ghost town.

Swinging the door open, I'm not prepared for the sight in front of me. And from the look of shock on her face, either is Kylah. The expression quickly turns to something else entirely though, as the color of her eyes morphs into a deep, dark blue.

"Hey," I say, watching as he takes me in, scanning her way down my naked torso until she lands on the edge of the towel, tucked in just below my belly button. She blinks as I clear my throat. "I wasn't expecting you so soon."

Kylah blinks a few times, as her hand comes up to touch her lips. She opens her mouth and then snaps it closed again. Wrenching open the door farther, I gesture with a nod of my head for her to come in.

We're standing just a few feet from one another and I can smell her fruity scent which now fills the room. My dick seems to realize the possibilities and perks up underneath my towel, reminding me of my current attire.

Her back is to me and as I adjust my growing erection, she turns and notices. Her reaction is priceless, the heat blooming across her cheeks in a display of both embarrassment and interest.

"I'm so sorry to come over so early without calling. I wasn't thinking straight. I can go...it's not a problem." She starts toward the door, her feet practically tripping over themselves, as my hand shoots out to grab her wrist, which is soft to my touch and sends a thousand watt jolt up my arm.

"It's okay. Really." I pull her back and she nearly topples into me. "Don't go. I'll just grab something to put on. Just...wait right here."

She seems appeased by this and I rush over to my bureau, yanking out the first things I get my hands on, leaving her in the middle of my room as I close the bathroom door behind me.

During the time it takes me to get dressed, it gives me the space I need to calm myself. I then consider how she looked when I opened the door to my room. Aside from the surge of lust that passed through her features, she appeared to be upset over something. Her body was strung tight; I could tell that. Her neck was corded, her posture stiff. I've never seen her so wound up and ready to lose it. But that's the sense that I got.

I open the bathroom door and slowly emerge. Cautiously. This is the first girl I've ever had in my dorm room outside of Lyndsay. A sudden rush of lust swirls through me. A tight ball of eagerness simmers in my belly. And then she turns around to face me and I realize I'm a goner.

Her lower lip is trembling and her eyes are glistening. If I thought she was upset before, it's ten times worse now. I've seen my share of crying women in my life and I know when the shit's gonna hit the fan.

"Ky."

I pull her into my arms and against my chest as the dam bursts open, the top of her head barely touching underneath my chin. I have no idea what has caused this sudden emotional breakdown, but something awful must have happened to have her crying this way. Nestled against me, she sobs into my shirt, her body shaking in jerky movements, as I simply hold her tight, whispering words of encouragement.

"Shh...it's okay. I got you."

Her tremors seem to lessen over the course of the next few minutes. The tears that had consumed her are now dissipating. I don't want to move her, but I know she's going to need a Kleenex soon. I pull away just enough to reach toward the box on my nightstand, giving her a tissue to dab at her face.

"*Thaaannnk yooouuu.*" She stammers between sniffles. "I'm sorry, Van. I didn't mean..."

One of my hands rests on her shoulder, as I move it to the back of her neck. The other I use to tilt her chin to look up at me. Those beautiful eyes of hers are now sea glass blue-green.

"Are you hurt? Did something happen to you?"

She shakes her head, eyes sliding away from mine and to the floor.

"I'm just stupid. I overreacted. I'm such a cry baby."

I can't stand the fact that she's cutting herself down like this. Kylah is nothing if not sweet and adorable. I've never seen her anything but happy and light-hearted. She's been a sounding board for me over the last month after everything that happened with Lyndsay. If anyone's a crybaby, it's me with my stupid life drama. She's been my rock.

I bend down to place a kiss to her forehead, my hand cupping under her jawline. When I open my eyes, she's staring at me with such awe. Longing and lust shoot through my veins, straight to my cock which doesn't give a fuck that Kylah's upset. All it cares about is that a beautiful girl is in my room and looking at me with lustful adoration.

She parts her lips, her tongue slipping over the bottom lip and slicking over it as I stand entranced by the action. I bend my head again, with the intention of kissing her cheek, but in a last moment decision, I zero in on her lips. The first kiss is just a peck. A friendly touch that's whisper soft and could hardly be considered the kiss a lover would give.

Because we're not lovers. We're friends.

And that's how it should stay. Instead, my body confesses it doesn't want to remain friends. It wants something more. And the breath of air she sucks in when I pull back says that she wants more, too.

The choice is taken out of my hands entirely when Kylah reaches up with her hands and grabs the back of my neck, pulling my head toward hers. Our lips meet with fiery purpose, sampling each other's mouths in exploration and conquest.

My God, she tastes incredible.

Somewhere in the back of my mind, I knew this would be good. I thought about her far too often and fantasized about what it would be like to kiss her. Touch her. Bury myself inside her.

Okay, I may be getting a little ahead of myself. But fuck. Her breathy sounds make me hard as hell.

Things start off slowly. We sample one another's tastes, our mouths meshing together as the momentum builds, climbing to a crescendo when I slide my tongue between her lips. She's hesitant at first, a little stiff, and I feel her pull back slightly, but I restrain her with my hands on her hips. The only thing between us now are her skirt and my shorts, which are doing little to cover up the heat I feel between her legs.

I haven't experienced a first kiss since I was seventeen, when I kissed Lyndsay for the first time behind the school library. Truth is, I don't remember it being this hot. My body is instantly consumed with the need to get naked with Kylah. With that thought, I realize I need to back the fuck off and slow my roll before things get out of control. I'm supposed to be consoling her, not mauling her.

It should be easier than this to stop this crazy rollercoaster, but the sensation of her small hands gliding down my back, stopping just at the bottom of my shirt feels too good. She tentatively fiddles with the edge and then slides them underneath until she's touching my bare skin. Every goddamn thought in my head freezes. Instead of doing the responsible thing and stepping back to give us space, I grab underneath her ass and pull her up in my arms in one swift motion.

"What are you doing?" she whispers against my mouth, her breath warm and intoxicating.

I growl as I move toward my bed. I know it's a bad idea. Some level of common sense still remains in my brain, even though all the blood has driven south to my cock, which pleads with me to continue down this needy path of foreplay.

Despite the fact that my subconscious is telling me that this is not a good idea, I can't manage enough strength to stop it.

I move toward my bed and when my knees hit the edge, I gently lay her down onto her back. Every muscle in my body tenses with anticipation as I look over her body. Her face is flushed a beautiful pink. Her wavy hair spills loosely across my pillow and I smile knowing that her scent will linger on my sheets long after she's gone.

A shy smile curves across her lips as I watch her chest rise and fall, pushing against the fabric of her dress.

"I've dreamt about this so many times, but I never thought it would happen."

Her hot and naughty confession is a huge turn on. My dick likes it. I like it.

I hover over her, my arms caging her in at her sides, as I dip my head to the crook of her neck. She's so warm and smells so damn good. I place my lips underneath her ear and begin to suckle, gently at first. Her soft, sensual whimper nearly does me in. I drop my full weight onto her, my thigh nudging between her legs.

She's wearing tights underneath her short dress, as my hand migrates down her hip to her thigh, tracing the thin material. I want to touch her everywhere, but want to feel her skin more than anything right now. I take possession of her mouth again, sliding my tongue inside as she lets out a lusty moan that vibrates right down to my cock.

Kissing Kylah is one of the most incredible things I've ever experienced. She's so eager, sucking at my lips with lust and fervor. Responsive every time our tongues meet and tangle together.

Her eyes are closed but pop open the minute my hand slides underneath her skirt to the edge of her tights. I'm not above begging if I have to, because I'm dying to feel her. To slip my finger between her legs and inside her, unveiling how wet she is for me. I know we won't go very far tonight. She's not ready for that, and either am I for that matter. But I want nothing more than to fool around and continue making out with her. All night long if she's willing.

"Is this okay?" I murmur, my lips sucking at hers.

I will stop if she says no. I'm not an animal, even though she brings out beastly instincts that I haven't ever felt before. The intensity between us is so strong. Maybe it's pent up sexual frustration because I haven't been laid in months. Or maybe it's just the pent up need for her. I've been dreaming about her since the day I met her. I tried stuffing those thoughts and images away all this time because they made me feel guilty. Like my mind was cheating on Lyndsay.

But she was the one who did the cheating. And now my dreams are coming true.

My thumb moves in a circular motion across the thin fabric of her tights as her hips cant in consent to my question.

"Yes."

It's now that I realize that whoever created tights was a sadistic bastard. They're better at protecting a girl's chastity than even the strongest of chastity belts. As I grunt and groan against the obnoxious material, we both laugh at the absurdity of the situation. Kylah tries to help by lifting her hips, as I sit up on my knees and yank them down her legs.

My entire body is hot and needy with anticipation, my heart rate skyrocketing with excitement as I slip them off her feet and throw them on the floor behind me. I return my attention to her smooth legs, sliding my knuckles up her inner thighs. She trembles under my exploration and my eyes roam from my hands up to her face. It's the sexiest sight I've ever seen.

Kylah's dress is bunched up at her belly, exposing her navel and the soft expanse of her stomach. Her mouth is parted in a slight 'O', head tilted to the side of my pillow, eyes shut as if she's trying to control her body's response. I am so turned on by the knowledge that I'm turning *her* on. And it only prompts me to move faster. To find out how wet she is.

Before I go any further, though, I want to make sure this is what she wants. I don't want any question because I know, without a doubt, this will ruin our friendship. Even if we don't have sex tonight, the heat between us is too hot to ever return to just friends.

My gaze floats down the length of her body to her panties. They're a light pink, with a satiny trim and a bow at the top. Sweet and sexy. Her legs are pressed together, primly. Uncertain. Bashful.

I kneel on the bed and lay down facing her, placing kisses along her jawline as her eyes flutter open. My hand briefly cups her cheek, caressing her softly. Slowly, but assuredly, my hand treks down her chin, neck, and then glides over her breast. She inhales deeply, her boobs arching toward the ceiling, fitting perfectly into the palm of my hand. I squeeze gently, my thumb brushing over the soft cotton fabric covering her erect nipple. My mouth waters to taste her there.

But I don't want to make any sudden moves and undressing her would definitely freak her the hell out. It's better to keep things this way. By keeping her tits covered, it will prevent me from taking advantage of our situation. Taking advantage of her. I don't trust myself right now, so slower is better. Even if it might kill me.

She squirms under my touch and I smile with anticipation, knowing exactly how much more restless she'll become once I slide my fingers inside her body. I nearly groan at the vision.

"Can I touch you, Ky?"

Her responding head nod is all that I need as I glide my hand down her smooth belly, circling her belly button. She gives me the exact reaction I expect by gasping loudly. I bend my head over her waist and smile, my tongue swirling around the outtie that she has going on.

And then my attention goes to the spot between her legs. My nose is so close to that coveted space and I can already smell her arousal from here. I inhale, reminding myself to take my time, and give my cock notice that we're not working to beat the clock tonight. You know, basketball reference.

My fingers hover at the edge of her panties and then tickle her softly over the silky material. Oh fuck. I can feel the dampness of the cotton panel and my body responds accordingly, arching into me begging for more. I practically dry hump her leg from horniness.

I stroke between her legs, a barely-there touch, but it's enough to warrant a small moan of pleasure from Ky. In order to continue my progress, and get a better vantage point, I press my thumb against her leg, prompting her to open her legs further for me.

She's hesitant, but widens her legs to allow me access, as my index finger returns to her center, circling around her clit now throbbing underneath my touch. The only experience I've had is with one girl; but I've fooled around enough, watched my fair share of porn, and heard many recounting of tales from my friends to know that a guy needs to start off slow with a girl. If you want her to come, you need to work up to a slow build up. Tease her mercilessly. Keep her hanging on at the edge of her seat until she can't take any more. Make her go crazy with lust.

Seeking closer contact, I wrench the edge of her panties aside and touch her bare sex. We both groan at the contact. I tease the tip of my finger over her clit, circling lightly before sliding it down to part her lips. She mumbles something incoherently and I take that as a good sign to continue.

Kylah tilts her hips upwards, practically right into my face, and I take advantage of the position to push my middle finger inside of her, lodging it in her heat. I'm rewarded by a sensation so intense that I'm close to salivating. Her intake of breath is the sexiest thing ever, as is the way her inner muscles clamp around my finger.

Kylah's pussy is impossibly tight. So wet. So hot. I'm about to pass out from pleasure as I move my finger in and out of her, creating a nice rhythmic momentum. I add another finger, stretching her a little as my thumb circles her clit. Her hip movements become more frenzied. More erratic as we both thrust together.

I want to use my tongue, to move in and replace my fingers with my mouth, but I don't want to move too fast. I remember our conversation a few weeks back and her response indicated an uncertainty over that. Instead, my place kisses at her hipbone as I watch the slide and pull of my fingers in and out of her body, relishing in the slick feel of her arousal. Pulling my finger out, I coat her sex on an upstroke as her body immediately tenses and seizes up. I turn my head back up to her face as I watch her expression morph into a vision of ecstasy.

"Ohhhh..." She cries out, her hips moving fast and furiously, as I continue pumping my fingers deeper and faster. I shift upward in a fluid motion, biting down on her mouth to swallow her sounds as she comes for me.

Her body relaxes a few moments later and a sweet, contented smile forms on her mouth. Her eyes are still shut, but she opens one to see me grinning down on her.

"You are so fucking sexy when you come." She snaps her eye closed again and turns her head away from me, but not before I get a glimpse of the rosy heat fanning across her cheeks.

I cup her chin and turn it back to me so our gazes meet. A brief shadow of doubt passes through her eyes, which has me worried. Was this a bad idea? Were we wrong to take it to this level?

Before I can blink or even voice those questions, she props herself up on her elbows, her eyes roaming down to my groin and gives my dick a thorough stare down.

Oh shit...I've seen that look before.

It means something really, really good is about to happen.

13

K ylah

HOLY GUACAMOLE.

What started out to be the second worst night in my life since my parents announced they were separating two years ago, has now turned into the most amazing night ever.

Van Gerard just gave me the first orgasm I've ever had from a guy. He had his fingers inside me, for heaven's sake! I'm honestly incapable of even speaking right now. It was so incredible. I had no earthly idea how good it would feel. It's like my body is floating out on a raft in the ocean, with the waves gently rocking me into a state of transcendental peace.

I've wanted this to happen for what seems like forever. Yet I never imagined it would feel this perfect. And now it's my turn to bestow the same type of attention on Van.

Truth time. I'm scared shitless that Van will laugh at me because of my inexperience. No matter how much advice my sister gave me on what to do when this moment arrived, I honestly don't even know where to start. How do I do it? Do I just tell him, "Hey, whip out your dick so I can fondle you."? Or am I supposed to be all Double-O-Seven stealthy, acting like it's no big thing and work my way into his pants?

Just great. I have no idea.

I bite down on my lip, probably hard enough to draw blood, as I lean up on my elbows and look into Van's eyes. They are a dark gray, his lashes fanning out in his desire-laden gaze. His hair is still damp from the shower. And oh my God...when he opened the door wearing only his towel, I thought I was going to faint.

His body is a chiseled piece of artwork. I used to scoff when my brother and his friends would make crude comments about how girls "creamed their pants" over them...but now I totally understand the euphemism. The moment I noticed his practically naked body, my hormones went on a total bender. I was insta-wet.

Leading me right up to this defining moment in my newly born sex life. I'm about to touch Van's perfectly sculpted body. Considering I'm still completely dressed, I make the decision to leave his shirt where it is, even though I'm dying to smooth my hands over his incredible pecs. Instead, I reach down to his shorts, which are the elastic-banded basketball shorts, and start to tug the waistband down. I'm startled when Van's own, very large mitts, grasp hold of mine to stop my progression.

I blink up at him inquisitively. Did I do something wrong already? Leave it to me to fumble before I even get started. His face holds a mixture of mild amusement, lust and concern. A heady combination, if you ask me.

"You don't have to, Ky."

He just broke the sexiness-meter. Never in my life would I have expected a star basketball player to be this thoughtful and considerate of me. If there was any possibility that I could like him any more than I do already, now's the moment.

I stretch my body up toward him and touch my lips firmly to his. He has a large mouth where I can get lost in its pleasures. Pulling back, I give him a coy smile.

"But I want to. It's all I've been thinking about for weeks."

He blows out a sigh of relief. "God...me, too."

I take that as a good sign and all the approval I need to continue my journey. He helps things along by lifting his hips and slides his shorts down past his knees, kicking them off so they land on the floor next to my discarded tights.

I'm sure I look like an idiot right now, as I stare doe-eyed at his package. His very, large and imposing package. I'm a little shell shocked. My mouth goes dry from the sight of it. His very thick and big erection stands straight at attention, reaching up as if it's trying to touch his belly button.

Now keep in mind, I've never seen a penis up close and personal. I may or may not have pulled up some dick pics on Tumblr once, maybe twice, just to get an idea of what they look like. But Van's cock puts the one's I've seen to shame.

I'm so enthralled by the beauty of his appendage that I don't even realize he's picked up my hand and moved it to his shaft. Holy moly...my mind goes blank and my hand begins to tremble. I am absolutely clueless as to what to do now. I'm trying to remember the instructions Kady gave me earlier.

"*Wrap your hands around it...stroke it from base to tip...circle the tip...use your tongue to slide up and down the vein of his shaft...lick...suck...stroke.*"

Okay. I've got this.

My hands instinctively tighten around his girth and it garners a growl from Van. Now we're getting somewhere. My shaky hand jerks it unsteadily up to the large, purplish head (I had no idea it would be *that* color). When I get to the top, I notice a bead of liquid. Did he already come? I think back to my conversation with Kady earlier.

"He'll probably have some pre-cum. It's his body's way of getting ready for the main event."

Curious as to what it feels like, I run my finger across the slit, spreading the warmth around the tip. Another moan from Van and my eyes flick to his. Van's head is propped up on a pillow, but his eyes are semi-closed. There's a look of pain on his face and it worries me that I'm doing something wrong.

"Is this...am I...does this feel okay?"

He mumbles a deep encouragement. "God, yes. It feels awesome. Keep going. A little faster."

His hand gently provides me a tutorial – which I appreciate, by the way – until my hand gets the motion, moving up and down, circling and twisting and he lets go. I notice now that Van's hands are clenched at his sides. Bending down, I decide to be bold and flick the tip of my tongue over the purplish head. The low growl he emits from deep inside his chest is the sexiest thing I've ever heard.

It emboldens me further. I nudge in closer and open my mouth wide enough to wrap my lips around the entire head of his cock. I tentatively suck him deep in to my mouth, my cheeks hollowing out, as I work to keep my teeth out of the way. I slide my tongue along the underside of his shaft, then swirl it as I hit the top of his dick. It's then that I feel his thighs tense beneath me and I lift my eyes to see him staring down at me. His reaction is confusing and I wonder if I shouldn't have done this. I've never given a blowjob. Maybe I suck? No pun intended.

Apparently, I don't suck – in a bad way. Because I have him in my mouth less than five seconds, my tongue swirling around the head, when Van mumbles out.

"I'm gonna come..." He pulls my head up – which surprises me, and I watch in complete awe as his dick twitches on its own accord and a ribbon of hot liquid shoots all over my hand and across his belly.

Although I didn't swallow, I did get a chance to taste him. Like Kady told me, it's very unique; unlike anything I've ever tasted before. A salty, masculine flavor. Not bad, but not something I'd want to bottle up and sell.

The thought has me snickering and Van's head pops up off the pillow to look down at me, his eyebrows quirked up inquisitively. And this makes me laugh harder.

Van yanks me up underneath my arm pits so my head is on the pillow next to him.

"What's so funny? Are you laughing at me because I was so quick on the draw?" He looks embarrassed, which is unbelievable.

"Oh my God, no. I'm sorry," I say, stifling another giggle. "It's just my stupid brain. I think weird thoughts at very inappropriate times."

"Oh yeah? What were you thinking, Miss Inappropriate?"

I shake my head and press my lips into a tight line.

"Come on...fess up." He prods me with his tongue, sliding it between my closed lips. I moan without realizing it. "I have my ways of getting it out of you."

I wiggle my eyebrows. "I don't doubt that."

"I will get you to tell me. But first, need to clean up." He gives the tip of my nose a quick kiss before rolling over on his side to grab a Kleenex from the same box he used to dry my tears not even an hour earlier.

How crazy it seems that my troubles literally disappeared the moment he kissed me. All of my worries over my life because non-existent while I was wrapped up in his arms. Pressed against his body. Climaxing from his fingers.

I sigh as he hands me a tissue and I wipe off my hands. The first time I've ever had to do that. I wonder if he knows I'm inexperienced? It makes me remember my conversation with Carver and I'm curious if he kept his word and his mouth shut or if he spilled my secret to Van. Now I'm more nervous than ever that Van is going to question why he's with me. I'm just an inexperienced, virgin geek-girl. He could do so much better. I've seen some of the girls that hang around the basketball parties. Flirting and working it to gain the attention of these guys. He could have his pick of any one of them and they'd all give him exactly what he wants.

And now that he's single, I'm sure the girls are swarming. Maybe he's even taken advantage of his situation over the last month and just hasn't mentioned it. God, I feel like an idiot. I should really get the heck out of here before he asks me to leave.

Van returns from the bathroom, as I watch him slide on his shorts over his strong, hairy legs to cover his now semi-hard dick. I'm curious as to what it'll look like when it's not erect. The whole science behind it is miraculous. I'm absolutely enamored with Van's male physique.

He climbs back on the bed and eyes me with uncertainty.

"Do you need to go?"

The question makes me realize that I have no idea of what the protocol is after you make each other orgasm. Kady mentioned that some guys get really tired and sleepy after they climax, and most guys don't want a clingy, needy girl. I do a quick analysis of how I feel at the moment, noting that I don't have a particular need to snuggle or cuddle in his arms, but I also don't necessarily want to leave him right now. Is that normal? I don't know.

I adjust the skirt of my dress, my legs dangling in front of me on the bed. "Um...do you want me to leave?"

He pushes his hair from his eyes and pulls it all back into his fist, wrapping a twistee around it to keep it out of his face. He bends down and kisses my temple – the same kiss that started this whole night.

"I want you to stay." He kisses me again, this time on the cheek. "In my bed." Now he kisses the corner of my mouth. "With me. All night."

Then he captures my mouth in a searing kiss that I feel all the way down to my toes.

"Okay." I whisper, wrapping my arms around his waist and pulling him flush against my chest.

WE END up watching an old movie that he says is one of his all-time favorites. *Rudy.* I admitted to him that I'd never seen it before and he just groaned and playfully smothered me with his pillow.

His dorm room has a couch shoved against the long wall, but we chose to prop ourselves up against his headboard. Our shoulders and hips touch, but aside from earlier, he hasn't made another move sexually. The laptop sits across his large thigh and honestly, except for a few scenes, I haven't really been paying all that much attention to the storyline. My mind has been on what we just did and how warm his body is sitting next to me.

I'm wondering what he's thinking. Because all I'm thinking about is his body.

I can't take my eyes off his legs. They're so powerful and strong. And so incredibly long. His feet hang off the bed. I'm fairly used to tall guys since Cade has always played ball and all his friends tower over me. I'm not particularly short, but compared to all of them, I'm a dwarf.

My face burns hot as images flash through my brain of our earlier make-out session. The way he held himself above me, his taut body hovering on top of me, his broad shoulders blocking out the light from above. His body is a massive rock of muscle. I'm disappointed now that I wasn't brave enough to divest him of his shirt so I could see him fully undressed...unless you count the few minutes I saw him in his towel.

Well, crap...now my insides turn molten, the flames of desire flickering low in my belly as I imagine straddling his nakedness. I'm embarrassed that I'm thinking these naughty thoughts, because he seems totally unfazed by me. I give him a sidelong glance and find that his eyes aren't even on the screen either – he's staring at me.

And whoa. His eyes burn with an unleashed intensity that sears through me.

Before I know it, he turns his head toward me, grasping the side of my neck to pull me into him, his lips locking with mine. My lips immediately open, granting him access as his tongue penetrates my mouth. He devours me like he's starving. And I'm more than a little hungry for more of him, too.

My hands tug at the bottom of his T-shirt, as I slide them underneath, splaying my fingers wide on his torso, which I ascend like a mountain. I wish I could describe the terrain of his abs. Peaks and valleys that are waiting for me to traverse them. I move my hand further north, because if I follow the little treasure map south, I'll surely land somewhere I probably shouldn't go at the moment. So I continue my journey up where I end up smoothing my hands over his pecs, brushing the curly swatch of chest hair in the center.

I feel, more than see, Van pushing the laptop off his legs to the side of the bed, as his hands reach around to grasp me at my hips, yanking me up over his lap. I straddle him, his erection pressing up into my heat. This is the first time I've ever sat atop a boy, but my body instinctively knows what it wants and what to do.

Our lips continue to mesh and mold together, as we suck

and kiss at each other, craving closeness. The grasp he has on my ass tightens, as he squeezes my butt cheeks, drawing me against him hard so I'm rocking and punching my pelvis in sharp orchestrations. My body comes alive under the movements, tiny sparks of heat the first signs of the fire building low in my belly.

My sex aches for more contact – more friction from him. My body wants to be filled by him and craves the kind of release its never had before.

Van releases me from his grip and pulls back, looking me in the eye expectantly. I have no idea what he's about to say. And I'm floored when he speaks.

"I want to see you naked...I want to touch you. We don't have to do anything you're not ready for," he says, his voice raspy like he's been chain smoking. "I just need to feel you. I'm dying here."

Yes, yes, yes.

I'd do anything for Van right now.

While I'm not sure how comfortable I am being totally naked in front of him, I also don't want to seem like a prude or a Nervous Nelly.

Instead of responding verbally, I grab hold of the dress sleeves and yank my arms up and out before I can second guess myself. I'm momentarily blinded as I slip it over my head. When I finally meet Van's eyes again, they are darkened with lust and I can feel their heat as he peruses over my skin. Thanks to Kady's help, I'm wearing a matching pink panty and bra set, with the clasp in the front.

I take a fortifying breath and reach to undo the clasp, but Van's quick reflexes stop me. I shoot my eyes to his and he gives me a sly smile, shaking his head.

"Let me."

Oh, okay.

His hands have a slight tremble, which is so endearing, as they fumble a little, but get it unfastened in relatively short order. With the flick of the clasp, the cups fall open, my boobs spill out in front of Van's face. It takes every bit of confidence I have to keep my hands from covering up my chest. But one glance into his eyes – the dark spheres that are hazy with appreciation and lust – and I capitulate.

My nipples harden as both his hands reach underneath to palm my breasts, squeezing them with reverence. I just about die from pleasure. His fingers – a little rough with calluses – scrape over my highly sensitive nipples and my body convulses in shivers. I feel so wanton as he kneads my flesh, bringing one nipple into his mouth to suck.

Holy cow...I never knew my nipples were so sensitive. Ripples of pleasure run through my back and down spine, hitting me square in my throbbing clit. I roll my hips forward, which only intensifies the feeling when he sucks my breast farther into his mouth.

His wet tongue flicks the small orb, as his other hand continues squeezing and playing with my other breast. We both moan in unison. His erection twitches between my legs, so I begin to move faster without much grace or finesse. I'm trying to chase this achy, throbbing feeling away with every forceful connection between us.

All of a sudden, I'm consumed with the need to feel my skin against his. I grab a fistful of his shirt and yank it up, unintentionally breaking the connection he has with my breast. He jerks his arms out of the sleeves and I whip it over my shoulder, as he resumes his devotion of my breasts. His body is bowed over me and I bend backwards, his arm slung solidly around my waist to keep me from falling, while allowing him room to devour me.

Due to the friction between us, I'm close to falling in another way. Over the edge of oblivion. I'm close to that precipice and don't quite know if I should continue. I'm worried that he'll expect sex, and I'm not entirely sure I'm ready for that quite yet. But I'm scared to say anything. I don't even know what I'd say or how to communicate what I want and where the line is drawn.

Instead, I run my hand between our bodies, pressing against his bulge and fingering the elastic waistband of his shorts, hoping he'll get the picture. His eyes widen in confirmation, yet he may not understand my full intent.

So I bite the bullet and spit it out.

"Can we...um, can we leave my underwear on?"

He agrees without saying a word. With no preamble, Van flips me over and pulling down his shorts in one smooth move. I'm actually a little shocked by his stealthy-fast moves as I land on my back, legs spread eagle, as he wedges himself on top of me. The warmth of his skin touching mine is exquisite, like the tropical trade winds of Hawaii licking over my body.

It's then that he aligns himself to my center, and his steely cock gliding against my cleft as I shiver from the pleasure. If it feels this amazing through the protective barrier of my underwear, I wonder what it will feel like when there's nothing between us? Just the thought alone has me reconsidering my decision. But this feels great, too. My body is certainly ready for him to make a woman of me, but my heart and brain are a bit more hesitant.

One step at a time.

Van bends down and kisses me hotly, groaning feverishly into my mouth, as he continues to bump and grind on top of me, each time drawing out an erotic grunt. God, it's so sexy. He's so sexy.

I reach for his butt, taking hold of his muscular ass and pushing him harder into my center. Apparently I need it harder and faster because I'm almost there. He changes tactics, as his lips leave my mouth and move to my neck, sucking at the tendon below my earlobe, causing even hotter sensations to spiral and swirl between my legs.

And when he bites my earlobe between his teeth, I go off like a rocket to the heavens.

I have no idea what I scream in the moment. I'm sure it's all mumbled gibberish. I'm temporarily blinded by a burst of white dots from behind my eyelids, my body being taken away on a wave out to sea. I barely register the low, resonating growl that Van lets loose, as he stills above me, his head buried in my neck, and I'm flooded with the warmth of his release across my silk panties.

Van collapses along my side, his breath coming out in sharp, quick spurts. My own heartbeat is hammering against my chest and I'm filled with the most serene sensation. It's such a heady feeling knowing that I made the guy I've been crushing on for months come all over me. In fact, it makes me insanely happy.

Curiosity sends my hand down to my belly to touch the evidence of his orgasm left cooling on my skin. My finger investigates the pooled moisture, swirling it around in a circular motion, making doodled artwork across my abdomen.

"I'm sorry," he says quietly, his breath hot against my ear. "Didn't mean to get you so messy."

"I like it." I admit softly.

Van groans and flops on his back, his arm crooked over his face.

"God, Ky. You're going to be the death of me."

I'm not sure what he means, but I certainly hope it's a good thing.

14

V an

CHRISTMAS at the Gerard household can be a crazy, chaotic time. My parents have always gone all out in celebration, inviting family and friends from their church over for big, elaborate dinners.

Tonight is no exception. My mom has the ham in the oven and I'm chopping up celery to add to the stuffing. Dougie sits at the table playing a video game, while Christmas music wafts from the Bose speakers. My brother loves holiday tunes – and although he can't sing along with them, he bangs his hands against the table in time – his own way of toe-tapping. I glance over my shoulder at him and smile, turning back to see my mom at the stove smiling, as well.

My parents are devoted members of their church and are very big believers in practicing what they preach. I can't recall a time when our Christmas dining table wasn't filled with at least three or four people who had nowhere else to go. Whether they had no family in the area, were going through hard times, or were recovering addicts – it was irrelevant. My parents welcomed them with open arms.

It made me proud that they cared for people in that manner. They could have turned into very cynical and angry people after Dougie was diagnosed. It's not been easy for them to watch their firstborn son go through the horrendously debilitating disease of cerebral palsy. Dougie is now completely confined to a wheelchair, has limited mobility with his hands, and requires round-the-clock care to ensure he's fed, bathed, clothed and his bio needs are handled. He requires assistance for caring for himself in every way because his motor functions are so lacking – ways in which others take for granted. Where I am able, he is incapable. Life isn't fair.

My mom's voice reaches me over the sound of the music and Doug's raucous noises. "How's school going, Donavan? How'd your finals go?"

I finish chopping the rest of the stalk and throw the pieces into the pot of melted butter, wiping my hands on the dishtowel next to me.

"Good, I think. It was a pretty easy semester, honestly." I shrug, returning to the pot on the stove to stir the contents.

"I'm glad," she says, drawing in a deep breath. "I know you were going through a lot that last month with Lyndsay. I was worried about you."

My parents obviously know that we broke up, but they don't know the entirety of the situation. No one else knows Lyndsay cheated on me and is pregnant. When we broke up, she begged me not to mention it to anyone. She hadn't decided what she was going to do or when she'd tell her parents, so I promised I'd keep it under wraps. And aside from Cade and Kylah, I haven't told a soul.

My mom stops what she's working on and turns to me, looking up at me with concern.

"We always liked Lyndsay, don't get me wrong, Van. But we thought you both were too young to commit to each other so fully. I think it's a good thing you have some choices now."

I know the underlying message is about sex. My parents, while not naïve, do not approve of premarital sex. Lyndsay and I were always careful not to fool around at my house, and I took great pains in keeping the details of our sex life under wraps. My dad was much laxer about it, since he was the one who had to have the 'talk' with me when I was sixteen. He didn't go into the actual details about sex, but discussed his expectations that I should always respect my partner. That sex should only happen when love is present and a commitment has been made. And outside of that, abstinence should be observed.

Which winds my thoughts back to the other night with Kylah.

There's a pang of guilt for letting things go that far with her. I don't want another relationship this soon after my break-up. For that reason alone, I had planned to avoid anything sexual and remain friends with Kylah. But when I saw how distraught she was over her mom, and how she broke down in my arms, I couldn't help myself. Believe me, it wasn't out of pity that I did what I did and kissed her. I've wanted Kylah for months. My resolve be damned.

Honestly, I was elated to finally let her know just how much I wanted her. It felt like the weight of a thousand-pound boulder was lifted off my chest when I wrapped her in my arms. Once I kissed her, there was no turning back. Screw our friendship. Fuck the fact that we'll have to hide this thing from Cade. I wanted her so badly, I would've sold my soul to the devil just for one taste.

The problem now is that my thoughts are consumed with

her. Wanting more of her. We didn't have sex with penetration, but we crossed the line and there's no turning back now. I know it's just a matter of time before things progress further.

And there lies my conundrum.

Do I let it continue? Do we start dating in secret so her brother doesn't find out?

Or should I squash my feelings for her and end it before it even starts? Before I do something to screw it up and she gets hurt.

I'm so confused and torn over this. What I definitely don't want is for her to think she's a rebound fling. If I wanted a rebound, I would have fucked a hoops hunny without a care in the world. But that's not who I am. I care for Kylah more than anyone and just want to protect her.

Well, fuck her. Then protect her.

So that leads me back to my mom's concerns over my well-being.

"Everything's cool, Mom. Don't worry about it. I'm in a good place right now."

I'm not ready to divulge anything about Kylah, especially to my mom, who'd be curious and would start poking me with questions. She is right about one thing – I do have choices now. My path, however, seems to veer toward Kylah. This connection we share is so strong – like some sort of Jedi mind trick – with a pull like the tractor beam on the Death Star. It's been leading me toward her since we first met. Even before I knew I liked her.

We finish getting dinner ready and I help serve our guests, as everyone around the table talks and chats amiably. I sit next to Dougie and help him with his dinner, giving my parents a break to enjoy their own meals. My heart is full, but I'm missing something. I want to share this with someone I care about. Someone like Kylah.

She'd mentioned that Christmas Eve they'd spend at their

dad's condo, but she didn't think Cade would be joining them, so it would just be her and Kady. I guess the rift between Cade and Mr. Griffin hasn't been fully healed yet – although I know they've been working on it. She mentioned that out of the three of them, Ky has remained closest to her dad after the divorce.

As I spend time with my parents tonight, I can't imagine what it would be like to have them separated. How different and lonely it would feel not having them both in the same room – hearing their laughter and enthusiasm for the holidays as they share it with others. I'm a very lucky guy and they've set a find example for me to live up to.

We have great family dynamics, despite the fact that Dougie is the way he is. Regardless of the workload that goes into caring for Dougie, none of us would have it any other way. He's a beautiful part of this family. I wish I could be more like him, because nothing ever gets Dougie down.

He's been my cheerleader on the sidelines ever since I started playing basketball in the third grade. He'd cheer, and yell, and pump his fists in the air – smiling the big, broad, toothy grin of his that made other people around him smile, too. As we got older, it made me sad to see the way people stared at him. How they talked behind his back and made fun of him. It hurt me to know that people could be so cruel and intolerant of things they didn't understand.

As we grew older, I became very protective of Dougie, who was two years ahead of me in school. Although he had limited mobility, he had mild cognitive impairment, meaning that his brain function was at a high functioning level so he could learn and excel at school with the help of student aids and electronic communication devices. There's no doubt that when someone like Dougie attends a public school, there are going to be ignorant assholes who make fun of him. And they did.

I was a sixth grader in middle school the first time I got into a fight defending my brother's honor. We were in the cafeteria and Dougie was having a meltdown at another table because his para-assistant wasn't doing something right, so he was babbling loudly. He did that when he got over-excited. On this one occasion, his hands flapped wildly as the para tried getting his lunch set up on the tray in front of him. Dougie's flailing hands must have hit the tray and sent the food sailing across the floor.

A boy in my grade sitting at the end of the table made a comment to another kid about Dougie being "*a loud-mouthed retard*" – and I just lost it. I jumped from my seat, came up behind the kid, pushed him off his chair and onto the floor, and started wailing on him. I had never been an aggressive boy and was taught by my parents to always turn the other cheek. That's all well and good in theory, but that boy deserved to be taught a lesson. And so did the kids sitting around him at the table, all laughing at my brother's expense.

I learned a valuable lesson that day. Thankfully, I was given leniency by the Principle because I was a good kid who'd never gotten in trouble before. My parents, on the other hand, grounded me, taking away all my TV and video game privileges for a month and in place made me volunteer down at the local mission, cleaning up the bathrooms and kitchen messes.

The lesson learned, however, was that I will never change someone else's thoughts, actions or behavior by beating them up. That goes without saying. But I did learn that it feels pretty fucking good in that moment when you're giving someone a bloody upper lip. Just saying.

Technically, that was the one and only fight I'd been in over Dougie. As we all grew older, the kids in our school began to accept him – especially my junior and senior high school basketball teammates. The last home game of my senior year of high school, they all made a special banner for Dougie, commemorating his contributions to the team. The coach also added Dougie to the roster that last game, threw a jersey over his head, and let me wheel him out on the court to shoot a basket. I've never seen Dougie smile as big as he did that day. His laughter and animated motions made it all worthwhile.

He's grinning from ear-to-ear now, too. All our guests have gone, leaving just the four of us in front of the tree. The Christmas lights blink in multi-colored unison, the fireplace flickers its radiant heat, and the tooting sounds of the train circling underneath the tree stand gives Dougie reason to laugh. He loves that fucking train.

My dad reaches underneath the tree to the presents stashed in the back. Handing one to me and another to Dougie, he prefaces the gift by saying, "It's not much this year. You're both at an age now where it seems kind of frivolous."

I nod my head in agreement, glancing over to my brother. "You go first, Doug. Let's see what Santa brought you."

A loud exclamation comes from his throat as he rips into his package. He holds it up like a trophy, reveling in the joy of receiving the latest video game. For having limited use of his hands, my brother can use a video game controller like no one's business. If his body wasn't restricted by this horrible disease, I know with one hundred percent certainty that he would have been an amazing athlete. Quick reflexes and a determined focus.

I take a peek at that labeling, even though I know what game it is, since I helped my dad pick it out. It's an Xbox Minecraft game. He is a whiz when it comes to building and creating things. His brain has a capacity for hugeness, if only his body didn't limit him. In some way, it's like he can build these worlds using this game where physical limitations mean nothing, and he can actually be free from his body's constraints.

"Nice, bro. That outta keep you busy for a while." I wink at him and ruffle his hair in the process, which garners a grin from him.

He uses his electronic voice to respond. "Your turn."

I give him a head nod and open my gift. My brother squeals in delight as I hold up the basketball jersey. It's a Phoenix Sun's team jersey with Steve Nash's number thirteen. He was my favorite player growing up – especially because he was a Phoenix ball player. Although I don't play point guard, Nash was an all-around dynamic player whom I admired as a kid. Whenever we could afford it and had the time, my dad would take me and Dougie to the games, maybe once a year. It was always a special event, and because of Doug's wheelchair, we always got really good seats.

"Hold it up. Let me get a picture." My mom cheers, pulling out her phone as I do as she requests. I bend down next to Doug's chair and hold it in front of us. Leaning over to Doug, I ask, "Did you help pick this out, bro?" He grunts and lifts his shoulders in a shrug.

We finish up the rest of the evening and I finally crawl into bed, exhausted and happy. I had left my phone charging on my nightstand while we were having dinner, so I haven't checked it for several hours. Opening up my text messaging, I see five or six different texts. The last one was from my mom, who sent me the pic of me and Dougie. I smile 'cause it's a great picture of us together. My dad is photo bombing us in the background, making a goofy face. It makes me laugh.

There's a few from my friends wishing me a Merry Christmas and asking about upcoming plans for New Years' Eve. The remaining two are from Kylah and Lyndsay. I debate which one I should read first. I'm hoping Lyndsay's will just be a quick one, so I open hers up first.

Big mistake.

Lyndsay: I'm sure I'm just being overly emotional. But this is the first Christmas we haven't spent together in a long time.

Lyndsay: I miss you, Van. So much.

Lyndsay: I'm so sorry I put you through all of this.

Lyndsay: I still haven't decided what to do about the baby. Cody doesn't want it.

Lyndsay: I have a present for you and your family. Can I stop by tomorrow? I really need someone. Someone I love and trust.

Fuck me. My emotions reel from the audacity she has to send me these messages. What the hell am I supposed to do with this?

Good for her – she found out her baby daddy's a loser. And what? She thinks she can come running back to me? Does she think I'm just sitting here, wallowing in misery, waiting with open arms for her to come to her senses?

She can go fuck herself if that's what she thinks.

My perfect, peaceful Christmas Eve has bit the dust because now I'm seething with anger. And truthfully, I'm confused. If I didn't still feel something toward Lyndsay, would I still be angry? Do I still have feelings for her after all?

I don't think so. But she's right. It is kind of sad not to have someone to share the holidays with like we used to together.

My brain buzzes and my blood boils with indecision. I'm not sure I should give her the opportunity to come over – but I can't shut her out, either. I'll feel like an asshole. Regardless of the circumstances, and the fact that she stomped on my heart, I do still care about her. I probably always will. She was my first love.

And like my parents always told me – turn the other cheek.

15

K ylah

IT's BEEN twenty-four hours and I still haven't heard back from Van.

In fact, since Tuesday night when I left his dorm, I have yet to hear from him.

I texted him last night to let him know my dad got me two tickets to the Twenty One Pilots concert as my Christmas present. I nearly jumped out of my shoes when I opened the gift box to find the tickets inside. I couldn't wait to tell Van about it.

My enthusiasm has waned, though, since he hasn't responded to my text. Kady's patience has worn thin with me, too, as she scowls from the end of the couch where her laptop is propped on her lap.

"Stop fidgeting. You're driving me crazy."

I shift in my spot and put my heels underneath my butt. I've been trying to read the new book my mom bought me but my interest lies elsewhere.

It's driving me absolutely crazy not hearing from Van. Maybe I'm deluding myself, but I really thought things were great between us. I mean, I practically dry-humped his brains out the other night and he gave me something no other guy has ever given me. So I suppose I shouldn't complain. But I'm worried. Freaking out that he just used me and now is done with me.

My heart sinks in recognition of the despair I feel.

Kady warned me this could happen, but I didn't believe her. "*Van isn't like that*", I told her, confident that he wasn't like other guys and wouldn't leave me hanging after we hooked up. I can tell she's thinking it, but doesn't want to rub it in by saying "*I told you so.*"

Now I feel like a complete and utter fool. What if we would have gone further the other night? I could've given him my virginity and never heard from him ever again. What a loser I am.

Now I'm just a broken-hearted virgin. One thousand times worse than just being a plain old virgin.

I guess I should be thanking him for not pressuring me to give it up. That's what I don't understand. When we're together, he is sweet and considerate. He asked for my permission at every juncture. Other guys would never ask, they'd just assume and take. Unlike some of Cade's other player friends, there is nothing about Van that screams 'player'.

I reread this damn page for the third time and finally decide to just give it up, sighing loudly as I snap the book shut and toss it on the end table. Kady peers up over her laptop, eyebrows practically reaching her hairline.

"Speak." She demands, closing the lid and stretching out her legs across the cushions, her toes touching my thighs.

"I think I did something wrong."

Kady jumps up onto her knees on the cushions between us, slapping them in the process as I shift from the sudden movement. "Whoa, whoa, whoa. Why the hell is that the first possible answer with you? Why would it have anything to do with what you've done or should've done? It's all on him, Ky. He's being the asshole if he's ghosting you. If he's too stupid to see what he has with you, then fuck him."

It's just like my sister to come to my defense. And I appreciate that. She always has my back. She's right, too. I do always take on the responsibility of whatever goes wrong. It's just part of my personality make-up. I can't help who I am any more than she is who she is. Kady's the lioness. And I'm the cowardly lion.

"Fuck him, who?" My brother chimes in, stepping in from the hallway adjacent to the family room.

We both respond simultaneously. "No one."

Cade rolls his eyes facetiously, glancing from one to the other. "*Riiiight.*" He plops down between us. "So who's having the boy problems? Maybe big brother can help."

His arms go around our shoulders and he squeezes us into him, as we both try unsuccessfully to squirm out of his hold.

"Go away, Cade." Kady says, shooing him with her hand. "You stink and you weren't invited to this conversation." She sniffs the air as if something rancid permeates it. She's just being a brat. Cade smells fine.

"Oh come on...I smell awesome. And who better to give you boy advice than me? Let me have it..."

I tilt my head in his direction. He actually seems sincere for once and I'm a little in awe over his genuine offer.

Kady obviously doesn't see it. "Why don't you go make out with your girlfriend, already, and leave us alone."

Cade takes it all in stride, removing his arm from her shoulder, but keeping it securely around mine. He knows where the love is.

His tone turns solemn. "Ainsley's busy today. I can't see her until later tonight."

Oh, my poor brother. So in love with his girl and feeling neglected. Cue miniature violin solos.

We all know how dedicated Ainsley is with the two jobs she works to support herself and her younger sister, all while attending nursing school. I've gotten to know her over the last several months and found her to be such a great person. She has been a great influence on my brother.

"So that means you're stuck with me today, girls. So...tell me what I can help with."

My eyes gravitate to Kady, who gives me a shoulder shrug and an expression that clearly tells me, "*it's up to you*."

I figure it couldn't hurt to share this with Cade. I won't mention Van or anything, but just my predicament in general. To get a guy's perspective.

I sigh, pulling my feet out from underneath me. "Okay...so here's the scoop. And don't go getting all judgey, okay?" I eyeball him. "I like a guy. I thought he liked me. We kinda hooked-up..."

His head snaps to me and his mouth opens wide. "Wait, what? Did he de-virginize you?"

I groan and Kady smacks him on the shoulder. "You idiot," she scolds. "That's not even a word and it's none of your freaking business."

He starts to refute this fact but she slams her palm across his mouth before he can speak. "Shut it, or she won't tell you anything more." She gives me a meaningful look.

His response is muffled. "Fine."

"So anyway," I continue. "I thought we were good...like *really* good. But now I'm questioning my instincts. I've heard nothing from him in nearly two days. So maybe he's decided he doesn't want anything to do with me. I don't know. I'm confused. And sorta hurt."

Cade grows quiet for once. He's normally a chatterbox,

always talking away to anybody and anyone. When I turn to face him, I see the frown and the concern etched across his brow.

"Since I don't know anything about this guy..."

Um, you kind of do. But I'm not about to mention that.

"I can't know what's causing the lack of communication. But generally there's two reasons a guy will ghost you. The first is simple. He lacks the balls to tell you face-to-face that he doesn't want to continue things. It sucks, 'cause we guys are notorious for this move. We figure if we quit responding to the chick's texts and calls, they'll just go away on their own."

He gives me an apologetic look. God, I hope that's not the case with Van.

My brother continues. "He might also be scared."

"Scared?" I spit out incredulously. No way would Van be scared about talking to me.

"Again, guys don't want to look like fools and rush in, only to get rejected. So the fear prevents us from doing the right thing and sharing our true feelings. We'd rather put a stop to things before they start so we can't get our hearts broken."

"Aw," my sister whines sarcastically. "Did our big brother get his heart broken?"

"Shut the fuck up." He argues, giving Kady a good-natured shove so she topples over laughing. Those two.

"Is that what happened between you and Ainsley?"

"Nah...my balls are too big for that." He snickers, grabbing between his legs crudely. "In our situation, it was kind of the other way around. But regardless, it probably has nothing to do with you, per se, Ky, and more to do with him. He's probably shitting bricks that you'll not like him the way he does you and he doesn't want to face that reality."

Kady pipes in. "That's exactly what I said!"

She peers around Cade's broad body to stick her tongue out

at me like a brat. "You just never listen to me, even though I'm clearly always right."

I give her the middle finger and we all laugh. It feels good to be surrounded by my family. I really love my siblings and I'm pretty lucky to have the relationship we have together. I know it'll only make it ten times harder when we all return to school in January, but for right now, I'll soak in all the love I can get from these two.

"So who's the guy, anyway? You want me to rough him up for you? Punch some sense into him?"

I actually think Cade might be serious about that. Which would only make it worse if he ever finds out it's Van that we're talking about. My goodness, that would be ugly.

I pat his hand gingerly. "Thanks, bro. But I'll figure this out from here. I appreciate the insight, though. It does help."

Cade leans down and kisses my temple gently. "Anytime, sis. But the offer's always good, anytime you need me."

My eyes well with tears at the sweet sentiment as his phone buzzes with an incoming text notification. Pulling it out of his pocket, he opens the box and I hone in on the sender name.

Van.

This reminds me of the last time this happened, and a stone of worry gathers in my stomach. I don't want to seem obvious, so I try to read it out of the corner of my eye, but he's too quick and shuts down the screen.

"Well, girls, I'm outtie. I gotta go pack up some leftovers and head home to hang out with the boys. But I'll see you on Friday at my place, right? We can do shots for your birthday."

First off, I'm more than a little curious about the text he just got from Van. Obviously his phone isn't broken, since he's texting my brother. And secondly, I'd forgotten about the upcoming party. It'll be all the usual suspects...guys from the team...some high school friends...Van. Me. Can you say uncomfortable?

"Oh geez...don't go spending too much on our birthday present, there, bro." Kady snipes.

"Hey...I'll have you know that I'm buying top shelf tequila for you two. So shut it, or you won't get any."

Cade clamps his hand together like a clam shell, before he leans down and gives us both quick kisses on top of our heads. He heads out, leaving me to put the puzzle pieces together over what's going on with Van and me.

My sister interrupts my thoughts. "Just let it go, Ky. He'll either respond or he won't. Either way, don't sell yourself short and don't keep sending him texts. You're not one of those desperate girls."

I know she's right. I know it. But I am desperate to know what's going on with him. It doesn't make it hurt any less. I just want to know what I did to make him disappear like this.

Goddamn boys. Why do they have to be so dumb?

an

It's Kylah's birthday today. December Twenty-ninth.

It's been over a week since I last saw her and a day before the concert she invited me to attend with her.

I left her hanging without any explanation and I hate myself for it.

I'm scum. I'm lower than pond scum.

The fact is, I didn't have the wherewithal to deal with anything else after the whole Lyndsay text. She threw me for a loop and my brain was just fried. Emotional overload. I didn't have anything I could give Kylah in the way she needed me.

Kylah's a sweet girl and deserves someone who isn't fucked up in the head right now. After Lyndsay dropped the bomb on me, it unraveled everything I thought I felt. I thought I was doing great until she told me she and Cody broke up.

The thing is, I don't love Lyndsay anymore. I know that. That level of connection was broken the minute she admitted to lying and cheating on me. There's also no way I'd ever get back together with her, regardless of what amends she tries to make.

The problem is that I lost a great deal more than just a girlfriend. I lost my faith in humanity. Yes, I realize that sounds extreme. I shouldn't take my displaced anger over Lyndsay out on the general population, but it's a little hard not to hold a grudge. It's difficult to let go and believe that not everyone is capable of ruining your trust.

Here's the kicker. I feel I'm doing the exact same thing to Kylah. We'd grown to be friends. We'd become close. Physically and emotionally close. She put her faith in me when she shared her confusion and unhappiness over her mother's engagement news. She let me comfort her and hold her...and then practically maul her after opening up to me.

And how do I repay her for that?

Shit. I'm a fucking dickhead.

Thankfully, we've had practices and strength training the last couple of days, so I've been able to push away my growing conflict over my predicament and focus on the art of basketball. Working out helps assuage my guilt to some level.

My biceps and triceps strain as I do bench presses in the weight room. Cade's spotting me, standing overhead in support, as he shouts out what should be words of encouragement. I know for a fact those encouraging words would change in a hot instant if he knew what I did to his sister.

"Come on, you pussy. My sister could press more than you, asshole."

Oh shit. He can read my thoughts. My eyes pop open at the mention of his sister and my arms struggle to stay above my head. They shake in their quest for relief and I grunt out for help. Cade grabs hold of the bar and helps me place it back in the rack.

I pull myself up to a sitting position, grabbing for the towel to wipe off the sweat that's dripping from my head.

"Jesus, Van. You okay? Didn't think you were going to make it through that last set."

Cade hands me the bottle of Gatorade and I gulp it down, giving myself some time to think about my response and to catch my breath.

"I'm fucked up, man." I confide, uneasy with sharing too much of my personal shit. Thankfully, I trust Cade. He's a good friend. And I know he's gone through his share of relationship hell.

"What's going on?" He takes a seat at the bench across from me. There's only a handful of guys left in the gym, and most are over in the far weight room.

I breath heavily. "I've met someone. I really like her."

Cade nods his head with enthusiasm, a smile growing across his face. "That's good to hear, man. You deserve it after all that shit with your ex. So what's the problem? She not putting out?" He chuckles at his joke, which he wouldn't find humorous if he knew it was Kylah he was unknowingly discussing.

I huff out a laugh. "Um, no, that's not the problem. It's Lyndsay."

His head whips back, as if he's been stung, his mouth in a tight grimace. "I thought you guys were done, dude. I didn't know she was still in the picture...after what she pulled."

"Yeah, it's not that. It's just...you know, I'm a little gun shy now because of that shit. And I'm not being fair to this other girl, who I really like."

Cade nods, his support evident, even though I'm only telling him half of the story.

"I feel ya, dude. I get it. It's like the past has a way of fucking things up for us when we finally meet the right one. But if you're into her enough, you gotta give it a chance. Show your cards. Be honest with her and let her know how you really feel. That's the only way." He leans over conspiratorially and whispers. "And let me tell ya...girls love it when you spill your guts and wax poetic. You won't be sorry and either will your dick."

He thumps me on the back a few times before standing up, lending me his hand to help pull me up, too.

"Hey, by the way, man. It's the twins' birthday today. We're having a few drinks over at our place. You're welcome to come over and hang out. I'm sure Ky would love to see you again."

I nearly choke on my response. I'm pretty sure she wouldn't.

How did I get myself into this mess? Shit, if I do by some miracle get Kylah to forgive me and give me another chance, it'll be like passing through Hell's gates when I bring it up with Cade. He's going to be one sorry mother fucker when he realizes the advice he gave me was about his sister and not some random chick.

Throwing the soiled towel into the bin as I pass through the locker room door, glancing over my shoulder at Cade. "Yeah, maybe I'll stop by. Should I bring her a present?"

Cade snorts. "Nah, man...'cause if you bring one present, you have to bring one for the other. And Kady's a picky woman. There's never any pleasing that girl!"

I make a sad attempt at laughter, but my mind fast forwards to the next time I see Kylah. I pray she is as mild-mannered and forgiving as I think she is. Otherwise, I'll be in the doghouse for a long time to come.

I DON'T ARRIVE EMPTY-HANDED. I brought a twelve pack of beer for the guys and two bouquets of flowers for Kady and Kylah.

In one of our many conversations over the last few months, Kylah had mentioned that she'd never received any floral delivery or arrangement from anyone outside her family. So I decided to go big or go home.

I bought a huge bouquet of rainbow colored roses and a big Happy Birthday balloon for Kylah. For her sister, I got a much smaller and friendlier bouquet of bright pink and purple gerbera daisies. I don't want to look weird coming in with a gigantic arrangement for a girl I didn't even know. This will already earn me a bunch of side-eye glances from the boys. But fuck it. I have to grovel, so this is a start.

I inhale deeply and blow it out as I open the front door of the apartment. I've been to their place more times than I can count, but this is the first time I've ever been anxious walking through the door. The nerves over seeing Kylah, and the possibility of getting my head taken off for not contacting her back, have me literally shaking in my shoes.

Stepping across the threshold, I hear shouts and laughter coming from every part of the room. Lance and Scott Wagner are over on the couch, munching on some popcorn and arguing over who gets to play the next game against Carver. And he's sitting on a chair, locking lips with some blondie who's practically down his throat.

Ainsley's on Cade's lap over in a corner chair, and they're looking at something on her phone and laughing. There's a few others milling around that I'm familiar with, but don't know personally, as I turn to the direction of the kitchen. There sitting at the table with her back to me is Kylah. Or at least, I think it's Kylah, because the look-alike currently staring at me has blue hair and is giving me the stink eye.

Yup. Pretty sure that's her evil twin sister and she is none too happy with me.

She says something directed at Ky, whose head suddenly whips around toward me. She's wearing her glasses and an expression I can't read. I watch her eyes as they glance down at what's in my hands and then they make their way back to my eyes, where I give her an apologetic smile. I know I'll have to do way more than that, but I see a start of a shy smile form in the corner of her mouth, before turning away from me.

I slowly make my way into the kitchen and round the table, stepping to the side so I'm facing Kylah. Her cheeks are red – from embarrassment or anger, I'm not sure which. But she doesn't look at me. Instead, she stabs the piece of cake in front of her with her fork and takes a bite, focusing her eyes down at the table.

"Happy birthday, Kylah." I need to start somewhere and that's the best I can come up with. "These are for you."

I hold them out to her but she doesn't take them. Doesn't even glance up.

I shoot a glance over to her sister, who is at the very least acknowledging my existence.

"And these are for you. Happy birthday, Kady. I'm Donavan. Most people call me..." She cuts me off.

"I know who the fuck you are."

I take a step back, for fear of losing a limb from the icy blade of her voice. Christ, she's vicious. Kylah mentioned they were opposites. And now I see the difference.

I place the arrangements down in front of each of them, but keep my distance as best as I can. It's probably comical, with me being six-foot-seven and two-hundred and fifteen pound, afraid of two little nineteen-year-old women. One of them bites, I can guarantee you that much.

"What are you doing here, Van?" This from Kady. Her tone razor sharp. "You're not welcome at our birthday party."

Hmm. Okay. How to proceed when the hound of hell is fiercely protecting her sister?

Be humble. That's what my dad always taught me. So here goes.

"I'm pretty sure you're right, Kady. If I were Kylah, I wouldn't want an asshat at my birthday party, either. Because I'm kind of a shit show right now and have obviously been a horrible friend to her lately. I don't have a great excuse, except that I was dealing with a lot of crap, stuff I'd like to explain to her in private, if she'll let me. But if not, I came here - invited by Cade, by the way – to apologize to Kylah for my behavior and for letting her down. I didn't mean to. And I just want her to know that I value our friendship, above everything else, and I would really like a second chance to make things right. If she'll accept my apology and forgive me."

My heart pounds a hundred miles an hour and I can just tell my face is getting blotchy and tinted red. This is way tougher than I expected it to be – especially with Kady giving me the death glare.

Laughter and music come blaring in from the other room, but I pay it no attention to it. All my focus – everything I see – is right here in front of me. My eyes don't veer from Kylah as I reach to grab her hand, bringing it to my mouth.

She jerks her stiff hand back but I hold tight as I place a light kiss on top, allowing my lips to linger there for a split second before placing it back on the table. She lifts her eyes to me which hold pools of tears welling in them.

I don't want to make a scene. All I want is to get her away from everyone so I can tell her how I feel about her.

"Ky," I murmur. "Will you come outside me with? Can we go for a walk so we can talk?"

Her eyes dart over to her sister, presumably for direction. I see an imperceptible nod of approval, as Kady stands from the table and picks up her plate. Just before she heads to the kitchen sink, she leans into me and speaks directly into my ear.

"Don't you dare fuck it up with her. I will hunt you down and have your balls for breakfast. And that's *before* my brother gets ahold of you."

I swallow thickly, blinking once as I flash a quick glance to see if Cade is still there, before I turn back to Kylah. She's nervously chewing on her lip, which is trembling softly. She gets up from the chair and we both head toward the door. I place my hand gently on her lower back to guide her out, just as Cade calls out to me. I stop in my tracks. Oh shit. Here we go.

"Hey Van! Glad you made it. Where are you two heading off to?" His smile is wide, but then he tilts his head when he sees Kylah's expression.

Shit.

And then she does the most incredible thing.

"He has the new Twenty One Pilots song that he wants me to hear. It's out in his car. We'll be right back."

They all just wave us off and we walk out the door, as I let out the longest breath. As soon as we're out of sight and ear shot, she shoves my hand off her back and stalks toward my car.

"Kylah. Please...you have every right to be mad at me..."

"You're goddamn right I do." She turns and stomps back over to me so I'm looking straight down at her. Then she slaps me hard against the chest. It doesn't hurt and I don't budge, which makes her angrier.

"Argh! You big ol' wall of stone!"

I can't help myself, I have to touch her.

I pick her up, wrapping my arms around her tiny waist, and hold her flush against me. She squirms and kicks at me, getting a few good shots in at my kneecaps - thankfully nothing close to my groin - until she finally loses steam. I inhale her fragrance that seems to have enveloped me when she was flailing around in my arms. I bury my nose in the crook of her neck and just hold her tight, hugging her as if my life depended on it.

One moment I think her body's gone lax, and then I feel her shaking – her sobs wracking her – wrenching a knife in my gut.

"Why?" she cries out, muffled by a sob. "Why did you do that to me?"

I go with complete honesty. I have nothing left to lose. "I panicked, Ky. I'm a total fucking coward. That's why."

Her body jerks with a cross between a sob and a laugh. She pulls away slightly, the lights from the street lamp shining on her, illuminating the tears that dazzle like crystals on her face.

"Why would you be scared? We were friends...I thought we were friends." Her voice is so tiny. So sad.

A few people mill around us in the parking lot, invading our privacy. I walk toward my car, to the passenger side door, and set her down, opening the door so she can get in. Once we're situated in the front seat, I resume our conversation.

"Ky, we *are* friends. But then all of a sudden, we became more. I fought myself the entire way because I didn't want to mess it up with you. I like you too much. My feelings for you were all over the board. One minute I want to kiss you...to sleep with you...and the next, I'm telling myself that I can't do it. I can't get into another relationship this fast."

She stops me. "I don't expect a relationship, Van. Honestly. I just...I want you however I can get you."

I reach for her hand and bring it to my heart.

"You're not a hook-up, Ky. And we're not meant to be friends with benefits. We'd be fooling ourselves to think there's not more here...because I feel it. I think about you every second of the day. I can't get you out of my head. But I'm also still so messed up from what happened with Lyndsay. She texted me on Christmas Eve."

I glance away, feeling guilty by just admitting it out loud.

"She did? What happened?"

"Nothing. I promise. It was late, just before bed when I read her text. She said she broke up with Cody. That she made a mistake. She wanted to see me to explain. To apologize."

Kylah drops her head and sighs. "Oh. I see."

My hands shake as I place them over her cheeks, drawing her face into mine so our foreheads touch.

"No, you don't see." My eyes search hers in a plea as I pull back, dropping my hands. She's still here with me, so that's a good thing. She wears her emotions across her face, so I know her anger has dissipated and now she just looks worried. Resigned. I've got to change that.

"Kylah, Lyndsay and I are over. My feelings toward her are nothing more than sympathy at this point. She clearly fucked things up with her life. And mine. But honestly, it made me realize that I had been trying to hold on to something that was no longer there. I made it work with her all this time because I couldn't let go...I was scared of the unknown. Of what I would be without her. She was the only one who really knew me deep down inside. Who I was. But the distance, her changing attitude – *your presence in my life* – helped me to see that things weren't healthy anymore."

I close my eyes, breathing through my nose as I settle back into the driver's seat. I'd had a lot of time to think about how I would explain this to Kylah, but it is still difficult to get it all out.

"You came into my life at the right time, Ky." I reach for her hand and loop my fingers through hers. "I needed you more than you could possibly imagine. Your friendship. Your positivity. Your support. Everything. And if you let me, I will work to prove myself to you. I've missed talking to you these past few days and I was a fool for shutting you out. I'm so sorry. If you can forgive me, I'll promise I'll never do that again."

Kylah sighs and her head bends forward as if in prayer. Maybe she's praying I'll leave her alone and never see her again.

Fat chance. If she doesn't forgive me tonight, I'll continue asking for it. I won't stop until I can make it right.

"Van," she whispers, and I can hear it in her voice. I've broken through. I think my heart skips a beat.

Placing my finger underneath her chin, I tilt her head up so I can see into her eyes. They gleam with unshed tears that she's been holding back.

"I don't want to be a rebound. And I don't just want to be your friend. I'm not sure what I want, because things will be complicated. Rushing into anything would be a really big mistake, I know that. But God, I've missed you, too. I've been miserable not talking to you. Both Kady and Cade warned me not to call you...to wait until you reached out to me, but it was so hard."

My body stiffens as soon as she mentions her brother. "Wait, your brother knows about us?" Jesus, I'm surprised he even let me into his apartment. Or hasn't beaten me to a pulp yet.

Kylah offers a small giggle at my outburst. "Heck no. He has no clue it's you that has me tied up in knots. But he might catch on soon if we don't head back inside and rejoin the party."

I nod my head in agreement. "Yeah, you're probably right." I reach out to place my hand on her cheek as she leans into my palm, a small smile forming across her lips.

"It'll be hell not to be able to touch you in front of everyone. To keep my distance. I'm dying to kiss you right now, Ky." My thumb strums across her jawline, stroking her softly. "Can I kiss you?"

"Mm-hmm."

I grin at her. "Thank God."

Slowly, with purpose, I lean forward, cupping her face in both hands, and place my lips across hers. Kylah's breath fans across my mouth, smelling sugary sweet from the icing on her cake. In this moment, she's the icing on my cake. And I devour her.

Although it starts off gently, our kiss turns heated within seconds. My tongue plunges into her mouth as I swallow her gasps and moans – which make me so fucking hard – as I suckle at her wet tongue. I'm not going to win any awards for finesse right now because I'm too wound up. I kiss, suck and lick everything my mouth can connect with – as I move my lips to her neck, puncturing tiny, wild bites under her ear.

Her hands feather their way into my hair, sifting through it before tugging tight. I groan against her skin. This is heaven. I'm not sure I can control myself for much longer and I'm certainly not going to take her in the backseat of my car while her brother or any number of friends could come out and see us at any moment.

While I'd love to throw caution to the wind, I come to my senses and pull back, ignoring my throbbing dick down below. It's screaming for more action, but it'll have to do without for now. Kylah's breath hitches, one of the sexiest, neediest sounds I've ever heard. I want nothing more than to dive back into those lips and find my way between her legs.

"We can't...not here." I glance around to our surroundings. It's dark and the only light is coming from the windows of the apartment complex, but it's enough to illuminate the interior of my car and anyone could walk by and see us.

She sags back into the car seat. "You're right. I know."

It kills me to let her down like this, especially on her birthday. I want to make her feel special. Give her a night to remember.

"We could...um, go back to my place." I'm hesitant to throw that out there because I don't want her to think that's the only reason I came here tonight. Although, fuck. I'd love for nothing more than to make her come right now with my tongue.

Shit. That is not helping my boner situation at all.

Kylah's mouth opens, like she's forming the words but they can't eject, and then it snaps shut. Fuck, I already crossed the line again. Now she does think that's all I want from her is sex. Which okay, sex is on my mind right now. Just ask boner down there.

"Sorry, that was dumb. Forget I asked."

She reaches to grab for my hand. "No...Van. Trust me, I want to go...but, um, I don't want my brother getting suspicious. If I took off with you right now, his radar would go off and it could get ugly. But tomorrow night..." She turns her head to look out the passenger window, embarrassed by what she's about to say.

Her resolve must kick in then as she turns back to give me a sheepish smile. "I'd still love for you to come with me to the concert. I'll tell my mom I'm staying at Cade's afterwards. I can... um, stay over at your place then."

Oh, sweet baby Jesus. Just thinking about her sleeping in my bed...or not sleeping, rather...has me about to blow my load in my pants like a horny teenager.

I nod my head, incapable of speaking at the moment.

She gives me her signature Kylah smile, her eyes glistening in the dim light, as she leans over to kiss my cheek.

"Good. It's a date."

17

K ylah

ALL MY WORRIES and anxieties I had prior to Van picking me up for the concert have flown out the window.

The concert was everything I'd hoped it to be and more. The crowd was insane – jumping and screaming along in rippling waves across the auditorium - the music and performance incredible, and being next to Van the entire night was better than I imagined it could be. Way better than my fantasies.

I am so gone for this guy I don't even know what to do with myself.

At one point in the show, we were stuck in the middle of the crowd and I couldn't see over the guys in front of me, who were all built like skyscrapers. So Van, being a chivalrous gentleman, picked me up and placed me on his shoulders. I was a little self-conscious at first, because on top of his tall, broad body, I towered over everyone. Thankfully I'd chosen to wore a pair of jeans and not the dress I had originally planned on wearing.

As they played the last song of the show - my favorite, *Trees*, we swayed to the music, singing along with five thousand other fans - Van slipped his hand through mine and brought it to his mouth. The light stubble on his lips and chin scraped against my skin and my heart fluttered in pleasure. I tipped my face up to him to find his eyes glistening in the strobe lights, telling me exactly what he was thinking. A swirl of butterflies took off in my stomach, leaving a wake of excitement between my legs.

Then, as if in slow-motion, he bent down and took possession of my lips. His tongue slid expertly into my mouth, hungrily dueling with mine, in a quest to show me how much he wanted me. Van's very large palm held me behind my head, pulling me him, as I

sunk...

sunk...

sunk into his kiss.

When he finally let me go, I was swimming with need – dizzy from lust. And then my body was doused with gasoline, the fire burning within me blazing in the pyre in my soul when he moved his lips toward my ear and whispered.

"You make me so crazy, Ky. I want you so badly."

Everything around me ceased to exist. All I saw...all I wanted...all I needed in that moment was Van. Without feeling the need to speak, I reached up to thread my fingers through his hair, yanking his mouth back to mine. I might have murmured "Yes" while I kissed him some more.

I thought I'd be more nervous than I am when the time finally came to lose my virginity. I prepared myself with a last minute conversation with Kady before I left tonight about the in's and out's of the whole process. What I should expect – the uncomfortable pain I might experience – the moment before where uncertainty might clog my thoughts – and the potential rush of gooey feelings afterwards that Kady told me to *"avoid at all costs."*

She says she's worried that because of my personality, there's potential for me to become too attached to Van, and heaven forbid, fall in love with him. And then, if that were to happen, she's certain a broken heart is inevitable. It's all doomsday and zombie apocalypse with her.

I'm not worried, though. Yes, Van will claim the title of being my first lover, which only means he'll forever hold a special place in my heart. But that doesn't guarantee he'll will feel any differently toward me. I'm very pragmatic going into this and understand the ramifications. There's also the little teeny, tiny fact that he's just getting over his ex and probably has residual feelings there that won't easily wash away just because he sleeps with me.

Aside from all those troubles, there's also one gigantic subject that I have yet to broach with Van. To my knowledge, and I know I haven't said anything, Van doesn't know I'm a virgin. Now, he's a fairly smart guy, so there's no doubt in my mind that he knows I'm inexperienced. And while I've tried to hide it through my dorky attempts at sexual prowess, it's relatively easy to conclude I haven't been with a lot of guys. A fact which I even shared with Van early on in our friendship.

But that was then and this is now. Shit's getting real now and time is of the essence. Van's told me he wants me badly, and I him, so there's really nothing left to lose - except the obvious.

As we enter his dorm room, he flips the light on his desk lamp in the corner, which casts a soft yellow glow across the floor, the shadows creating dark blankets throughout the room.

His voice is low, almost bashful when he speaks. "I got you a birthday present."

My head pops up in surprise, mouth slightly agape. "You

did? Oh wow. But you got me flowers yesterday. I didn't expect anything, Van. You shouldn't have."

He projects a shy smile. "It's nothing, really. Trust me. But when I saw it, I knew I had to get it for you."

Van stops in front of his chest of drawers and pulls open a drawer, reaching in and grabbing a small wrapped package. It even has a bow affixed, slightly askew. This boy is so thoughtful.

"No card, though. Sorry."

I take the gift from his hand, waving him off like he's full of nonsense. The package is fairly small and floppy in my hands. I sit down on the bed and begin to open it; carefully. With purpose.

Van chuckles at my meticulous process, and I laugh, too. This is the way I've always been, even as a young child. Where Kady would go hog wild and frantically rip at her gifts, I took my sweet time. Savoring in the quest – allowing my imagination to grow wild with possibility.

"Just rip it." He encourages, taking the bow from me and placing it on top of my head. "That's a good look. You could start a new trend."

I shake my head. When the paper is completely undone, I unfold the gift and hold it up in front of me to get a good look. It's a white print tee, similar to the ones I typically wear. Except this one is a *Deadpool* print with the slogan *Did someone say Chimichangas?*

I burst out laughing because we had this very debate over the phone a few weeks back about which is better – tacos or Chimichangas. He likes tacos, and you guessed it, I'm a Chimichanga girl.

"Oh my gosh, Van. This is perfect. I absolutely love it!"

I spin toward him and wrap my arms around his back, pulling him into a hug. My face is nestled in the crook of his neck and his skin is radiating warmth, along with an intoxicating scent of a light, spicy cologne, and something distinctly Van. He turns his face so his nose is buried in my hair, just at my ear.

"I'm glad you like it."

Van Gerard could have given me a box of rocks covered in mud and I would've thought they were made of gold.

"Are you going to try it on to make sure it fits? Maybe give a little twirl." He says in a humorous manner, using his finger to demonstrate the movement, but there's a different meaning hidden under the surface.

"You just want me to take my shirt off for you." It's a statement, not a question, meant to tease, but I swallow the heavy lump in my throat. There's a serious implication there, too.

His voice is deep and raspy, his eyes narrow as he watches me. "Maybe."

This is what I came for, I remind myself, as the nerves begin take shape inside me. My hands tremble lightly as I set the shirt down on his knees and begin to unbutton the blouse I'm wearing. I watch as his eyes as they track my movements, starting at my collarbone and working their way down to the last button. I give my bottom lip a bite, as I peel back the shirt tabs, exposing my belly and my bra-covered breasts.

I'm standing within reaching distance of him, as he raises his hand, the tips of his fingers spanning out against my sternum. I suck in my belly with my gasp. He draws a path toward my center with his calloused index finger, circling my navel before he leans forward to lick it. My breath hitches in a gasp as he moans against me.

"I love your outtie. It's so fucking sexy."

His compliment has me consumed with need as the weight of his hands circle my waist, pulling me toward him, his legs opening into a V so I can wedge between them. He's a little more than eye level to my breasts and he takes full advantage. One hand dutifully cups my lime-green demi-bra, his thumb skimming over my nipple which immediately pebbles under his touch.

In order to aid things along, as well as keep my hands occupied, I reach behind my back to unclasp my bra, letting it fall down my arms and onto his lap. We both look down at the discarded lingerie, briefly staring at it, until he lifts his heavily darkened gaze again to my naked breasts. The warmth and admiration in his eyes has me shuddering with pent-up need. I wonder if it's possible to come from just a look.

I'll never know the answer to that, because he resumes his adoration of my breasts, both hands now playing with them. Squeezing, plumping, lifting, sucking. All of it makes my legs shake from the exquisite feel of his touch. I arch my back when he bites my nipple between his teeth and the movement presses me further into him, one of his hands splayed wide in the middle of my back to support me and keep me pinned. I can now feel the steely hardness of his erection hidden underneath his shorts.

I slide my hands through his hair and sift through the soft waves, his moans telling me he likes my touch. He returns his mouth to my lips, his tongue sweeping in and claiming me. We kiss for several minutes with unrestrained lust, my heartbeat dangerously ratcheting up to unprecedented heights. A throbbing ache has begun a slow build between my legs, which I desperately try to eliminate by rocking my hips against his erection. My sex clenches in anticipation, wetness pooling in my panties.

I feel like I'm in some dream, where his beautiful dark eyes hungrily drink in my nakedness. My body is suddenly left standing on its own as he releases his hands from me and grabs the back of his T-shirt, yanking it up and over his head. I can't help the small gasp of air that leaves my lungs as I look at him in wonder. I'm still amazed that this gorgeous boy wants me. After all these months of waiting, dreaming and hoping he could one day be mine...I finally get my wish.

"What?" He asks, raising his eyebrow at me salaciously.

My words come out in a stuttering breath. "You...you're just so hot." He gives me a soft chuckle.

His chest is a golden tan still, even though we're in December. The small patch of dark chest hair between his pecs is begging for attention, so I sweep my fingers through it, lingering at the hollow of his collarbone, running over the ridge there. I trail my palm down over his pec, rubbing the perfectly round nickel-sized nipple. His body jerks under my touch and I dart my eyes back to his, where I find his eyes closed, a contented smile across his face.

He hums. "Mmm. I like that."

I don't know how I got so lucky to end up with Van – our friendship blooming and transforming into something decidedly more. And now here I am, nearly naked with him in his bedroom, preparing to do the most intimate thing there is between two people. It just amazes me and I'm in awe.

I trail my hands around his chest as he continues to give me encouragement. I'm sure we are going much more slowly than he usually does or wants to go, but he hasn't said anything to the contrary. He's patient and willing to give me time to explore, seeming to sense that I want to take my time.

I haven't mentioned my predicament to him yet. I honestly don't know how to bring it up. I mean, how does one go about that? He hasn't asked, and it's not like I'm just going to blurt out at some random point, "*Oh hey, by the way. I'm a virgin. I'd like you to pop my cherry. Thanks.*"

But I don't want him to feel duped. Maybe he's one of those guys who doesn't sleep with virgins. I've heard that's a real thing with guys. And if I don't tell him, he may not go as slow as I need him too, and then it might hurt a lot worse.

Gah. I'm just stuck.

The other uncomfortable discussion is how to bring up protection. Does the guy automatically take care of that? I do have a condom in my purse – Kady of course gave me one from her endless supply. I'm also pretty sure I could've stolen one from Cade's room, too, if I had to. I don't know if it's needed, though, since I've been on the Pill since I was sixteen, mostly because my mom wanted both her girls to have that back-up protection...especially in light of Kady's free-spirited nature.

All of this leaves a heavy weight on my conscience. At what point are you supposed to talk about these things with your partner? Maybe I should just take the bull by the horns and bring it up. But I'm embarrassed. I don't want to bring this incredible evening to a grinding halt because of my internal debate. I figure if Van feels it necessary to use a condom, he will. And if not, well, I trust him to know he would never put me in danger. I'm sure he got tested after he found out his ex was screwing around with another guy. Right?

Oh geez, now my brain is all screwed up with a never-ending supply of worry. Van seems to notice, as my hands have stilled on their own accord just above his belly button, my body stiffening.

"Hey, what's going on?" The concern in his tone has my tongue-tied and thick.

"I, um...I'm on the Pill." I blurt out.

Stupid. Stupid. Stupid.

Van chuckles, both hands cupping my cheeks and his mouth giving me a soft kiss on my lips. I feel him smile against my mouth, and my relief is evident as my entire body relaxes.

"Good to know," he reassures, placing kisses along my cheek, down to my neck. "I can still use protection, if you want. I'm clean, though, and got tested after...well, after everything." He clears his throat. We both know what he's referring to.

Shit. It appears he's leaving this decision up to me. I wish mental telepathy was a real thing between twins, because I'd call out to Kady for help. *Kady, what should I do?*

"Oh, uh...I'm good with whatever you want." *Brilliant. Very confident, Kylah.*

Chuckling again, Van leans over to the bedside table and pulls out a condom wrapper. Giving me a wink, he says, "We'll play it safe."

My heart melts. He's the most upstanding guy I've ever met in my life.

I should use this moment to bring up my virginity. I should... but I can't. I don't want him to look at me with anything other than the desire he holds in his eyes right now.

So I shut down my brain, and climb on his lap, straddling him so that he's forced to lay back on the bed. We begin making out again, our naked chests now plastered together, our lower halves still covered with denim, but rubbing in all the right places.

My patience is waning. I pull back with a sound of frustration, scooting my butt down and over his erection, which elicits a long groan from Van. I begin to unbutton his shorts. He lifts his head and watches me with interest as I pretend to know what I'm doing. Things are going well so far until the zipper gets stuck, because honestly, his hard on is so big, there's not a lot of room down there.

I'm determined to do this without aid as I pull the material away, loosening the gap, and gingerly glide the zipper down. Success! Van leans up to lend a hand, as I have to sit up on my knees to give him room, watching as he pulls the waistband down and kicks his shorts off onto the floor.

My mouth literally waters at the sight of his erection jutting up toward his navel. It's so crazy to think that some girls don't like the look of penises. Everything about the male body – Van's in particular – is utter perfection. And knowing that his dick is hard and throbbing for release because of me is the biggest turn on ever.

Van covers my hand with his and brings both up to his heavy cock. I follow his lead and allow my fingers to wrap around his length, as we both begin jacking him off in slow, even strokes. Van's fully erect dick is wide and long, my fingers straining to hold all of him. I watch our joined hands, the smooth move-ment, as he twists our hands around his shaft.

He lets go, leaving my hand in control of his pleasure, as his eyes close and his head returns to the pillow. The only sounds in the room are our heavy breathing, along with his low murmurs of pleasure.

"Yeah, that's so good."

"Just like that, Ky."

"Mm. Right there."

None of this is rushed. He seems to relish in the teasing rhythm of my slow hand job. Determining to move things along just a tad more, I lean my head down and lick the tip of his head. The pearl of liquid sits against my tongue as I swallow it down, reminiscent of the first time we were together. The penetrating growl precedes the sudden change of position, as he flips me over onto my back. My gasp is drowned out by his mouth, which opens in a hot kiss to my lips.

His hands begin working at my jeans, unzipping and yanking them down my thighs until they get stuck at my knees. We both laugh as he fights with the material, my legs trying to shimmy and kick them off. Finally relieved of the offending constriction, my body lays open and exposed to him, as his eyes and hands peruse over me.

I've never been ashamed of my body. I'm not stick thin like

some girls, or as curvy as others. My legs are fairly long, my butt nice and round, my belly not as flat as I'd like, and my boobs a happy B cup. I close my eyes, enjoying the sensation that his calloused fingers provide as they flutter over the tips of my nipples, caressing the underside of my breast, down my middle. He circles my belly button and continues lower. As soon as he hits my center, my hips begin to move on their own accord and he chuckles, but I don't open my eyes.

I inhale as if I've been submerged in water and have just come up for air as his finger slips in between my lips, working through the wet recesses between my legs. He teases and tickles, dipping a finger inside and bringing it back out to sweep across my clit. I moan loudly – squirming under his ministrations. Wanting the torture to end, but hoping it continues. He knows exactly what he's doing to me and I love that.

My eyes are still closed when I feel him shift and the warm breath he releases at my apex has my head rising to look down at him. It's the most erotic sight I've ever seen in my life. His hair fans out around the tops of my legs, his lips are shiny and he wears the most salacious, sexy grin.

"Open up for me." He commands, pushing my legs wide as he plants his face at my center.

I squeal as the first onslaught of his tongue licking its way through my sex. He hums against me and it reminds me of that first naughty conversation we had over the phone where he admitted to the fact that he loved to eat pussy. And now, here he is, eating me out. Going down on me. Giving me lady-head.

Holy shit. It's so good.

And then he adds a finger and I'm done for.

With his index finger pushed deep inside me, he swirls his tongue lightly against my clit, and I absolutely lose it. My hands reach for his head, unbidden, and I literally push his face down harder, grabbing chunks of his hair and yanking tight. His lips clamp onto me in silent delight, as I arch my back and come all over his face.

My body continues to convulse with the aftershocks of my release. My head feels woozy, like I'm drunk, even though I've never been more sober in my life. I'm lit up like my mom's Christmas tree, the electricity charging through my veins. I consider what just happened. Van ate me out and it was the best mother-effing thing in my life. He's really good at that.

Just like that, jealousy courses through me, sending an even stronger vibration through my blood. If he's good at that, it's because he's probably done it a million times before with his ex. I know I shouldn't think about that, or picture them together, because that's creepy and not important. He's here with me now – not her. And according to Van, he's completely over her. There's no going back.

Van's head re-emerges from down below and his face shows an expression of bewilderment.

"Ky, are you okay? You're crying."

I am? I lift my hand to my eyes and sure enough, I blink back the tears that cling to my lashes. What the heck is that about?

"I...uh...I don't know why I'm crying. That was just intense."

He sighs, dabbing away a teardrop with his finger with a soft smile.

"It *was* intense. You taste fucking amazing." He wipes his hand over his mouth, briefly hiding a gigantic smile.

Oh my God. I can't believe he just said that to me. Before I have a chance to consider why that's an embarrassing statement, Van presses his lips against my mouth and I can taste myself all over his tongue. Whoa. That's the hottest thing ever.

No...not quite, but almost. Van hovers over me, slipping a condom on his steely cock, and that is surely the hottest thing ever. I watch him with unfettered lust as he checks the fit, pinching the top to make sure there's room. And then he plants both hands on the bed right next to my head, as I feel the tip of his latex-covered cock nudge at my entrance.

I swallow thickly, my eyes closing tight, waiting for the pain.

Oh Lordy...this is really going to happen.

"Ky, open your eyes and look at me." His voice is gentle, yet commanding and I do as he asks.

My fears subside as my eyes lock with his. He bends to kiss me again, our mouths fusing together, working to get closer. His tongue submerges, slowly sweeping and circling mine, making a promise to me about how good this is. How good it will be.

"Are you ready?"

I've been ready for you all my life, Van.

I nod my head, and realize that the truth I need him to know still sits unspoken on my tongue.

"Van, wait...there's something...."

The rest of my confession remains unsaid as he pushes inside of me.

With one swift, hard thrust, my virginity is gone.

an

TIGHT.

She's so fucking tight. And wet. Holy shit, I might lose a nut right this second.

I suck in a deep breath, as I slide back out of her to the tip, getting ready to plunge right back in. Instead, I take a moment to look down at my cock first, which is sopping wet. The image, along with the incredible feeling of being buried deep inside Kylah, has my balls drawing up tight, ready to blow.

I need to slow my roll, otherwise this will be one quick fuck, which under normal circumstances might be fine, but this is my first time with Kylah. It feels like something I need to savor and appreciate.

My eyes linger at the erotic image of our joined bodies before trailing up her stomach to her chest. I land on her breasts, which heave in and out, pushing air out of her lungs in quick succession. I suck a nipple into my mouth, slicking my tongue over her tit before releasing it from my suction. I glance up to find her mouth closed in a tight line, an expression of pain etched across her face.

Then her words sink in. Just as I was sinking into her, she started to tell me something. She said, "wait." Oh fuck...I was so wrapped up in the moment, so eager to penetrate into her warmth, that her words didn't even register in my brain. Until now.

It takes everything in my power to refrain from pushing back inside. Instead, the tip of my cock remains poised at her entrance.

"Kylah," I murmur, coaxing her attention back to my face. Her eyes snap to mine, her lips parting in an "O". "What did you just say?"

She shakes her head, too quickly, her eyes looking away like she's guilty of something.

"Am I hurting you?"

That's the last thing I'd ever want to do. I have to admit, I was so undone as I slammed home, and the bit of resistance that I was met with...oh God. Oh shit.

Oh no. Did I? Jesus, Mary and Joseph...did I just deflower her?

I hold myself still, even though my cock twitches for more action. I'm trying to recall if she ever told me about her first time. I'm guessing the reason she never brought it up was because she'd never had one. Until now.

Just to test the waters, I slide back in an inch and she sucks in a deep breath.

I stop my movement. My voice croaks. "Ky? Were you a virgin?"

She nods her head in confirmation.

"Fuck."

Oh holy shit. How did I not know this? Goddammit, I'm an

oblivious idiot. Somehow on a deep, subconscious level, I knew. I just didn't want to admit it. Being someone's first has so many ramifications. Consequences I don't think I'm capable of handling right now. That's not to say I wouldn't have gone through with it with her – because I really wanted her - but I would have made a much better effort at getting her comfortable. I would have gone more slowly. We would have talked it over – we would have talked things through.

Instead, I just plowed right on through her hymen.

"Shit, Ky. I'm so sorry."

I'm about to pull out, eject myself from the game and go take a seat on the bench – to use a basketball metaphor – when she clamps onto my ass cheeks and pulls me forward.

"Oh my God, Van. Don't you dare. I'm sorry for not telling you, but please don't stop. I've wanted this with you for so long. *Please...*"

What should I do?

My dick is telling me to get back into the game, and my brain is on the fence. But what she does next breaks my resolve and solidifies my strategy. Kylah tilts her hips so her wet pussy connects with my cock, reminding me how fucking good she feels wrapped around me. How wet and tight she is for me. That her virgin-pussy has only had me inside it.

I stare at her, all the questions written all over my face, as she smiles tentatively and pulls me down with her hand on my neck so her lips can touch mine. We're fused together, her mouth opening for me in a way her body just did – giving me all of her. I kiss her back, telling her without words how much this means to me. That she trusts me enough to give me this gift means more to me than anything.

I nip at her lips, licking the moisture there. I can still taste her essence on our lips and it's fucking incredible. "We're gonna talk about this later," I warn, as I thrust back inside her. "But right now, I need to fuck you."

It has been over three months since I've had sex, unless you count with my own hand – so Ky's tight virgin pussy, and the burning ache and need to release, has me losing myself again in seconds. Her sweet little moans don't hurt, either. If the building was in flames or the sky was falling right now, I don't think I'd have the wherewithal to leave the nirvana that I've found in Kylah's slick heat.

It's maddening how good it feels and every time I push back inside, she lets out a sexy little gasp. Her hands have found their way down my back, stroking my skin to my ass and back up again.

"Wrap your legs around me."

She does as I ask and I immediately find myself deeper, the position hugging me to the hilt. We both moan in unison. My arms begin to shake as I hold myself above her and the low prickly tingles at the base of my spine indicate that I'm about to erupt and shoot off like a geyser.

I rise above her, slamming into her with punishing thrusts, our skin slapping together, causing her breasts to jiggle in time with the movements. I pray that I'm not hurting her too much, but I couldn't stop now even if I tried. My body tightens and I come with a hoarse cry and a grunt of release.

My weight collapses on top of her, my face planted between her ear and her shoulder. The fruity scent of her shampoo or perfume, whatever it is, envelopes me in the most serene state of existence. Everything around me fades as I practically pass out on top of her.

It could be seconds, minutes or days – I don't know – but she finally lets out a little laugh, shoving at my chest.

"Van, uh...are you alive?"

I literally have to make myself pull out of her with a disgruntled groan, sliding out of her comfort and warmth, gripping the condom as I do. Now on my side, I have an opportunity to look her over, starting at her face.

What I see in her eyes tells me that she feels exactly as I do. Content.

I can't help but smile, giving her a wink at the cute grin across her face. She's adorably mussed up, her hair in tangles, fanning across my pillow.

"I hope you feel as good as you look." I take a piece of her hair that curtains her face and tuck it behind her ear. "Because you look beautiful."

Kylah's cheeks turn pink, as she raises her arm to drape across her eyes, tilting her head away from me. It gives me the opportunity to lean over her and kiss her breast which just happens to be exposed to me at the moment. I suck happily on her nipple for a few seconds, lightly running my fingers underneath the underside of her breast.

She moans softly, dropping her arm behind my shoulders, rubbing gently. "Thank you for...well, taking care of me. That was perfect."

My heart swells at her praise, because honestly, it's an ego-booster. There is nothing better for the male ego to hear that he made the woman he's with feel good, especially for her first time.

"Hold that thought," I instruct, popping her gently on the nose with my index finger, before turning over and off the bed. "I need to take care of this."

It's times like these that I love having my own bathroom. Heading in, I close the door behind me and take care of business. Standing over the sink as I wash my hands, I look into the mirror at my reflection. My own hair is tangled and messy, signs of a thorough fucking. My lips are puffy and shiny, from all the kissing and sucking I just did.

God, that was so hot being between Kylah's legs. It had been a while since I'd done that. I think the last time was sometime in the summer with Lyndsay. Now I know why she pushed me away every time I tried to go down on her this fall before our break-up. She didn't want the intimacy that it brings.

I shake my thoughts free of my ex. Fuck her. Grabbing a washcloth from the stack underneath my sink, I get it damp under the faucet and wring it out. Heading back into my room, I find Kylah sitting up in my bed, my sheet pulled up to her chin. She looks uncertain. Nervous.

She blinks, guilt darkening her irises. "I'm sorry, Van." She glances down at the spot on the bed where it's stained a dark red. "I didn't think..."

Shit. She's worried about ruining my stupid bed sheet? I probably got it at Target for less than fifteen-dollars. Screw the sheet. In fact, would it be weird to frame it?

I lean down on the edge of my bed, handing her the wet cloth, which she takes wearily.

"Kylah...that means nothing to me. Big deal. It'll come out. Are you okay? Did I hurt you?"

My hand is drawn to her hair, where I slip my fingers through the soft, silky strands. She sighs, flashing me a shy grin.

"I'm fine. Seriously. That was better than I ever imagined it would be."

"Why don't you go clean up and I'll get us something to drink, okay?"

Kylah nods in agreement and gingerly moves off the bed. I watch her walk toward the bathroom door, admiring her perfect little ass that I just had my hands on. My flaccid cock decides that he likes my hands on her ass, too, and starts to perk up again. I have to find something to keep my mind off that, 'cause I know we aren't going to be getting it on again tonight. I'm sure she'll be sore for a few days.

Grabbing two Cokes out of my dorm fridge, I open them with the bottle opener attached to my door and place them on the nightstand. I look around the room in search of my underwear. Locating them on the floor with my jeans, I yank them on and look back at the bed. My sheets are crumpled and I notice the stain again. It's small, barely visible, but it holds an enormous weight in its size.

The question on the forefront of my mind is why didn't she tell me she was a virgin before we got that far? Was she worried I would treat her differently? Maybe I would have, I don't know for sure. Obviously, I've only been with one other girl in my life, and we both lost our virginity together – fumbling, inexperienced sex.

I hoped that Kylah at least experienced something more than what Lyndsay did her first time with me. The difference between a seventeen-year old me and the twenty-two-year old me should account for something.

The light in the bathroom flicks off as Kylah walks out to find me sitting on the couch. She'd grabbed her panties and the T-shirt I'd given her and she's wearing them now. She looks well-fucked and incredibly sexy. I pat the cushion next to me and she joins me, scooting over so our hips and legs touch, my arm wraps around the top of her shoulders.

I can't keep my hands or lips off her, as I place soft kisses on her neck, my fingers lightly strumming over her shoulder and arm. She tastes and smells so good. Like sex and sugar.

"Why didn't you tell me, Kylah?" I ask, pecking kisses along her neck, nuzzling behind her ear with my nose.

She turns her head toward me, breaking our connection. "I should have, Van. I'm sorry for making it so awkward. I just felt... stupid, I guess. I didn't want to turn you off with my inexperience."

Kylah draws her legs up in front her, folding them up like an accordion and wraps her arms around her knees, chin on top. My hands can't help their automatic need to touch the smooth, satiny skin of her legs, as I reach over and glide them over her shins. The feel is exquisite and I go to a semi-hard state again.

Down boy. Ain't gonna happen again tonight.

I slide my arm underneath her knees and scoop her up, placing her on my lap. She gives me a small snort of laughter, but burrows into my chest. She's warm and soft, melding into my body. I touch the top of her head in small kiss.

"While I wish you would've been honest with me, I can understand your hesitation. And for the record, it wouldn't have detracted from anything that I feel for you, Ky. Not one bit. I'm incredibly grateful that you thought highly enough of me to let me have this part of you. It was an experience I'll never forget."

She shifts on my lap, her ass moving across my groin, awakening my cock once again. I try my best to forget that she's sitting on my dick, only in her panties and a T-shirt, and concentrate on her beautiful eyes that stare up at me through her dark lashes.

"You made it everything I ever wanted it to be. You are amazing."

We cuddle for a few minutes, take a few sips of our Cokes, and discuss the upcoming New Years' Eve party at her house. I don't know how she wants to handle things with her brother, but I'm willing to take the fall and talk to him about us if she wants me to.

"About the party this weekend," I begin to say, just as she interrupts with her own train of thought.

"We can't tell Cade about us."

I lift her chin so she's looking directly into my eyes. "Why don't you want him to know?"

Her shoulders sag, as if it's a lost cause. "He won't understand. He'll tell me it's just a rebound fling with you and he won't like it."

I capture her face between my palms. "I'm going to say this as many times as you need to hear it, Ky. You are not a rebound for me. I've been into you since the first time we met and my feelings have only grown stronger. And I don't give a flying fuck about Cade's opinion. He's my friend and your brother, but it doesn't matter what he thinks. It's what you think that matters. How do you feel about me?"

A resigned sigh leaves her mouth but a smile replaces it. "Isn't it obvious? I like you, a lot."

"Good, because I feel the same about you. We're attracted to each other. We have a solid friendship to back it up. I want you – you want me...I don't see the problem. Let's just keep going and see where this leads."

There is a part of me that is worried what will happen when Cade finds out, but I'll cross the bridge when I come to it. As for the rest, everything will work itself out. I still have another week with Kylah before she has to head back to California. It's only four hours away, and while I absolutely hate the fact that I'm getting right back into a long-distance thing, I don't want it to be the end of us. My attraction to her is too strong to let her go just because there's a few hundred miles between us.

She snuggles comfortably on my lap, as I flip on the TV across from us. Letting all the other worries go for now, I concentrate on the silky glide of her hair as I run my fingers through her strands.

A bubble of contentment exists around us right now. I know it won't always be like this, because I've learned that people change and make choices that hurt others.

But for now, this thing with Kylah is perfection.

19

K ylah

OUR NEW YEARS' Eve party tradition began over twelve years ago. My parents would host these lavish parties for their friends. As we grew older, the dynamics changed and more and more of Cade's friends showed up, leaving the grown-ups to a small portion of the house and all the young adults to the basement and party room.

Now that my parents are divorced, and we're all in college, this year's party will solely consist of our group of friends. My mom and John, her new fiancé – which I've slowly become accustomed to and let go of my anger - went on a mini-tropical cruise to the Bahamas, leaving us to the party planning.

Well, technically, party plans have fallen on my shoulders. Cade basically told me how many people he invited and expected, offering to pick up the keg and booze. Kady went to the party store to pick up decorations and all the necessary party supplies to ring in the new year in style. As for me, I was left with all the grocery shopping, planning out the hor d'oeuvres and making all the Jell-O shots that all good parties should include.

I am measuring out the vodka and rum as Kady strides into the kitchen, taking a peek at the various kinds of Jell-O I purchased.

"Ew...you're making the green kind? That stuff is nasty. The flavor tastes like snot."

I want to ask her how in the hell she'd know what snot tastes like, but I don't get a chance, because in her next breath she catches me off guard.

"Someone's glowing like she got her cherry popped." She exclaims, ruffling my hair as she walks toward the refrigerator to grab a soda. "How was it? Did he make you orgasm? Did you do it doggie-style?"

I snicker, slapping at her from behind me. "Shut up. Don't be crass."

Kady maneuvers herself up on the barstool across from the island where I stand, mixing the concoctions before I pour them into the little plastic cups to freeze. She leans down on her elbows, batting her eyelashes at me.

"Me? Crass. Ha! If I were trying to be crass, I'd ask if he fucked your asshole after wetting his dick in your pussy."

"Oh my God, Kady, you have the mouth of a sailor. You're worse than Cade sometimes, you know that?"

She throws her head back in hysterical laughter and I just bow my head in disgust. How in the world can the two of us have shared the same womb? I love her to death, but sometimes she is a lot to handle.

"Sorry," she ruefully apologizes. "I promise to be good from now on, as long as you give me all the dirty deets." She locks up her mouth with a pretend key and gives me an eyebrow raising smile.

"No way. Not gonna happen."

She mumbles a *"please"*, but it sounds more like a meow. Kady jumps from her chair and corners me at the sink, wrapping her arms around me and shaking me in a giant hug. I laugh, because it reminds me of the scene from *Despicable Me* where the little girl shakes the carnival toy with such adoration. I wiggle from her hold, and concede to her request.

"Fine. It was great." Sticking my tongue out at her, I place a tray of the shots in the freezer drawer, shutting it closed.

"Uh-huh. More...I know there's more."

Kady is not going to let this go, that much I know that. But there are things I don't feel like sharing with her right now. Maybe because it feels good to have it just between Van and me. Our little secret.

Which is how I want to keep things for the time being from everyone, must importantly my brother. Telling Cade that I'm sleeping with one of his teammates will not start my New Year off on the right foot. Despite what Van said about not putting stock in what others think, I don't want to be scrutinized by others. I am not an attention-seeking girl, and it would be like living under a microscope if others find out.

So at least through the party tonight, Van promised me he would keep his distance and there would be no PDA. Which will probably kill me. But he did warn me that at the stroke of midnight, he was going to drag me into a closet somewhere and kiss the hell out of me.

That promise, and the implications of it, has me bubbling from the inside out with anticipation – like I'm the champagne in the bottle and the cork is about to pop. It makes me yearn for his strong hands clasping onto my hips, pulling me into him as he kisses the ever-loving life out of me.

"Woohoo!" My sister snaps her fingers in my face to gain my attention back. "It's written all over your face, so you might as well spill the beans. Or the pork-and-beans..." She laughs at her own attempt at a scandalous joke.

I clean up the kitchen counter as she trails closely behind me. Finally, I spin around to meet her, nose to nose, toe-to-toe. "You know, if you're going to follow me around like a little stalker, you could at least help me clean up or something."

"I'll be glad to be your taste tester for the Jell-O shots. I'm very good at that."

"I'm sure you are."

"Speaking of good...come on! Tell me about it, Ky. You know you're dying to." She gives me an angelic smile and I finally capitulate, sitting down on the stool she vacated.

Sighing wistfully, I begin. "Van was amazing. Even when he found out I was a virgin – after he deflowered me-"

"You're shitting me! You didn't tell him beforehand? Holy mother of Judas."

"Shoosh," I chastise her interruption, putting my finger in front of my lips. If she wants to hear this, she's going to have to keep her trap shut for more than two seconds.

"No, I didn't get around to telling him before he, uh...slid home." A whoop and a gasp come out of her mouth. "But oh my God, Kady. He was so sweet and tender. I couldn't have asked for anything more."

I'm sure my face has an annoyingly dreamy expression all over it right now, but Kady doesn't care. She's smiling along with me. That's what sisters do. They celebrate the wins with you and commiserate the losses.

"Oh my God, Ky. Did he make you come?"

My cheeks flame red, even though it's only Kady I'm spilling my secrets to, it's still a little embarrassing.

"He, uh...used his tongue and fingers. It was...I can't even describe how good it was."

Kady props her chin on her fist, elbow on the counter as she leans over at me, a look of approval sweeping across her beautiful face. "Very nice. I'm so happy for you. Are you glad you waited?"

I snort with self-deprecation because it's not like I ever really had a choice in the matter. Unlike Kady, who had boys chasing her around as a teen. But yeah, I'm really glad I waited to have sex until I found someone I really cared for. And it doesn't hurt that Van's older and has a ton more experience than me, so he knows what he's doing.

Nodding my head, I say, "I am glad. It was so worth it. But it also makes me a little jealous."

Kady's forehead wrinkles in confusion. "Jealous of what?"

I scratch my fingernail over an invisible spot on the granite counter, trying to distract myself from the way I feel.

"As they say, practice makes perfect, right? Well, it's obvious he perfected his game because of all that practice with someone else. And it just makes me..."

"No, stop right there." She admonishes, slapping her hand on the counter next to me. "No self-talk or self-doubts. It doesn't matter if he practiced every day on one girl or thousands before you. What matters is that he's with you now. He cares about *you*. He went down on *you*. He fucked *you*. Not anyone else. So get off the jealousy train, Ky. It's not worth the ride."

Tipping my head, I take in the identical face of my sister staring back at me. It's funny that when I look at her, I see a beautiful girl, even when I don't see myself in that way. I always feel relatively plain next to her gigantic persona. She's fiercely loyal. Protective. Supportive. I'm so lucky I have someone like her to share this with. Otherwise, without her uplifting encouragement, I'd probably be wallowing in self-pity and deconstructing all the reasons Van shouldn't be with me.

"And..." she continues. "Not a lot of guys would be that unselfish to spend time getting a girl off before the main event.

The fact that he did tells me he's a decent man and cares about you."

"Yeah, he's a really good guy. I like him a lot."

Kady once again comes around the counter top and envelopes me in a hug. "I'm so happy for you, sis. You deserve this. Now...let's go upstairs and decide what we're going to wear tonight. Preferably something low-cut and easy to get off in the heat of the moment."

She wiggles her eyebrows and grabs my hand, as I swat her arm away, but let her lead the way anyway. Truthfully, I want to look sexy and hot tonight for Van. I may even let her convince me to wear heels.

PEOPLE START SHOWING up around ten p.m., milling around in our spacious formal living, dining and family rooms. We've blocked off the stairway so that no one can go upstairs, but all the entertainment is through the door to the basement. We were kind of spoiled as kids growing up, and have a plethora of fun games and tables downstairs, including a pool table, air hockey, ping pong (which is set up for beer pong tonight, per Cade's direction), and even a shuffleboard table along the back wall. I was never one to play those games, only for the reason that I'm terribly uncoordinated.

Ainsley and her friend, Mica, have arrived and are in the family room talking to a few of the dates belonging to some of the players. Lance, Cade, Carver and a few other teammates I only know peripherally, have all gone downstairs where the keg is set up out on the patio of our walk-out. I can hear them all shouting and yelling at one another good-naturedly over some tournament game they played recently.

As I set out the appetizers and various plates of cheese and crackers, I feel a warm pair of hands wrap around my hips, pulling me back into a solid wall of muscle. My startled yelp is loud, but no one except us can hear it over the noise of the music. The next thing I know, Van's mouth is at my ear, his voice low and filled with desire.

"You're lucky there's people around, otherwise I'd have you stretched out across this countertop, eating you as my appetizer."

Wow. Van's a dirty-talker. Never thought that would turn me on, but I can already feel its effects working their way through my body. My neck and face heat up, and I'm sure I'm a flowing beacon. I glance around surreptitiously to see if anyone is looking. My body flushes at his dirty words, my insides going molten at the sound of his low, sexy voice.

I'm thankful everyone is preoccupied and we're the only ones in the kitchen. No one else can see where his hands are from behind the privacy shield of the counter, but even still, I'm very aware of how close he is in proximity to my body. If anyone did wander in or turn to look our way, they'd definitely know what is going on.

I attempt to wiggle out of his hands, shimmying my hips, but he simply holds his ground, adding more pressure with his fingertips.

"Van." I lamely protest, even though one could argue it sounds more like a plea. "Stop, someone could see us."

He bends over me, pushing me forward, his heavy erection fitted nicely between the crack of my cheeks, as he emits a low growl. "I know I promised, Ky. I'll be good. But it's been two days since I've seen you, and you look amazing in this dress. It's going to be so *hard*," - he accentuates by pressing further into my backside – "to keep my hands off you."

An involuntary moan escapes me unbidden, and I let my

eyes fall closed as if he's put me into a hypnotic trance. Good heavens, this man.

To make matters worse, his hand now skims the bottom of the skirt of my dress, sliding his hand up the back of my bare leg. Kady pressured me into wearing this outfit. I was planning on wearing jeans and a nice shirt, but she insisted that this would drive Van wild tonight. I should be thanking her right now because it definitely seems to have done the trick. Already. Now all I can think about is how and when I can get Van alone.

Cade's voice interrupts us as he rounds the corner of the kitchen. We both gasp, as I feel the immediate absence of his hand and his body when he jumps back about five feet, making the distance between us appear more appropriate.

Thankfully, Cade seems somewhat oblivious, as he swings his head over his shoulder to ask Ainsley a question.

"Babe, what can I get you and Mica? Whatcha drinking tonight?"

He takes a step into the kitchen, turns his head to both of us, and welcomes Van with a huge-ass smile that only Cade can give.

"Bro, you made it!" He slaps one hand on Van's bicep and the other he uses to do some complicated bro-handshake. Silly boys.

"Yo, Cade. What's up? Thanks for the invite."

Cade leans down into the fridge and rummages through the many bottles lining the shelves. "No problem, man. Good to have you here. I wasn't sure if you'd be able to make it tonight or if you'd be back home in Tucson with your family."

He grabs two Mike's Hard Lemonades from the fridge and closes it behind him, turning his attention back to us. I've begun nervously rearranging the cheese platters, hoping to remain inconspicuous and avoid Cade's scrutiny. My breathing is still erratic, sounding choppy and practically asthmatic. I'm not sure

I could even form a sentence right now from the adrenaline rushing through my veins over the fear of getting caught.

"Van, will you tell my little sis not to stress out about the food and just come have a good time with us?" He bumps my butt with his hip as he passes by. "Kylah needs to loosen up a bit and learn to have some fun. Hey, speaking of fun, did you invite that guy you like?"

Van sounds like he's just choked on the beer he'd just taken a sip of and I have to white knuckle the edge of the counter to keep myself from collapsing to the floor.

If only my brother knew that he was the one who invited that "guy I like". And lookie, lookie! Said guy is standing right here, waiting for you to leave so he can maul me with wet, hot kisses.

My hands shake as I wipe them with a dishtowel, trying to dry the perspiration that's gathered on my palms. I keep my eyes plastered to the counter so I don't have to look my brother in the eyes.

"Oh, uh no. He had something else going on tonight. Maybe some other time."

Cade seems to accept that answer but then adds. "Well good. Van here can keep you company tonight. Maybe he can be your partner in a game of shuffleboard or something."

He then laughs, waving the hand that's holding a bottle at me. "Never mind that. She sucks at it. But if you partner up with her in a game of Trivia Pursuit, you're bound to emerge the champions."

Oh, brother. Literally. As if this isn't embarrassing enough, he has to make wise cracks at my expense. Cade gives us both a casual wink as he heads out toward his girlfriend, drinks in hand. Just as he hits the carpeted room, he glances over his shoulder and says to Van, "Keep a watch on her, though, bro. Don't let her have too many of those Jell-O shots she made. She's not much of a drinker and doesn't realize that they go down easy, but come back the hard way."

Van tips his head as my brother rejoins his girlfriend, as we simultaneously release a sigh of relief.

I wipe away the remaining sweat and tip my head up to Van. "Okey dokey, then. That was a close call."

Van chuckles, stepping into me once more, presumably to set down his beer on the counter in front of me. Anyone else looking from the other side would see that he appears to be browsing the selection of meats and cheeses over my shoulder, but I know the truth. His hand is once again making a beeline to the hem of my dress, inching it up so he can touch my bare skin on my leg. I shiver in response.

"Cade or not, I don't think I can make it to midnight to get my mouth on you tonight, Ky. Can we go somewhere? I need to kiss you so bad right now. I don't think I can wait."

I maneuver my body around so my lower back hits the edge of the counter. We're so close I can feel the hairs on his legs brush softly against mine. My body lights up at the contact.

"Third door on the left at the top of the stairs. Give me five minutes."

I feel like a sexy Nancy Drew with my covert Ops suggestion. The excitement rips through me in waves.

It appears that I'm going to be ringing in the New Year with a whole different kind of fireworks.

20

Van

I AM SO FREAKING TURNED on right now. Maybe there is some-thing to be said about a secret, illicit rendezvous. It makes me horny as fuck.

Or it could just be Kylah.

I'm doing my best to hide the very large bulge in my pants as I meander through the living room, trying to inconspicuously work my way toward the staircase the leads upstairs. I'm stopped no less than three times by either people coming through the front door, waving their hellos and greetings, checking in on how I'm doing, congratulating me on the games we've played this pre-season so far, etc. It takes me damn near fifteen minutes to even get up to the second floor landing.

Once I do, I count the doors as I pass, coming to the third door. Turning the handle, I step into the darkened room. Kylah's room.

I'm immediately hit with her tropical fruit scent, leaving my mouth watering and my semi-hard dick perking up once again.

I find the light switch on the wall and flip it on, scanning the room that's now visible. There's a wall with a white-painted bookcase, filled to the brim with books, books, and more books. I smile at the knowledge that my girl likes to read.

My girl.

Whoa. That happened fast. Yet, in a way, not really. It feels more like it simmered to a boil at a low temperature, progressively increasing in heat and intensity as time went on; until it finally blew the top off the lid.

I nose around a little bit, perusing the pictures and posters hung on the walls – mostly artwork in various forms. There's a portrait of their family, possibly taken several years back, as it includes her dad, and the girls look much younger. So does Cade, with his cocky, toothy grin and a much shaggier, Justin Bieber-esque hair style. I laugh out loud and remind myself I'm going to have to give him some hell over that.

Something large catches my eye in the corner of the room, near her closet. It's an instrument, in a zipped case. By all appearances, it looks to be a cello. Interesting. Kylah is a musician. I had no idea. I envision her performing on stage, her delicate fingers playing the notes, as she glides the bow across the strings, the cello vibrating between her legs.

Ah shit. Now I'm thinking about what's between her legs. And wonder if she's wet. Whether she'll vibrate with need as I slide inside her pussy.

Now I'm the one vibrating with need as I suck in a ragged breath, trying to ease the tension from my body. I'm restless and growing more and more impatient with every passing minute. The thrill of knowing we'll be together soon, hopefully, naked on her bed, has me amped up and anxious for her arrival.

I'm looking down at my phone when I hear the click of the

latch, and I turn to face the door. She stands with her back to it, as her hand quickly locks it behind her. I stalk over to her, taking three large steps until I tower over her. Boxing her in. I see a glimpse of excitement gleam in her eyes, as I place my hands on both sides of her head. Keeping her where I want her.

"What took you so long?" I nuzzle at her neck, my lips sucking in at the tender skin. I love the way she tenses, letting go of a full-body shudder.

"I got stuck talking to Ainsley and Mica. I had to make an excuse to come up here."

"Mmm." Is all I can say, as I begin placing open-mouth kisses down her neck, to her collarbone and across to the other side, sampling the flesh over there, too.

My teeth bite down, suck the skin, suctioning hard right at the base of her neck. Kylah jerks her head back, her hands lightly pressing at my chest. She tastes so good and it's driving me wild. Fumbling for her hands, I capture her wrists and swing them over her head, locking her into me.

"I'm so hard for you, Ky." I bring one of her hands down to my crotch, grinding her palm against the thickness hidden in my pants. My breath lodges in my throat at the exquisite feel of her touch.

I capture her lips with mine, my tongue slipping through her lips and probing the warmth and wetness there. I've never fucked a girl up against a door before, but I'm more than willing to in this moment if she is. Kylah has other plans, though, as she wiggles her hand free from my grasp, still being held hostage above her head.

Tearing my mouth away from hers, I marvel as both her trembling hands undo my button and pull at my zipper, yanking the tabs away so the outline of my dick is prominently displayed. It pulses in anticipation, as she runs her fingers down the length, tracing a sensual path as she burrows in. My body is swamped with desire, and I press my pelvis forward into her small hand.

I swallow hard as I watch her hand move over the protruding appendage, my body shifting and punching into her grip. I pull at her lips, giving her another drugging kiss. She tilts her head, allowing me to ravage her as I mouth fuck her into a frenzy. I've barely had one beer tonight and yet the effects Kylah has on me makes me feel stumbling drunk. I'd lose my balance and fall if I tried to move right now.

My virility is off the charts and I'm a stallion ready to unleash its beastly instincts, rocking against her hand. Just then, Kylah drops to her knees in front of me, taking my pants and boxers with her as she slides them down on legs. I kick them off and barely notice as they go flying across the floor.

Before she does the unimaginable, she drops her head back and stares up at me with these wide, beautiful eyes. Without uttering a word, her gaze tells me everything. She wants me. She's with me. She's all mine.

Then she blinks a few times before closing her eyes, leaning into my stick straight cock to swipe it with her tongue from base to tip. My chest rumbles a fiercely masculine sound. In order to keep myself upright, I have to lean forward and place my hands against the door.

Her tongue roams around my rigid shaft, testing and touching it with light, whisper-soft strokes. God, I could come just like this. With barely a touch.

I'm thinking I should find a way to direct us over to her bed when she wraps one hand around my cock, the other placed securely on my ass cheek which clenches under her touch. It's then that the world stops spinning for a moment and the earth stands still. Kylah sucks me in deep.

She whimpers against me, the sound so X-rated that I'm about two seconds away from losing it in her mouth.

Do I want that? Oh, hell yes. The idea of shattering open and pulsing down her throat is what my fantasies are made of. Then again, I also want to unleash myself while I'm in her tight sheath, between her thighs.

I take a calming breath and do the unthinkable. Dropping my hands to her head, I slowly dislodge her from my dick. Holy shit...if her sucking me wasn't enough to have me shooting off like a rocket before, seeing her swollen, saliva drenched lips is truly the hottest thing I've ever seen.

"Am I doing something wrong?" She asks sweetly, with reservation, licking her lips that were just filled with me.

Groaning, I shake my head, helping her to a standing position.

"You were perfect, Ky. It was so good...but I want to fuck you. I want to come inside you."

She was just sucking me like a wanton woman, and yet she blushes like a virgin bride at my words. Such a contradiction, this girl of mine.

"Without a condom?" Her question is eager. Hopeful.

Fuck. Shit. Damn.

There's no way I could say no to that. I trust her. I know she's been with no one else before me. It's crazy, though. I never fucked without a condom, even with Lyndsay. We were always too scared something would happen and we'd be saddled with an unwanted pregnancy. How comically ironic can that be?

And now here I am, only my second time hooking up with Ky, and I'm already throwing caution to the wind.

Because fuck me, I want to feel her dripping wet pussy clenched around my dick.

I growl, flexing my arms and lifting her up in my arms to walk us over to the bed.

Setting her down on the edge, I quickly dispose of my shirt over my head, before staring into her soulful eyes.

"Are you sure, Ky? Is that what you want?"

Her eyes drop down to my dick, which is casting its vote as a definite *Hell Yes*, and then back up at me. She nods her head, a coy smile on her face.

"I want to feel you inside me."

Her fingernails flutter across my belly, tracing a teasing path through the patch of hair below my navel, sending squirrely sensations throughout my nerve endings. My dick twitches with excitement it can't contain, making the Kylah's innocence even more pronounced as her breath hitches at the unbidden move-ment. I see her nipples harden underneath her dress, prompting me to get this show on the road.

The dress is a V-neck jersey-like cotton material. I slip my hands under the material at the V and yank it down to expose her bra. She's wearing a skimpy lace, see-through black bra which makes me wonder if her panties match. Noticing the front latch, I unsnap it and her tits pop free. She's fucking perfect. Her pretty pink nipples are small and rosy, and right now they're engorged, so ready for me to suck then into my mouth. Which I do.

Bending over her chest, I pull one taut nipple into my mouth, delighting in the scent and the erotic little sounds of Kylah. She tastes so good and smells divine. I take one little nibble and she cries out.

"Ah...*ooooooh*." I take that as a good sign and continue on.

I get my hand into the game and begin fondling the other breast, flicking my thumb nail across the aroused flesh. I continue doing this for a bit, settling in between her legs, which are stretched out wide to accommodate my large frame. As I continue to suckle and sip at her flesh, her pelvis rocks against mine, seeking friction at her center.

I'm now fairly certain that if I were to move my hand down underneath her panties, I would find them drenched. So this is exactly what I do, but not before I pull off her dress over her head. Her lush, pale-skinned body lays naked before me, except for the panties covering her sex. My eyes drink her in, a greedy, animalistic need flooding through me to take her hard and fast so she knows how much I want her.

Tilting my hips to the side to make room, I allow my finger to glide across the slinky material. Sure enough, she's so wet she's seeping through the thin fabric. Touching her lightly at first, she stirs in response, moaning out a sexy breath. My own dick leaks when I peel back the edge of her panties and feel the moisture pooled between her legs. And then I sink my finger inside and all thoughts leave my head completely.

I'm perilously close to coming when she begins to gyrate her hips in time to the rhythmic finger-fucking I give her. One of the surprising aspects of Kylah is that once she gets into it, she loses all inhibitions. She just seems to let nature take over, letting go of any and all insecurities she might have had.

I'm pretty sure she's close to orgasm, as I use my fingers to spread her wetness across her swollen clit. Her breathing is ragged, as her chest heaves with exertion, each time her heavy breasts lift and fall with short puffs of air. I take a swipe of her tits with my tongue before tasting her mouth once again, kissing her hard. Reveling in her taste. She tastes like cherry Jell-O.

My thumb sweeps across her clit and then settles into a pattern of slow circles when I feel her body begin to stiffen. Her inner muscles tighten and flex, as she spasms around my finger finding her release, letting go with an intense cry.

"Ohhhh." It's the most beautiful monosyllable word I've ever heard spoken.

Her hands, which had been gripping the bed cover, are now relaxed, spread out in a windmill of sorts, her head lazily flopped to the side. I grin with satisfaction because there is no better feeling in this world than getting your girl off. Well, I guess it's a close second next to getting off *with* her.

As she remains still, I lift myself up allowing the space to slip down her panties, which are still on. When I look back up, Kylah is smiling at me, a sexy, wanton smile lighting her face.

"You ready for me?" I ask, knowing that without a doubt, she's wet and ready to take me in.

Kylah nods her head, her eyes half-lidded with lust as she spreads out her legs and arms out like a temptress in an open invitation to fuck her.

I don't need any more encouragement than that. I grab my dick, slide between her luscious thighs, and poise the tip at her wet entrance. I think about our first time together, Kylah's first time, and how I just slammed home, without taking my time. With slow and controlled movements, I push my cock inside her dewy folds just inch and then I stop.

The suction of her tight pussy engulfs me in flames from her radiating heat. Pulling the tip back out, she sucks in a breath of air, which this time doesn't seem to include any pain. Hopefully only pleasure.

I sink back in, this time to the hilt, undulating my hips, gyrating them so my pelvis hits her clit each time our bodies meet. I'm zero to sixty in less than two seconds, my balls drawing tight, ready to launch any minute.

"Fuck...you feel so good."

My strained voice is drowned out by the sounds of a jiggling door handle.

We both stop – neither of us breathing – our eyes locked in wide-open terror. We search one another in silent question. Fear of being found out. The thrill of being caught fucking.

"Ky? Are you in there?"

Shit. It's her sister.

I watch in fascination as Kylah's face contorts from worry to amusement, her eyebrows shooting up, a small grin appearing on her mouth. I can't help myself, I bend down and kiss the corner of her mouth, before capturing her lips in a hard kiss, at the same time slowly gliding in and out of her.

The knock on the door stops my progress once again. Now I'm growing impatient.

"Does she know?" I whisper. Kylah nods her head once.

"Go away, Kady. She's busy."

Kylah throws her hand over her mouth, hiding the wide grin and amused expression.

We can hear her sister on the other side of the door bark out a laugh.

"I'm sure she is, Van...but tell her that Cade is looking for her. And he'll be up here soon if you don't hurry it up." She pauses as I keep my eye on Kylah. There is nothing worse for a guy than being cock-blocked in the middle of blowing a nut. I did not want to suffer through blue balls all night, but if I had to stop, I would.

"I'll do my best to keep him distracted for a bit...might give you another fifteen minutes or so. But be quick about it..."

There's a few moments of silence and we hear Kady's retreating footsteps, as our collective sighs echo in the room. I could laugh at the circumstances, but when I feel Ky's grip tighten on my ass and the hip jerk she gives me, my attention resumes to her naked body underneath me.

My cock, which deflated slightly at the interruption, roars back to life with a vengeance and a desire to continue where it left off. I yield to Kylah, who pushes me over so she's straddling me. My palms grasp her hips, giving her some instruction, but otherwise, I let her have free reign.

"I heard this position is...um, good for the girl." A classic statistical comment from my scientific girl. She projects her pelvis forward, hitting a spot that seems to do the trick. "Oh my God, yeah...now I see why."

"You just needed empirical proof, huh?" I laugh.

Her breasts jiggle in front of my face as she bounces and sways on my dick, and I can't help but reach up and latch on with my hands and mouth. She looks so sexy on top of me, moving with the intention of getting us both off. I'm pretty close already, but I want her to come again, too.

I reach for her wrist and bring her fingers to her pussy, her eyes popping wide to look down where we're joined. She doesn't say a word, just lets me guide her fingers through her folds, stroking her clit with every pass through. She mewls every time we hit the right spot.

Kylah's movements become hurried, jerky; until she's twerking against me, her hand working at her clit in lightning speed.

"I'm getting...close." She purrs softly. And fuck yeah, so am I.

I grip her ass cheeks, pulling them apart hard, as she cries out. It thrills me to know that my fingers and thumbs will probably leave bruises. Her ass hits my thighs each time she comes down on my dick, and I begin to push my own hips upward in quick, successive thrusts.

And then I feel it. Her inner muscles tighten up as she spasms around me, choking my dick like a vice. Two more thrusts and I'm shooting my load inside her, filling her up as I grunt out my release.

Kylah allows her torso to fall down across my chest, both of us heaving in breaths of air, panting from the workout we just gave each other. I can feel the remnants of my release dripping out of her, and although it kills me to move, I know we have to get cleaned up so we can rejoin the party.

"Van, will you stay with me tonight?" She asks tremulously, pressing herself up with her hands on my chest. My dick, which is still inside her, twitches at the thought of sleeping with Kylah in her bed, waking to find her naked and warm, rolling her over so I can fuck her again.

I move her to the side, pulling out, instantly feeling the loss of her heat all the way to my toes. Propping myself up on my elbow to face her, I glide my fingers over her hip bone, reveling in the goosebumps I leave behind.

"What about Cade?" I ask because that's the only reason that would deter me from staying the night. With her mom gone, she and Kady have the house to themselves.

Kylah bites her lip and smiles coyly. "He said he was spending the night at Ainsley's. She has to be home for her sister."

"Okay." I agree, because why wouldn't I want to wake up in the same bed as Kylah? "That sounds like a great way to start off my New Year...with you."

21

K ylah

BEST. FLIPPING. NEW YEARS' Eve. Ever.

We didn't have much time to cuddle after Kady's warning to hurry up, we cleaned ourselves up and got dressed. The only problem that seemed to throw me for a loop was the big hickey Van left on my right boob.

I had no recollection of him marking me like that while we were making out, but when I turned on the bathroom light and saw my reflection in the mirror, I gasped in delight. I traced the small, circular bruise with the pad of my finger, relishing in the memory of Van's mouth, lips, and body all over mine.

That reverie quickly dissipated as I realized where the mark was located. It just so happened that my V-neck dress wouldn't hide it all from prying eyes. I didn't have a lot of make-up tricks to use but did my best to use the concealer I had to try to tone down the purplish mark. I figured the lights in the house are low enough and no one would notice anything to do with my chest, anyhow.

Van and I decided to head down separately, with him going the front stairway and me taking the back, which leads down to the kitchen. I think it took us about five minutes to finally separate from one another, as we kissed hungrily at my doorway, the din from the party downstairs filtering up through the hallway, barely noticeable over the sounds of our heavy breathing.

"Okay," I say, pulling away reluctantly, placing my hands on his chest to push him away. His hands wrap around my wrists, holding me to him. "We need to get back downstairs."

He drops his head to me, his hair falling over our faces, kissing the tip of my nose.

"I don't want to go." He whines. It's pretty cute. I pull one of my hands free and slip a section of his hair back behind his ear.

I've always been curious as to his hairstyle and why he has long hair. "Can I ask you a question?"

"Sure. If it's, 'do I want to fuck you again?' Then the answer is an unequivocal yes."

I giggle at his audacity and his sexual appetite. I know if I brought my hand down to his crotch, he'd be hard again. The thought thrills me and sends frissons through my body – specifically to my nether regions.

I give him a good-natured eye roll but am secretly elated that he wants me again so soon after we just had sex. I've had to pinch myself so many times over the last few days to make sure this thing is all real and not a dream fantasy of mine.

I'm having sex with Donovan Gerard! Holy moly.

"Later." I admonish lightheartedly, sweeping my hands up to his shoulders, behind his neck and bringing his head down to mine, where I kiss him on the mouth. Just one little kiss before we part ways. My question that I wanted to ask him about his hair is lost in a sea of kisses.

"It's almost midnight. Since I can't kiss you downstairs, that will have to do until later tonight."

He grumbles, but relents, releasing my hands as I move toward the end of the hallway. Just as I get to the top of the steps, I glance back to find him still staring at me, not having moved an inch.

Scrunching my nose, I ask, "What's the matter?"

Van heaves a heavy sigh, bowing his head and shaking it back and forth. "Nothing. You're just so fucking sexy. It's gonna be a long night."

My head is on Cloud Nine after that compliment. I've been told I'm pretty before by my family, but it never meant much. I didn't really feel beautiful. But hearing it from Van, it's just too much. It's hard to believe that he'd find me attractive.

As I bound down the stairs, I try to hide my all-too-big-smile that's plastered on my mouth so no one notices. Just as I round the corner at the landing, I run into Ainsley, who is on her way up. Probably to use the upstairs bathroom.

The look on her face tells me she heard what Van said to me just now. Oh dear.

She says nothing, but her grin and sapphire eyes twinkle with delight. She knows.

I shrug my shoulders innocently as we pass each other on the stairs and she brushes my hand with hers, stopping me in my tracks.

"Van's a good guy, Kylah. He'll treat you right."

My smile widens, my feelings validated by a girl I admire and respect. But that girl is the same one who dates my brother. And probably shares all her secrets with him.

She must realize what I'm thinking because she shakes her head. "Don't worry. I won't tell Cade. It's not any of his business. You guys will tell him when you're ready."

The relief washes over me, sluicing like water down a river.

"Thanks, Ainsley. I appreciate that."

"No problem. Now hurry up and get down there. We're just about to open the champagne and turn the countdown on!"

She rushes up the stairs, as I head in the opposite direction. When I finally make my way down to the basement where everyone is congregated, I'm greeted by Kady, who stands next to a tatted guy with piercings and a trucker hat covering most of his eyes. She wiggles her brows at me and hands me an empty champagne glass. She leans over to whisper.

"Nice hickey."

My hand slaps over my exposed chest and she just laughs. Brat.

I move through the crowd, the noise of laughter, music and shouts of those mingling around adding to my already amped up excitement. I'm sure I'm grinning like a fool and my cheeks and neck are still flushed from my earlier down-and-dirty with Van. It's a good thing I checked myself in the mirror when I was in the bathroom because my hair looked a fright. What had been nice and smooth, was sticking up in every direction. The miracles of a flatiron when you need it.

There's a number of people I've never met before all milling around, some I recognize, and some I only know peripherally. Kady invited some of her high school friends, with whom I'm acquainted, but they were never my clique of kids. Kady was the artist and hippie funkster, who actually wore dreads for a large portion of our junior year. The kids she hung around all looked like they were in need of a bath and smelled of patchouli oil – a scent I could definitely live without.

I wind up in corner of the room, my back to the exterior doorway that opens to the patio. The slider door is open and there's a few smokers out on the patio lighting up. I hold onto the empty champagne flute I was given (plastic, of course), and scan the room to find Van. My eyes latch on to Cade, Lance,

Carver and some girls who are playing beer pong, but no sign of my tall, dark and handsome man.

My gaze shifts left toward the large screen TV that hangs on the wall, the Times Square ball drop on replay, as it hovers with just about one minute to go. I'm about to give up on finding Van when I feel his hand gliding up the back of my leg, similar to what started our sexcapades earlier in the kitchen.

Van is close – close enough for me to catch the scent of him – as he leans down to my ear. His breath is warm and inviting. "In case I didn't say it earlier, you look beautiful tonight."

If one can die from a compliment, I think I just did and am now in heaven. The room does this shift and sway thing – or maybe it's just me on my unbalanced feet. My face flushes and I close my eyes, feeling him brush my hair away from the back of my neck.

Someone from across the room yells out, "Everyone quiet down! The countdown is starting!" The room instantly turns to a low buzz of hushed voices and murmurs of excitement. I can't contain the wide smile on my face, as I hold out my plastic flute for the girl that's coming around to fill them. Since Van is standing behind me, I can't see him, but I hear him tell her, "No thanks."

Turning my head and shoulders, I notice he has a beer bottle in his hand, which he lifts up in a toast. And then the counting begins from voices surrounding us.

"Ten. Nine. Eight. Seven. Six. Five. Four. Three. Two…"

With a quick yank of my elbow, the champagne in my cup sloshes over the sides slightly, as Van pulls me toward the opened door behind us, gently guiding me around the corner of the patio. Once we stop, his hand slips behind my head and he pulls me hard into a deep and urgent kiss. I lose my breath as his tongue plunges into my open mouth, which was still gaping from the surprise of his action.

Forgetting about everything and everyone around me, I let myself get swept away from the touch of his lips, the sounds of his moan. I have to stand on my tip-toes and clutch one arm around his neck, keeping our connection as close as possible. We're so lost in one another that we don't hear the footsteps, but the shocked gasp does register. As does the very loud exclamation.

"What the fuck, Van?" I tear my mouth away from Van's at the sound of my brother's angry voice.

While our mouths no longer fused together, we still have connection as Van's hand remains on my waist, giving me a squeeze of reassurance.

My eyes bounce between Cade and Van, assessing the tension between the three of us that's growing by the second. The vein in Cade's neck is corded tight, and I can tell he's on the verge of blowing a gasket. He's going to lose his shit. I subconsciously take a step back, but Van's firm grip keeps me in place.

"Cade-" I begin, but Van interjects.

He's soft-spoken, but composed. "Kylah and I are together."

My brother practically sputters in disbelief. "Since when?"

He moves forward, posturing himself against Van, his chest puffing up like a sentinel on watch. Van doesn't move or back down. He simply stands there, brooking no argument over his position. All I can think of at this moment is, *Holy Shit, we've been outed.*

"It's really not any of your business, Cade. I understand you might have an issue with..."

"You're damn right I have an issue with this." His finger juts out and pokes Van hard in the shoulder, but does little to move the impenetrable wall he's created. Then Cade's eyes land on me.

"Is Van the guy you've been talking about? The one who you

hooked up with and then left you hanging? Who made you feel like shit cause he didn't contact you for days?"

My eyes go wide with embarrassment that Cade is spewing all the salacious personal details about us, as a small crowd begins to gather at the door, curious as to what all the ruckus is about.

Van looks at me sharply, asking me with his eyes if I shared this information with my brother.

Oh God, this is awful.

I'm sorry...I've already fucked this up for us.

I need to find the biggest rock and crawl under it right this minute.

Van's arm drops from my waist, leaving me feeling like I'm drifting without a life preserver in choppy waters. Self-protective instincts have me crossing my arms around my chest, shielding me from the verbal blows that are sure to be dealt.

He steps forward a fraction of an inch, creating a barrier between me and my brother. I do not want this to get ugly or draw any more attention than it already has. I hate drama, especially at parties, where the alcohol just adds fuel to the fire. From the looks of it, Cade's a little more than buzzed, too, which means he's not thinking clearly.

"Cade, maybe we can go inside and talk about this in private. Don't make a scene and embarrass Ky like this. She doesn't deserve it. If you're mad, be mad at me, bro."

Cade scoffs angrily. "I'm fucking livid, is what I am. How dare you take advantage of my little sister. If you wanted a rebound, you could've found a hundred other girls willing to sit on your dick. Not my baby sister."

God, the way he makes it sound, you'd think I was a twelve-year-old. Geez. Give me a little credit, would ya?

I think Van recognizes the anger seething through Cade at the moment and does his best to extricate me from the situation.

He turns toward me and begins to usher me back through the open doorway, pushing past the crowd blocking our way. But Cade wants to hash this out now, so he does what many drunken, angsty young men do. He throws a punch.

Well, maybe he didn't mean for it to turn into a punch, but it looks like an intentional swing. Cade leans in, grabbing hold of Van's shirt collar, as Van tries to get loose from his grip. Cade's hand flies up and hits Van in the face.

And then all hell breaks loose. Someone in the crowd yells, "Fight!" The crowd shifts and tightens around us. Lance and Carver come stumbling out onto the patio, along with Kady and Ainsley, who are both slack-jawed at what they are witnessing.

Ainsley screams at Cade to stop. Van stumbles back slightly, but then rights himself, but not soon enough as Cade careens into him with full body impact, tackling him as his arms curl around him. They both end up on the ground, Van shouting and trying to shove Cade off of him. Cade is off the rails and is scaring all of us a bit. He's never been one to start a fight or act belligerently toward anyone – especially not one of his own friends.

I'm just about to bend down to help remove Cade from on top of Van when Kady pushes in front of me and jerks me back a few feet. Carver and Lance have grabbed hold of Cade's arms and are prying him off of Van, who looks stunned. And really pissed.

The guys are still scuffling a bit trying to calm Cade down, with Ainsley fuming at Cade, her hands on her hips and her scary stare ready to shoot fireballs at my dumb-ass brother.

"Will someone please tell me what happened?" Ainsley asks, looking between the three of us. She knows I'm the reason the fight started.

Van stands up, immediately moving to me, planting his hands on my shoulders and pulling me tight against his chest.

"Are you okay? I'm so sorry this happened, Ky..." he whispers. My sweet, lovable guy is apologizing to *me* over a situation that my own family member caused.

"Stop, Van. It's not your fault." I create some distance so I can look him in the eye. "Are you okay? Did he hurt you?" My eyes dart around his face and my hands gently probe around his torso to see if he's been injured anywhere. He shakes his head and reaches for my wrists.

"I'm fine. No biggie. But I think we should go inside and let him cool down a bit before we talk to him. Is that okay?" His eyes are full of worry and regret. It makes my heart ache.

"Yeah, that's cool. Go upstairs to my room and I'll let Ainsley know. I'll be right up."

He walks away, glancing back at me reluctantly. I know he's worried about leaving me out here alone. Cade would never do anything to hurt me like that. He's just angry that I didn't confide in him about Van. It's all my fault for keeping it a secret, even though Van was of the opinion that we should tell him.

Stepping up alongside Ainsley, I place my hand at her elbow to grab her attention. She turns to see it's me and we move off to the side of the patio, away from the chaos. Kady decides to join us.

"What is up with your brother?" Ainsley asks me, hoping to find out the answers. "I've never seen him this crazy upset. I just can't believe him. He and I are going to have a serious talk when this thing blows over."

I bow my head, chewing my lip in guilt. "It's my fault. I should've told him about me and Van so he didn't find out this way. But I didn't want him to interfere with things. It just started to get serious recently. Nothing happened before..." I give Kady a side-long glance. "Well, it's new."

Ainsley smiles knowingly. "I'm happy for you, Kylah. I'm sorry your stupid-ass brother ruined it by being a *dickhead*," she yells out toward him. "Listen, I'll work to get him straight and we'll talk later if you want. Otherwise, I'll just tell him to let it go and let you be happy." She places a soft, gentling touch on my arm, squeezing me lovingly before dropping her hand.

"Thank you. I appreciate it. I'm going to go find Van. I'd hate myself if this ruins Van and Cade's friendship. I never wanted to do that."

Kady chimes in. "Fuck that. It was all Cade and his arrogant, over-protective arrogance. What a douchewad." She slams the last gulp of her champagne, wiping off her mouth with emphasis. That reminds me that I haven't even had a sip of mine yet.

I bring the cup to my lips and swallow – the first taste washing down, the effervescence tickling my throat. Fortified with a little liquid courage, I set the empty cup down on the patio table and turn to go find Van.

I just pray that this stupid drama won't ruin the rest of our New Years' Eve celebration.

22

Van

I'M PACING the floor like a panther ready to pounce when Kylah opens the door to her bedroom.

My footsteps stop as I watch her hesitantly approach me, a remorseful expression etched across her mouth. Without hesitation, I step toward her, encircling her in my arms.

I place a kiss on the top of her head as she molds her body against mine, as relief seems to overtake her.

She cries silently. The only reason I know this is because I feel the dampness her tears leave on my T-shirt.

"Shhh. Baby, it's fine. No harm, no foul. Just let him cool off for a bit. We'll talk it through when he's ready and things will be good as new. I promise."

I've thought a lot about what my relationship with Kylah might do to my friendship with Cade. Personally, it's none of his business, but as I don't have a younger sister, I can't put myself into his shoes. He has his reasons for being protective of Kylah, so I don't begrudge him for getting pissed at me and acting like a raging bull when he saw me practically mauling her outside. But that doesn't condone his actions.

I didn't expect Cade to go ballistic on me and throw a punch. He didn't hurt me physically – because I can hold my own – but we're like brothers, on and off the court. He knows who I am. So the fact that he would think I would do anything to hurt Kylah cuts me deep. I thought he respected me enough to acknowledge that if I am with Kylah, I'm all in.

She's not just a hook-up, or a fling, even though he seems to think that's why I'm with her.

That's the furthest thing from the truth.

Maybe I'm over-romanticizing this thing between us, but there is a deep connection we share – it's been there like a magnetic pull since the first time I met her. She helped pull me out of the dark place I was in over the end of things with Lyndsay. She is the reason I wake up happy every day and reminds me to enjoy every moment.

Even my brother noticed a change in my demeanor this past week, giving me some good ribbing over being so easily swayed by a girl. While he's never had a girlfriend, he definitely has been interested in some girls from school in the past. He knows what that emotion feels like.

Kylah squirms in my hold. "I feel awful, Van. That shouldn't have happened. And now everyone is going to know about it. I *hate* drama."

My palms glide across her back, rubbing the tension away for both of us.

"I hear that drama on New Years' Eve is good fortune. It means you have a full year of joy ahead of you."

She looks up at me skeptically. "Where on earth did you hear that? That sounds made-up."

"Ancient Chinese secret." I grin deviously, placing a kiss on her forehead as she crinkles her nose at my bold lie.

"You're full of it." She laughs, her hands gripping my ass and squeezing.

"Maybe." I laugh. "Hey, by the way, I haven't had a chance to say it yet. But Happy New Year, Kylah." My hands cup her cheeks and I kiss her slowly, but soundly. Her sexy murmurs of response heading straight to my dick, which is growing by the second.

"Happy New Year, Van." She whispers, her champagne breath painted warm and delish across my lips.

I was really looking forward to staying the night with her in her bed, but now that the shit hit the fan, I'm not so sure that's a great idea.

The knock on the door startles us both as we quickly release one another, Kylah jumping about two-feet to the left of me like a scared bunny.

Carver's voice calls out from the hallway. "It's me. Can I come in?"

Kylah looks at me in question and I just shrug, uncertain what Carver's interest is in any of this.

"Sure, come on in."

The door cracks open and he steps in. I glance behind him to see if Cade's with him and he shakes his head, acknowledging my question.

"Cade's still downstairs talking to Ainsley. He's chill now. It's all good."

Kylah sighs softly and I reach for her hand, entwining it with mine and pulling her next to me. I feel better when I'm touching her in some way or another. Like I'm not whole when I can't feel her. Which has me worried, because what the fuck is going to happen next week when she has to return to school? I'm right back to where I started from and in another long-distance relationship that will surely drive me insane.

Carver pulls out Kylah's desk chair, whips it around and sits down backward on it, staring at us with keen interest.

"Thought you two were just friends." He uses air quotes. "You left out the 'with benefits' part."

Carver stares at our joined hands and then back up at me. I can't quite tell what he's thinking. Is he mad? I don't see why he would be, this has nothing to do with him. And I don't feel it necessary to have to explain myself to him, for that matter.

"We were friends, but it turned into more," I say, acknowledging the truth about our relationship.

He nods his head appreciatively, his lips pursed as if thinking this over.

"So what, you're like a couple now?"

He doesn't state it in a condescending way, but it still pisses me off that the thing between me and Kylah is anyone else's business. Can't people just get their own lives and not worry about others so much?

"Yeah. What of it, bro? Why is it such a big deal to you?"

Carver's head hangs low, his arms crossed over the back of the chair, as he taps his fingers against the wood. When he lifts his head again, he gives me a cursory glance before moving to Kylah, his expression morphing into tenderness.

"I just don't want to see Ky-Ky get hurt."

"Duly noted."

Kylah, who's been silent up 'til now, jumps in.

"Van would never hurt me." She grips my hand tight, giving it a quick squeeze before releasing it. "I appreciate your concern, Carver, but I'll be fine. He's not like...*others* I know." It's an attempt at humor, a little jab at the player in front of us. Carver seems to understand she's poking fun at his man-whore status and laughs.

"Okay then." Carver stands, pushing in the chair under the desk and then turning toward us once again. "I'm happy for you. Good luck with things. Now, if you don't mind, I'm going to resume my role as a party favor to all the single ladies downstairs who want to start their New Year off with a *bang*." He snickers and waggles his eyebrows to show off his lewd intentions, then pats me on the shoulder as he leaves the room.

Kylah giggles, smooshing her face into my bicep, as I roll my eyes and watch Carver strut out the door. That man has such an inflated ego, but he's been a good friend and great team captain.

"So you think Cade is going to make a reappearance tonight? Or can we assume Ainsley has things handled and we can proceed worry-free with the rest of our night together?"

I unwrap her from my hold and walk her back to the bed, where we sit next to each other. I take a good look around her room again and am reminded of the cello in the corner.

"You play the cello?"

"Yeah. I know, I'm a nerd."

I grab underneath her knees with one hand and place another behind her back, and in one fell swoop, I lift her onto my lap, the sound of her little yelp filling the otherwise silent room.

"You're not a nerd, Ky. The cello is a beautiful instrument. Graceful. Melodic. Gorgeous. Just like you." My mouth finds hers, placing a swift kiss across her lips. "I want to hear you play."

She tilts her head with curiosity, her eyes gleaming as they take in my sincerity.

"You do?" She asks with a hint of incredulity.

"Yes, of course." I give her a bite on her earlobe, loving the gasp I procure. "And it would be even hotter if you played naked. Your thighs spread wide, your knees hugging the wood, as your hand wraps around the neck of the cello..."

I'm pretty sure she can feel my cock straining now against her ass. That image is never going to leave me – whether I do or don't get to see her play it for real. Just the fantasy is enough to get me going when I jack off in the future.

There's a sharp sting from the swat she gives me across my right pec. "You're a naughty boy, Van. But I like it." She bites down on her lip and gives me a coy smile. Damn this girl has no idea how naughty I want to get with her. She's the perfect mix of sexy and sweet, and I love both sides of her.

In fact, I love *all* of her.

I'm just about to capture her mouth when another rap comes at the door. *Jesus*, I mumble under my breath, because can't anyone leave us alone? Kylah freezes for a second and then jumps off my lap. She runs to the door and cracks it open. Apparently satisfied that it isn't Cade, she swings it wide to invite Kady inside. Instead, she waves a hand toward us both and remains outside the doorway.

"I just wanted you to know that Ainsley and Cade left. They went back to her apartment for the night, so you're free to get to fucking each other like bunnies."

"Oh my God, you're so terrible," Kylah says exasperated by her sister, but then gives her a hug. "But thank you for letting us know."

It's so weird to see them right next to each other. Although Kady has a unique look, while Kylah is classically beautiful, their features are identical, except for their eyes.

I've heard stories where guys will date a twin and they get duped somewhere along the way with the old 'switcheroo'. That makes no sense to me, because even if the twins look exactly alike, there are certain characteristics that just can't be duplicated. Voice, for example. Kady's voice is huskier, sharper than Kylah's, with sometimes a serrated edge to it. Kylah's voice, though, has this lyrical quality. Soft and breezy, like the sound you hear from the ocean at dawn.

Their eyes are also different. Nothing can compare to Kylah's wide-eyed, innocence. Her sister's have a much harder edge, a very deep blue, that look an awful lot like a tempest sea. I can get lost in Kylah's gaze. When I stare into her eyes, I see longing, trust, and adoration there. And maybe something more, but I'm too chicken shit to find out.

Kady waves in our direction and is just about to leave when she says, "Hey, don't worry about being loud tonight. I'll have my own action going on, if you know what I mean." Her voice has a slight lilt and lots of sass as she closes the door behind her and we are once again alone.

Kylah stands a few feet away from me, her hands twisted in worry.

"Come here." I reach out and wind my hand around her tiny wrist, pulling her to me.

"Wow, what a way to cap off a New Years' Eve." She heaves a huge sigh, allowing me to drag her over to her bed. "I'm glad it's over for now and we can have the rest of the night together." Her sly grin finds its way to my soul.

Sliding my hands through her hair at the side of her temples, I tilt her head to look up at me. Her expression is confusing. Still deep with worry, it also holds a profound mix of shyness, lust, and desire.

"There's nothing I want more."

Gently lowering her down to the bed, she stretches out underneath me, allowing me to languorously and sensually devour her body.

I count my lucky stars that I can start off the New Year with this sweet girl in my arms.

23

K ylah

Four Weeks Later

Studying for a chemistry quiz is hands down the most unappealing thing in the world, especially when the only thing I'd rather be doing is Skyping with my boyfriend.

Boyfriend.

Holy shit. I'm Van Gerard's girlfriend.

It still amazes me when I think about it too much. Which, if I'm honest, is all the darn time. He is on my mind constantly. When I'm awake. When I dream. When I daydream instead of figuring out the calculated atomic weight and number for each element.

Before I began my relationship with Van, school was everything to me. It was my focus twenty-four hours a day. Sienna would constantly harp on me because I never had any "fun" with my friends. But honestly, my friends were the same nerdy, geeky college kids like me. They were my tribe – and even when

I did get together with them, we'd usually just discuss school-work. And when we got really crazy, we'd eat pizza, drink Red Bull drinks, and delve into the unifying principles of life science. Ooh...the things we could tell you about the life of an academic nerd.

Since I returned to school after the holiday break, I've lost interest in all of that. I've been somewhat of a hermit. And have suddenly become a huge basketball fan.

Crazy, right? I mean, I attended many of Cade's games when he was in high school, and my dad would take me to his college home games, too. But I never cared too much about the actual sport and tuned out my brother half the time when he'd go on and on about a particular team, or game, or his stats.

My interest is insatiable now, and I can't wait to hear every-thing about a game from Van. That's what I'm doing right now; waiting for him to get back to his hotel room so he can Skype with me. Tonight they are in Seattle playing an away game against the Washington State Huskies.

I remember going to Seattle when I was in sixth grade with my family because of Cade's high school tournaments. We did all the touristy things, like going to the top of the Space Needle (not my idea of a good time. Found out I'm deathly afraid of being in very tall structures when there is a strong possibility of it collapsing in an earthquake). We rode the Ducks – one of those land/water vehicles that take tourists through the various landmarks around the city. Kady made fun of me because I actu-ally used the lip-duck-quacker thing they handed out to all of us.

Anyway, a feeling of melancholy has descended upon me because I want to see him so badly it feels like my chest is going to break open. The only thing that has given me a little bit of lift is knowing that in a little over two weeks from now, it'll be Valentine's Day. Van doesn't know it, but I'm going to go home and surprise him. I know the team has a home game over the President's Day weekend, so he'll be there. The only one who knows I'm coming to visit is Cade, whom I've enlisted to help me pull off my big surprise.

Once Cade cooled down after the New Year's debacle, we talked things over before I returned to school. His concerns had nothing whatsoever to do with Van as a person. In fact, he thinks Van is one of the most decent guys he knows. It turns out, Cade was just pissed off for being left in the dark. Upset that I didn't confide in him and tell him the truth upfront. And maybe there was a little mixture of big brotherly protectiveness, too, but he'd never admit to that.

In the end, it all worked out. We went out on a double-date with Ainsley and Cade two days before I returned to school and he's been very supportive ever since. Apparently, however, he did tell Van in a private *mono e mono* conversation that he'd kick his ass for real if he did ever hurt me. Aw, brotherly love.

My thoughts return to the present when my Skype app pops open and I see Van's gorgeous face appear on my screen. Clicking on the Accept button, I adjust my glasses and lick my lips in anticipation.

"Hey, baby." He murmurs, looking utterly handsome in his travel suit and his hair still damp. But then, as I get a really good look, I notice something terribly alarming.

Holy moly.

His signature Van-bun...it's gone. His long hair, which was normally pulled back into a bun, which I started calling his Van-bun, as opposed to man-bun, which I found terribly hilarious of me – has been chopped off. His dark tresses are now cropped shorter on the side with a long sweep over his brow.

Instead of greeting him properly, I let out a screech. "Oh my God, Van. Your hair! What did you do?"

He grins sheepishly, in the sexy way that he does, his fingers coming up to comb through the top, which falls a little out of place. Then he scratches at his chin which is covered with a day's growth of stubble. Mm. God, I love that. It makes my fingers twitch with jealousy.

"Meh, I was tired of the hassle. The guys always gave me a hard time about it...and I don't know. Honestly, I was ready for a change. Plus, I didn't want to be mistaken for one of the hipster Seattle-lumberjacks while I'm in town."

We both laugh as I watch him undo his tie and remove his jacket, making the camera jump around with his movements. He must be using his phone instead of his laptop.

"Wow...okay. It's just such a shock You look so different. But you look really good. You're still the hottest guy I've ever known."

He really is. I don't know how I ended up getting so lucky. Van is just amazing.

Moving from the hair subject, I redirect the conversation because I'm interested in how the end of the game went from his perspective.

"So how was the game? I saw the score after the first half and you were down by six. Unfortunately, I had to go to my study group and just got back about fifteen minutes ago, so I didn't see the final. What happened?"

"We won. I made a couple of three-point shots, and Carver really went balls to the walls. He was on fire tonight. A triple-double. I'm not sure what caused it, but he was the MVP of the game, that's for sure."

"That's awesome." Something in my brain clicks about my knowledge of Carver's background. "Hey, isn't Carver from Washington? I think I recall him saying he grew up there. Maybe his family came to see him play or something."

Van scratches his beard again like it's itchy. "Yeah, you're right. He grew up in a suburb of Seattle, I think. Maybe he was playing his heart out because he had family there to see him. I don't really know, though, because Carver is as tight-lipped about his past as they come. Never talks about his family, or his childhood, or anything."

I can see the movement of a shoulder shrug, but can't see his entire body in the phone frame. He's too broad and the camera angle is tilting up to his face.

"I miss you." I blurt because it's so hard to be away from him for so long. Even though if I were in Phoenix, I'd still not be able to see him when he was on the road, but it's just really difficult.

"I miss you too, Ky. All the damn time. The last few days, especially. I haven't gotten to talk to you as much when we're on the road. It sucks."

"Can I ask you something?" It's out of morbid curiosity that I want to know the answer to this question. I probably shouldn't ask, but I'm dying to know.

He brings his head to his ear, his dark eyes narrow on me. "Of course. What is it?"

Now I'm on the hook and I'm scared to ask for the truth. "Was it...well, was it like this when you were with Lyndsay?" I swallow down the ball of fear that's lodged in my throat. It shouldn't matter what he felt when he was with her, but it makes me feel guilty for putting him in the very same predicament that he was in with her. Another long-distant relationship that creates more hardships than benefits.

Van closes his eyes and takes a deep breath, the tone of his voice a warning. "Ky..."

"Never mind. I don't want to know. Forget I asked. It was stupid." I wave at the screen and then cover my eyes with my hand, trying to avoid his gaze.

"I swear to you, Ky, this is nothing like what I was in before. Honestly, now that I have distance and space to look back at it, I think the reason Lyndsay and I stayed together as long as we did was because it was safe. Going away to school was scary. Dealing with changes in our lives. Stress and pressures of college and sports. And then for me, there's Dougie and the challenges that brings my family. Anyway, what I'm trying to say is that with Lyndsay it was familiar. Easy, maybe. But over the last year, we just realized that safety net was pulling us down rather than lifting us up."

I consider what he's saying, and wonder if that will happen to us. "I'm thinking about transferring."

Van's head snaps back against the headboard like a rubber band, nonplussed. "What? Why?"

My face crinkles up because I thought he'd be happy to hear that. I've actually put a lot of thought into it over the last few weeks. Being back at school, after spending time at home over the holidays had me reassessing the whole going away to school thing. Even though Van is a factor in my consideration of a transfer, I was homesick well before we got cozy together. A few nights ago, over pizza and Diet Cokes, Sienna and I had had a conversation and she actually pressed me to seriously consider it.

"A lot of reasons. For one, I'm homesick, Van. I'm not made to be far from my family. Although Kady is in Colorado, my mom, my dad, Cade, Gramps – they're all in Phoenix. I don't like being so far away. It's been really rough on me this year. I tried to make it work, get out of my shell a little more – because I knew I needed to experience being on my own for once. But I realized it's not for me and I don't like it."

My voice shakes with diffidence as I continue. "And of course, there's you."

The words hang out there in the ether between us. At first, I'm so nervous that he'll think I'm a flake, and a naïve girl to consider a decision to move back because of a guy. I mean, we really haven't talked about it, so who really knows if this thing has legs and will go the distance. But I don't think my moving back will cause a problem. Even if we don't stay together long-term, I still want to be in Phoenix. It's what I know and I feel comfortable there.

He's too quiet for a moment, his eyes focused on a spot over the top of the phone.

"Kylah. Wow. I don't know what to say, or how I feel about this. It's strange because part of me feels you'd be crazy to give up a bright future at Harvey Mudd, with a world-class science program that will only be an asset in your quest to become a leading female scientist someday. I'd hate for you to give up on a program like that."

His voice trails off, and his eyes follow the same path, looking away from the phone. My heart plummets, falling to the floor like a dying star. Then I see a tiny smile form on his face, lighting me with hope.

"I don't want you to make this heavy decision because of me. I don't ever want you to regret doing something because you just wanted to be closer to me. I won't let you do that. You know I'll be graduating in May, and who knows where I'll end up with a job next year."

I want to crawl in a hole and die. Everything he says is a crushing blow. Like taking a wrecking ball to my heart. I can read between the lines. He's prepping me for the inevitable. It's obvious he isn't treating this as a long-lasting thing. I'm just a rebound fling for him.

God, I feel so foolish. I just want to get off the phone now and sob into my pillow for being so dumb. All this time, I thought he cared for me with the same intensity and degree as I do for him. I've fallen hard for Van, but apparently, we're not on the same page.

"Oh." Is all I can muster.

Now I regret saying anything at all. I should've just kept my mouth shut and never mentioned anything to him. I'd done all the prep work with my program administrator and counselor, as well as contacted ASU's admissions department to find out more about their programs. I was so excited to share this news with him. The only thing I hadn't done yet was tell my mom and dad. I didn't want them to fret over this decision quite yet.

Van's next comment has me blinking back tears...of joy.

"On the other hand, if I stay in Phoenix after graduation, it would be amazing to be able to see you all the time. We could get an apartment..."

My eyes flutter, finding his over the connection and the grin he wears has me beaming. My heart does an internal shimmy and happy dance, jumping around in elated leaps inside my ribs.

"An apartment, huh?" My mom and dad would freak, but that couldn't stop me. I'd be staying in an apartment off campus, anyway.

"We'll have to see about that, Mr. Gerard. It depends on how good of a roommate you are." I give him a little wink, conjuring my inner minx. "If you leave the toilet seat up or towels on the floor, there's no deal."

He blushes a bright shade of red. Adorable.

"I'll admit, I'm not the greatest with laundry and I like to leave my dirty socks laying around. But my mom always made me make my bed at home, so I'm kind of a stickler with that routine."

We laugh and talk more about the possibilities of what living together might look like. After another thirty minutes, I can tell he's exhausted from the travel and the game, so we say our good-nights, which tack on another five minutes to our phone time because it's so darn hard hanging up from that beautiful face.

Just before we hang up, he knocks me off my feet and recon-firms what I mean to him.

"Kylah," he murmurs, laying back against a huge stack of pillows behind his head.

"Yeah?"

"I love you."

Jaw, meet floor.

You know that feeling you get when you're at the top of the rollercoaster, after you've just climbed the long hill, hearing the clickety-clack of the tracks underneath you and the swarm of noise surrounding you? When you just hurdle over the otherwise, plummeting down in a blaze of glory?

Yeah, that's how those three words feel to me.

Exhilarating. Momentous. Life-changing.

"I love you, too, Van. Good-night."

Needless to say, I won't sleep a wink tonight.

24

MY COLLEGE BASKETBALL career is nearing the end. The second week of each February marks the countdown to the last full month of regular play before things get interesting. It's the calm before the storm, when all eyes were focused on what is ahead of us, in hopes that we'd wind up in the championship tournament.

Even those who aren't college basketball fans have heard about March Madness. It's the culmination of a hard work and sacrifice when a total of sixty-eight teams head into the post season NCAA tournament, also known as the Big Dance. Some teams get there by their conference championships and wins, and others are selected on the aptly named Selection Sunday when we are slotted into seeds and brackets. It's every gambler's dream - March Madness is the Holy Grail for betting types.

I'm both excited and a bit mournful over the upcoming month of play. I want to take it all in, remembering every aspect of each game played, locking it away as memories for my future life. It's difficult to imagine when play is finally done, I'll no longer be a basketball player. My final game will definitely be bittersweet.

Some of the guys on the team will be entering the draft come June. Two for certain are Carver Edwards and the other center on the team, Christian Lancaster. They both decided to remain in school and graduate before announcing their interest. A lot of players in the league dropout somewhere between their freshman and sophomore years, hoping to capitalize on their youthful physicality, agility, and vitality to make it in the big leagues. For me, that was never in my field of vision.

What has been in my future plans is making my parents and Dougie proud of who I am and what I could become. I'm not going to make a name for myself in finance, but I think someday I could be a good leader and maybe CFO. Every business needs one of those. Coach Welby has always told me to *"step up and use my natural born leadership skills"*. I'm not an in-your-face leader like Carver, who is gregarious and overly-confident. I'm more of the laid back kind of guys who quietly assert my opinions and ideas without blasting it in your face.

Like tonight's game, for example. We were down by twelve points going into the second half. Carver went out with an injury to his calf, so our other point guard, Kenyon Lyons, a sophomore from Missouri, stepped in. He's a good kid, but a little like a skittish bunny. So during one of the timeouts, I slapped him on the shoulder, grabbing the scruff behind his head, and gave him a little pep talk.

"Look, bruh. You're doing great. No one expects you to be Carver. Be yourself. Trust your instincts. You got this, dude."

After that, the stars started to align and we began making baskets, finding the open holes and taking the shots that got us the lead. I ended up making two three-pointers from the perimeter, and a couple rebounds while under the basket. We won the game by one point.

Everyone went out to celebrate afterward, but I left early so I could get home for my Skype date with Kylah. Tomorrow is Valentine's Day and I had shipped her a care package with a bunch of stuff I knew she would like.

Included in the package was a pair of polka dot panties I found at Victoria's Secret. I might not be able to see her wear them this weekend, but I'd definitely get a chance the next time we were together. Or maybe in our Skype session tonight I'd ask her to try them on for me.

Fuck, my cock is hard just thinking about the possibility of her laying out on her bed dressed only in her panties. I wonder if I could convince my shy little sex kitten to do that for me?

I can't wait to get her online to see her. I've missed her so much I can barely stand it any longer. I just want to hold her in my arms. Kiss her dewy lips until they turn swollen and puffy from my attention. Touch her body in all the places I know will make her squirm with excitement.

I open the door to my dorm room and the first thing I notice is that my desk light is on. I don't recall leaving it on. Weird. And then I catch a long-forgotten, yet very familiar, scent.

My eyes snap to the bed, where laid out nearly naked, in only a lacy bra and panties, is not Kylah...but my ex.

"Lyndsay."

Her name echoes off the walls of my small room, as I instinctively take a step back, planting my butt against the door. My hand firmly on the handle, as if my mind already knows I'll need a quick escape.

My immediate thought is that I need her to leave. I don't know what the hell she's doing here – practically naked in my bed – but she is an uninvited and unwanted guest. And that's a liberal term since she's not even a guest. That would imply that I'm the host of this little party, and that I certainly am not.

My eyes can't help but peruse her body. I've seen her in my bed a hundred times before. I know the feel of her body. The taste of her skin. The scent of her...

Fuck.

My tone is harsh and lacks any form of welcome. "What the hell are you doing here, Lynds?"

Lyndsay's eyes narrow on me, in an appraising glance, her penetrating stare sweeps over me as she makes her way seductively toward me on her hands and knees. Her lips curl into a licentious smile.

"Do you know what today is?" she asks, now kneeling at the edge of my bed, her tongue darting out to lick her bottom lip. It's supposed to be seductive, but it makes me want to throttle her.

"No, and I don't care. I want you to leave."

She moves with the speed of a gazelle, jumping off the bed and landing softly with a thud within inches of me. I try to back up, but I'm as far against the door as I can possibly go. I'm trapped. So I do the only thing I can do, I place my hands on her bare shoulders to hold her at bay.

"Van," she coos, tilting her head, chin down so her lips meet the top of my hand, which she kisses. "You don't remember? This is a special night for us. It's the anniversary of the first time we ever had sex. On our camping trip up at Coal Springs. God, it was such a great night."

My heart remembers. Damn it. She doesn't play fair. Of course, it was a great night. She was my first. We fumbled and stumbled together that first time, trying to figure out how to put a condom on and where and how to fit my dick inside her. It's almost comical to think back on it now.

But I don't want to think about it. It's not laughing matter. There's no room for history between us. It's done. Over. She fucking cheated on me, got knocked up by another guy and dumped me. And now I'm in love with another girl. I've moved on and so has she.

So why is she even here?

I drop my hands to my sides, like they have lead weights on them, and ball my hands into fists.

"You have exactly two seconds to tell me why you're in my fucking room, Lyndsay. And then you're going to leave."

She sticks her lower lip out in a pout. "I thought you'd be happy to see me."

"You thought wrong."

"I've missed you, baby." She reaches up to drape her arms around my neck, which I try to shrug off unsuccessfully. They pin me like a vice.

"I don't see how you can... I mean, what would Cody think about his pregnant girlfriend missing her ex-boyfriend?"

That apparently did it, because she drops her arms and takes a step back, her eyes meeting the floor.

"We're not together anymore. He broke it off after I lost the baby."

Here's the deal. When you've been shit on by someone you once loved, you want nothing more than to get revenge at some point. Love, when you've been fucked over, quickly turns to hurt, which then turns to hatred. And when you hate someone, all you want them to do is suffer exactly like you've suffered. Karma is a bitch, and all that.

However, being raised in a very Christian household, where I was taught to love everyone and turn the other cheek, yada, yada yada...it makes it a bit difficult to want someone I once cared for to suffer. Just looking at the anguish written all over Lyndsay's face I realize she has experienced a very difficult loss. Whether that was in breaking up with Cody Leach, over miscarrying his baby or both.

"I'm sorry, Lyndsay. That must be awful." And I truly mean it. I can see she's hurting.

She wraps her arms around her waist protectively, her head still angled toward the ground. As she slowly raises it, a start of an apologetic smile appears on her face.

"Don't you want to tell me I deserved what I got? That you're glad karma found me?"

Moving over to my desk chair, I reach for the hoodie laying over the back of it and hand it to her for her to put on. I'm a guy, after all, and having a girl – especially my ex – nearly naked in my bedroom does weird things to my brain. She accepts the offer and slips it over her head.

Once she's covered, I lead her to the desk chair and have her sit down.

"That's not what I would say, and you know it."

"I know."

"Is that why you came here? You thought showing up and trying to sleep with me would make things better?"

She winces at the severity of my words.

"I'm sorry, Van. It was stupid. But I just feel so lost. Everything that's happened over the last few months, the path I chose...letting you go. It was all...I made bad decisions. I fucked up. I know that now. It's just been really hard."

I no longer have the same feelings I once had for Lyndsay. Those are all gone. But seeing the tears spill down over her face, her head hanging in defeat, makes me want to show her she's selling herself short.

I hold out my outstretched arm to her, palm up, inviting her to take hold. She does and I yank her over to the side of the bed where we both sit. I wrap her up in a hug. It's not sexual in any way. It's meant to be comforting. She cries softly into my dress shirt, which I'm still wearing post-game.

"It'll all work out okay, Lynds. You're strong and smart. Don't get down on yourself. You'll be fine."

Her cheek is against my chest, chin resting lightly on the top of her head when there's a knock on my door.

"Yo, Van. Open the door. I've got something for ya."

It's Cade. Shit.

Lyndsay jerks back a little, her head popping up to look at me, my eyes wide with concern. This would not be good if he sees her in here with me. Not that easy to explain away.

But before either of us has a chance to figure out a plan or the best approach, the door swings open and Cade, and then Kylah, both appear.

Oh, fuck. Fuckity fuck fuck fuck.

The looks on their faces tell me everything I need to know.

Joy.

Surprise.

Betrayal.

Kylah squeaks out a loud gasp, as she covers her mouth with her hand, her eyes wide with hurt. The way she stares at me – the pain evident across her face – shatters me. I know exactly what she sees, even though it's conveying a completely different message. My eyes – my heart – my everything – beseeches her to know the truth. To realize this isn't what it seems.

Cade protectively throws an arm out in front of Kylah, blocking her entrance. He turns his head behind him and speaks low in her ear. I can't hear what he says, but I see Kylah nod her head and backs up and out of the room.

"Cade...it's not...we're not..." I ping-pong between Cade and Lyndsay, whose tears have dried up and she looks confused. She doesn't know I've been dating Kylah, and to my knowledge, has never met her. But she knows Cade. And I'm sure she sees the severity of the situation.

"You fucking asshole," he yells, charging me from the door.

In three long strides, he's pulled me up by my tie and collar, his fist ready to make contact with my jaw with the slightest provocation. "Give me one reason why I shouldn't fucking kill you right now."

Lyndsay jumps to her feet, lodging herself between the two of us.

"Because it's not his fault. He did nothing wrong. You should know better than that, Cade."

Cade grumbles, his hand tightening and then loosening as he decides whether or not to trust what Lyndsay is saying is true.

After a few moments, he gives me a quick shove and drops his hand, stepping back to assess the situation. He takes in the hoodie Lyndsay's wearing, covering only to her mid-thigh, otherwise naked underneath. He sees I'm still fully clothed and maybe he even notices the genuine concern in my eyes. All I want to do right now is fly out that door and track down Kylah.

She gave me no indication that she was going to visit this weekend. We both talked about how busy we were with classes and my basketball schedule. There seemed no way that we'd get a chance to see each other. A kernel of dread now pops through my veins, a heavy mixture of anxiety skirting around my brain. I need to find her.

Cade seems to read my thoughts and shakes his head.

"No...I'll go talk to her. But you need to fix this. You just pissed on her parade in a really big way, man. It's not going to be easy to come back from this."

"Yeah, thanks." Is all I can think to say. I'm at a loss for words.

I've lost big games before. I've lost my temper on several occasions. I've even lost my way a few times.

But losing Kylah. That I can't live with.

25

K ylah

I RAN out of Van's dorm room and down the stairs faster than I've ever run before. In fact, I missed a step on my way down and nearly collided into a guy coming up on the opposite side. I may have mumbled an apology, but I'm not a hundred percent certain.

All I know is that my heart shattered up in that room and I seriously wonder how I'm still alive and breathing.

Pushing through the building doors, I have to move to the side as a group of kids are walking in, all laughing and chattering. I wish I were them right now – high on life and happy. Instead, I'm devastated. I'm left hanging by a thread, unable to make heads or tails of what I just witnessed.

My plans for my first Valentine's weekend with Van have been completely obliterated. I had enlisted my brother to help me get into the dorms because I don't have an access badge. Showing up unannounced was risky enough, but to do it without certainty that I could get in the building was a difficult prospect. Cade was happy to help, knowing how much it meant to me. We'd planned on meeting right after the game at his place and then he'd bring me over to campus.

I brought a picnic dinner of sorts – filled with decadent chocolate desserts, white-chocolate covered strawberries, because Van loves white-chocolate – and a bottle of bubbly. Cade bought that for me since I'm not legal.

The picnic basket is still on the floor upstairs in the hallway where I dropped it and ran. So are my hopes that this weekend would be one to remember. My first Valentine's Day with a guy. With someone I loved and who told me he loved me, too. I believed him. I had no reason not to.

Now all my thoughts are running rampant, thinking back over the last month that we've been apart and wondering if I'd been played? Has Van been two-timing me along with Lyndsay? Although I've never met her in person, I know it was her. When we first became friends, he shared with me some of their pictures together.

I feel dizzy and unstable, as I finally stop to look around at where I'm at. I'd had no real direction in mind when I came running out of the building. Glancing around at my surroundings, I realize I'm in the middle of the quad, the street lights illuminating the pathway, casting shadows across the grounds.

Catching my breath, the loud pounding in my ears softening to a dull roar, I hear my name called from the not-so-far-off distance. My head turns in various directions to see where the voice is coming from. And then I see him jogging toward me. My brother.

"There you are." His long legs get him in front of me in three long strides. Due to the shape he's in he's barely breathing hard at all, while I am panting like a pig at a marathon.

I don't say anything. I *can't*. What could possibly be said at a time like this? I'm humiliated beyond words. Van has made a fool of me. He's exposed how stupid, ignorant and naïve I am. I'd given him my heart and soul, and he played me like a Stradi-varius violin.

Cade places his arm around my shoulder and tugs me into his chest. His touch is protective and gentle. God, I love my brother.

"It wasn't what we thought, kiddo. It looked bad, for sure. But I believe Van. He was ambushed by her. Lyndsay told me she showed up uninvited and tried to put the moves on him. Van had nothing to do with it."

The tears that had been stuck like a silent scream are now streaking down my cheeks and dripping off my chin onto Cade's T-shirt.

"But he...she was practically naked in his lap...on his bed." I hiccup.

Cade turns me to face him and props my chin up with his finger.

"Believe me, sometimes things appear one way but aren't representative of what's really going on. Did you ever hear about the time Ainsley showed up at our house party and found a hoops hunnie on my lap?"

I squint up at him, eyes narrowing in disbelief. Cade used to be a player, so it's very probable he'd have a girl attached to him.

"Seriously," he continues, unperturbed by my skepticism. "I was wasted, wallowing in my sorrows because Ains had broken my heart. Anyway, the girl sidles up to me, plants her ass down and starts trying to get busy with me. I didn't encourage her in any way. In fact, I was trying to dislodge myself from her grip when Ainsley walked in and saw us. If I were in her shoes and saw it from her perspective, I wouldn't have believed my inno-cence either. But that's the point. Without the whole story, it can be damning for the innocent."

I huff out an incredulous breath. "So you're saying is that I shouldn't believe what I just saw? That Van he wasn't getting busy with his ex? He looked pretty guilty by my standards."

My mind flashes back to the image of the two of them on his bed. My heart quivers in recognition of the hot anger that it sparked inside of me not fifteen minutes earlier.

"Yes, I believe him. Van doesn't lie. He has more integrity than any other guy I've ever known. And I know he's into you. He wants to fix this, Ky. I can't tell you what to do, but I think you should give him a chance."

I'm so confused. My brain can't disassociate the image of Van with his arm around Lyndsay. Or the panicked *'caught in the act'* expression in his eye. What am I supposed to do with all that? It's too fresh. The wound is too raw. The humiliation hurts too much.

"Maybe. But not tonight. I need to go home. I can't see him right now."

"Okay. I'll take you back home. Then I gotta get home to my girl."

He winks as I give him a teary smile. Even though I'm more than reluctant now, it is awfully encouraging to know that true love exists in the world. It may not be in my world this weekend, but at least it's out there.

As soon as I get home, I FaceTime with Kady.

"Are you fucking kidding me?" she bellows out when I tell her what happened tonight. "Holy shit. If it were me, I would've rushed over to that ho and bitch-slapped her punk-ass face. Then I would've kicked him in the balls."

I cringe at her violent proposition, because I would never have considered doing any of that. So I guess there are some positive aspects of my twin's differing personality traits. She's a bit rash and explosive – taking shots and then asking questions. I'm more of the little turtle – pulling into my shell to avoid conflict and drama. Hence the reason I ran. I'm a bit conflict averse, to say the least.

"It hurts, Kady. It hurts so much."

I see my mirror image looking back at me through my phone, her blue hair pinned back from her face, dark smudges underneath her eyes.

"It's okay, sissy. I know. Love fucking sucks. Sex can be great, but outside of that, guys are just assholes. That's why women should all be lesbians. Hey, speaking of which...did I tell you about my kiss with Leesa the other night? Holy hotness...that whole "I experimented in college" thing is for realz."

I know this shouldn't shock me hearing Kady confess something like this. She is anything but subtle and will try anything once. But holy cats – she kissed a girl? She made out with a chick? This is not something I ever expected to hear. I don't even have words...

"Uh." See? No words.

Kady snickers, her brightly painted fingernails moving to rub across her lips.

"I know...it freaked me out at first, too. I've actually never thought about it before, but it's no biggie. It's not like we fucked or anything. I didn't even get to cop a feel. It was more of a joke. We were at a party when someone dared us to kiss. Leesa is in my Interpersonal Relations class...so who better than to relate with?" She laughs boldly at her attempt at humor.

I roll my eyes at the absurdity of this conversation. This is what she always does. She somehow always manages to maneuver a conversation from whatever the topic is to direct the focus on her. I appreciate the redirection this time, though. It keeps me from thinking about...

Just then, a text pops up on my phone, as Kady continues to regale her 'I kissed a girl' moment.

My eyes stare in fascination at the words.

Van: Please, please, please

Van: Don't let this be over

Van: You're everything to me

Van: I LOVE YOU

Van: Please believe nothing happened

Van: I swear. Nothing was going on

Van: I need to see you

Van: Can I see you?

"Hey. What are you doing? You're obviously not listening to me right now."

Kady's voice dislodges me from my head, where I'm ruminating over Van's pleas. Except for my father when he left my mom, I've never been in a position to forgive a man. Am I supposed to make him sweat it out? Or give in right away?

I think about the remaining time I have this weekend. It's already late Saturday night. I have to leave back for school on Monday evening. The drive is four hours and I have a class bright and early on Tuesday. So if I don't want this entire weekend to go to waste, I need to decide now.

"Van's texting me."

Kady grumbles. "Duh. I figured that. What's he saying?"

I read her the texts.

"So? What should I do?"

"I'd personally make him wait. But that's just me. Maybe he did and maybe he didn't have anything to do with Lyndsay's impromptu visit. She could've been sneaky just like you and shown up announced."

Now that I think about it, I kind of feel bad for putting Van in that position tonight. If it's true that he was cornered by Lyndsay, and then pounced on by me out of the blue, I can only imagine what that might do to a guy. Of course, he appeared guilty. He had no control over the situation or circumstances.

"I do believe him. I just don't know how to move forward. How can I trust him?"

She shrugs her shoulders. "You either do or you don't. I guess it depends on how much you want to be with him. If you're going to make it work, you're going to need to talk to him about this, get it out in the open, tell him how you feel and tell him how it's going to be in the future. Find out from him where he stands with Lyndsay. He can't be your boyfriend and remain friends with her. I'm sorry, that shit just don't fly. He should sever ties completely."

"But, am I in a position to give that ultimatum? They grew up together. They were together for a long time. He's only been with me for a little over a month. Seems a bit drastic."

"I'm just saying that's what I would do. You, Kylah, have a much bigger capacity to love and forgive than I do. I doubt I'd even give a guy a second chance. But you, sissy, are a whole different breed. And not in a bad way. As long as you don't let him walk all over you. Just listen to your heart."

Hmm. My heart. It screams for Van.

"You make me sound like a stupid sap. I may be shy and quiet, but I'm not a doormat. I do stand up for myself when the occasion calls."

"I know. You're a tender-hearted badass. And that's why I love ya." She winks and flips me off at the same time. Ah, sisterly love.

"Now get some sleep tonight. And tomorrow, go have hot, off-the-charts makeup sex."

I snort.

I'm still too confused and tired to think about what that entails right now.

But it'll be fun to check another item off my sex bucket list this weekend.

26

IT'S noon and I still haven't heard from Kylah.

Shit. If I lost her because of Lyndsay's unwelcome visit, I will never forgive my ex.

I didn't sleep at all last night. Tossed and turned all night, checking my phone every five minutes in the event she called or texted me back. There was only silence. And it made me fucking insane.

I had to stop myself from going nuts with the apology texts. I could've continued, but felt like a crazy stalker and had to put a cap on my lame-ass appeals for reconciliation and forgiveness. When she hadn't responded within thirty minutes, I gave up and went to bed. There was no use in continuing to look like a loser. It's kind of like when you get called for a foul out on the court. You state your case to the referee, trying to get him to see your side, and when they make their decision, you accept it and move on.

That's what I'll have to do if she doesn't forgive me.

I woke up around ten, antsy and fidgety. Full of piss and vinegar. I've been moping around for the last hour or so and finally decided I had to do something. So I get on my workout clothes and run to the student athletic building on campus. Might as well get in some cardio and strength training today.

As I enter the gym, a number of people greet me with high-fives and hellos. I make my way back to the weight room where I see a few of my teammates hanging out. Carver's at the leg press, Scott and Lance at the bench press, and Christian is doing some deadlifts. They all shout out my name as I enter the little alcove in the back.

Carver gives me an evil eye as I walk toward him.

"Didn't I tell you not to hurt her, dude? Now I'm required to kick your virginity-stealing ass."

I raise an eyebrow at him. "How'd you know about that?"

Carver scoffs. "I know all, bruh. I heard Cade talking last night to Ainsley, in between rounds of fucking. Jesus, that girl is a screamer."

I blush, which is stupid. But I can't help it. It feels wrong to know about Cade's girl in that intimate manner.

"How'd you know about Kylah's virginity?"

"She told me." He says nonchalantly, puffing out his chest with a grunt through a set of leg curls, the sweat dripping down his chest.

I glare at him and he continues. "The night you two went to the movies. She asked for sex advice."

I choke out a cough. Wasn't expecting that.

"And exactly what advice did you give her?" I pick up a couple of hand weights and begin some bicep curls, curious as to their conversation about sex.

"Well, initially I told her that her best bet was just to fuck me because she wouldn't get a better experience anywhere else."

When I glare at him, Carver laughs, his shoulders shaking ruefully. "Eh, calm down bro. You know you're the one she wanted and I don't do virgins. Too bad you couldn't keep from running back to your ex long enough to be the guy Ky-Ky needed."

I throw down the weights and have him by the throat in under a second. The ruckus has all heads turning to see what's up.

"That's not how it went down, Edwards. Don't go talking about shit you know nothing about again."

Sometimes Carver pisses me off with his trash-talking, loud-mouth ways. Normally I let the things that come out of his mouth slide, but not today. Not in my current pissy mood.

Christian is suddenly at my side, gripping my arm that I let fall from Carver's neck.

"Fuck this shit. I'm outta here." I shoulder past Christian and head back outside, breaking into a jog to my dorm.

When I arrive at my building, the air conditioning hits my skin, instantly cooling my sweat-soaked flesh. I sprint up the steps, turn the corner, and then the wind is knocked out of me.

There sitting at my door is Kylah, knees bent so her chin rests on top, head bent as she plays with her phone. My sudden intake of breath catches her attention as her eyes flit to see me standing here at her side.

"Ky." Her name on my tongue sounds like home.

My hand darts out to help her up, as she pushes to her feet, but continues to stare down at the floor. It's like we're both teenagers at our first dance, uncertain of where to put our hands and our feet, fearful of tripping each other with our awkwardness.

I make the choice to open my door, leading the way inside as she follows behind me in silence.

"Do you want something to drink?" I ask, uncertain as to what I should say.

Her gaze flashes to the picnic basket sitting on top of my mini-fridge. She left it here last night when she dashed out of here. I haven't opened it to see what's in it. I felt too ashamed. Too upset. Too worried about what happened.

"No, thank you." She says politely, like a debutante at a ball.

"Ky-" I start to say as she says my name at the same time.

"Van...I-"

"You go." I oblige, gesturing for her to proceed.

Kylah gives me a worried glance, wetting her lip with a nervous lick. The same spot I've licked and kissed a dozen times. She takes a seat on my couch, picking at the frayed knee in her jeans.

"I guess we were both surprised last night when I showed up." Her lips quirk up into a sheepish grin. God, she's so sweet.

I laugh awkwardly. "God, Kylah."

I squat down in front her, tentatively placing my hands on her knees. I can feel the warmth emanating from her skin and it sends a shiver down my spine. "I'm so sorry you walked in that mess. I had no idea Lyndsay was here. She had a key...I never got it back from her. She showed up out of the blue. I haven't talked to her since Christmas. I'd never do that to you, Ky. Never."

Her soft, satiny palm lands on top my hand, sending electric currents through my arm and zapping me in the heart.

"I know that, Van. I believe you. It was awful to see you with her, regardless of the circumstances. It really hurt me. The pragmatic side of me knows it wasn't intentional. I know you aren't cheating on me. The irrational side of me, though, feels burned. I can't help that."

"I swear to you, Ky. Nothing happened and nothing ever would. I'm in love with you. It's you I want to be with. Not her.

Never again. I was so mad at her last night. I threw her out of my place. I told her I never wanted to see her or talk to her again. And I meant it. She broke me so deeply when she betrayed me. And honestly, I wasn't really sure I could trust again. But then you came along..."

As if a part of the iceberg is chipping away – melting from my admission – my heart begins to beat again. She stares at me, holding my gaze, her eyes pool with unshed tears. And something else. Recognition. Of the love I have for her. I'd give her the world if she'd accept it from me. What I need first, though, is her forgiveness. I need to know we're solid. That we can go back to the way things were before last night.

She chews on her lip, eyes averted again. "Thank you for that. I don't want to give you an ultimatum – her or me. I don't think that's fair. But if you want to continue..."

I adamantly nod my head in confirmation. "Yes, I want to continue."

Kylah gives me a smile. "We both need to trust each other if this is going to work. I need to know that when I'm at school and not with you every day or week, or after a game, you will be faithful to me. And I know you feel the same way. I don't care if you have female friends – that's normal. I have guy friends at school that I hang with. But I don't kiss them. I definitely don't touch them or let them up to my dorm room. I expect the same thing from you."

It's then that I realize the hang-ups I had over a long-distance relationship are no longer a problem. They were an issue when I was with Lyndsay because I was holding on too tight to a love that no longer existed. Kylah and me...this is what it means to be true. To be real. A mature relationship where there is trust and forgiveness.

I flip my palm over and bring her hand to my lips, kissing

her softly. I haven't shaved today, so the bristle of my days' old beard creates visible goosebumps up her arm.

"I love you, Kylah. I want to make this work. I'm so glad you came into my life when you did. I don't deserve you, but I want you. I want you so much."

The heat in her eyes causes a rush of lust to shoot straight down to my dick. Holy hell, I'm not sure what's on her mind, but if it's what I'm thinking, I can totally get on board.

"Are we good again?"

She reaches out to wrap her small hands around my neck, dipping her head down to meet my lips.

"Yes, we're good." She murmurs against my mouth, as I inhale a deep sigh before capturing her lips with mine. It's been a month since we've kissed. Since I last held her in my arms. Four weeks of abstinence and pent-up desire, with only dreams of burying myself deep inside her.

Suddenly she releases me and sits back, tipping her head toward her shoulder.

"Looks like you need a shower."

That might be a tactful way of saying I smell...after all, I was on a run and haven't showered yet today.

"Yeah, I do. Will you wait..."

Before I can finish, she begins to tug at her shirt sleeve, yanking her arms out and overhead, flinging the shirt off toward the corner of my room.

"I need a shower, too. That way I can check two more boxes off my sex bucket list." She giggles when I quirk my eyebrows at her.

"Sex bucket list?" I don't know what that is but damned if I'm not going to act as her willing participant.

"Yeah. Makeup sex and shower sex. I need them both. Now. With you." She says, standing and tugging me to my feet, leading me into the bathroom.

And who am I to refuse such a sweet offer from this sweet girl?

The End

EPILOGUE

Mid-May

"Do you have any idea how much shit your parents will flip when you tell them that you're going to live with Ky-Ky?"

I give Carver a sideways glance, wincing a little as I lift my end of the couch. He's helping me move out of the dorm and into my new apartment in Scottsdale.

It's crazy to think how much has changed in my life in the matter of a few short months. We went into the post-season on a winning streak, ended up making our way into the NCAA tournament, but were eliminated in the Regional semi-finals when we were clobbered by Gonzaga. It was a pitiful game.

We were playing in Seattle at the Key Arena, and were up by five when Carver went in for a lay-up and was elbowed in the face by another player. Ended up breaking his nose and knocking out one of his front teeth. He had to be rushed to an emergency dentist during the game and never returned to play. Needless to say, he was uncharacteristically sullen and angsty after he got patched up and we made our way back to Phoenix. I knew it had to be more than just the game, but I didn't know what.

"Telling my parents will be difficult, and they will definitely have an issue with it based on their religious beliefs, but they also know and love Kylah. And I'm an adult, with a degree and new career. I have my own life to lead now. The harder conversation will be with Allan and Kristine Griffin."

Over Spring Break, Kylah made the decision to transfer from Harvey Mudd to ASU in the fall. She'd met with the admissions counselors and gotten everything in order. The only remaining discussion was to tell her folks she was transferring and that she wouldn't need to live at home or in the dorms come fall. Her mom and new stepdad, John, were throwing a summer graduation bash for Cade next week and we'd decided to tell them all then.

The good thing about the timing was that it would be overshadowed by another announcement. Cade had already informed us that he was going to propose to Ainsley at the BBQ, which would certainly take the heat off of Kylah's announcement.

With sweat dripping down our backs, we hoist the couch into the moving truck. A few more items to pack up and then I'd be driving it to my new apartment where Kylah was already organizing dishes in the cupboards. It made me smile knowing in a few months it would become her kitchen, too.

"I don't know what you're grinning about, dude, because we've still got a few loads before we finish. And then you promised me a twelve-pack."

Waving him off, we head back up the stairs to my room.

"So what do you think about Cade? Isn't it crazy that he's going to be a married man in the next year?"

Carver lets go of a scoffing laugh. "Idiot. Why the fuck is he rushing into something like that? No man should settle down this soon after college graduation."

I lift my eyebrows at his disparaging remark. I take what Carver says with a grain of salt. He's always been anti-love, anti-relationship. I don't really know why. It just seems like there's a story there. But for him at this time in his life, I get it. He's getting ready for the upcoming NBA draft day.

"He's in love and wants to settle down. I get that. Not like you...you'll have tons of hot females following you around once you go pro."

"Damn straight I will. Getting pussy anytime I want, in every city I go." He winks suggestively.

As we wait for the elevator to return so we can move my desk, I ask him the question on my mind lately.

"You going up to Washington for a visit before draft day? Don't you have family back there?"

Carver's back stiffens noticeably.

"Maybe. Not sure. Next question."

"Don't you have to go back to that oral surgeon for the veneer or whatever the hell you need to get for your teeth?"

When Carver got his tooth knocked out, they replaced it with some sort of temporary bridge or something like that. Carver had to go in to have the permanent structure secured and didn't have the time until he was done with school.

"Technically, I can have the work done anywhere. But yeah, I have an appointment for next week."

"So, you are going back to Seattle. But you're not going to see your family?"

I know I'm digging, and I'm not really sure why. Maybe it's because I feel like I don't know Carver as much as I do my other friends. He only shows us certain aspects of his character. The captain of the team on the court, and the player off the court. And now that we'll all be going our separate ways, and Carver most likely being picked up on a professional team, our friend-ships will be scattered in every direction.

The elevator doors open up and we set the couch down, both stretching out our backs and necks in the process. Moving is hard work, even when you're athletic.

Carver tilts his head and glares at me.

"What's your deal? Why so interested in who I'm going to see when I'm back home?"

I shrug. "I don't know. It just seems like you're hiding some-thing, man. You never talk about your family. I mean, you know everything about mine – even Dougie. But I don't even know if you have siblings."

"I don't. So drop it."

"Okay. Chill out, bruh. Sorry it's such a touchy subject. But you definitely have an issue there. I noticed it after that last game. What happened?"

Carver sighs deeply. "Fuck, man. It's complicated, okay?"

"What's so complicated about it?"

Carver rubs the back of his neck as the elevator opens up once more and we lift the couch again, heading toward the truck.

"I ran into my old girlfriend back in March. Turns out she is the dental assistant at the oral surgeon's office I was sent to for the emergency repair."

"Wow. That's pretty weird, right? Small world and all that. How'd it go with her?"

Carver laughs with a sardonic undertone.

"Had she had her way, I think she would've knocked out all of my remaining teeth instead of fixing them."

"So I can assume things didn't end well between the two of you?"

He shrugs a shoulder, looking off in the other direction. "I honestly don't know. One day she was just gone; vanished. And I haven't seen or heard from her until that day at the dentist."

READ what's next in *Pivot* (Carver and Logan's story) – Book 3 in Courting Love Series

IF YOU ENJOYED THIS BOOK, please consider providing a review on either Goodreads or the retailer where it was purchased. Thank you for your support!

ABOUT THE AUTHOR

Since writing and releasing her first book in 2014, Sierra has found her creative passion writing about the fictional characters that live inside her brain, who constantly shout for their own love stories to be told.

Sierra frequently indulges in what some might consider to be an unhealthy dose of reading, dark chocolate goodies, and way too much coffee. She hates cold weather, scary movies and reality TV shows, and frequently finds herself traveling around the U.S. to see her favorite musicians.

Sierra resides in the Pacific Northwest with her husband of twenty plus years and her long-haired, German Shepherd. She is currently working on her next book.

Your feedback means the world to me! Please consider leaving a review where you purchased this book. (((HUGS)))

You can stay connected with Sierra through her newsletter, website and other social media sites.

Go to: www.sierrahillbooks.com

Or Follow ME on BookBub (it's FREE) to receive automatic updates each time I have a new release! https://www.bookbub.com/authors/sierra-hill

Made in the USA
Columbia, SC
24 March 2024

33542270R00153